I070244?

Lord of Goblins

II

Michiel Werbrouck & Hadi Y. Bendakji

TABLE OF CONTENTS

GLOSSARY

Lev/Gherm: Assassinated during his victory speech. Lev was forcibly torn from his world during his moment of triumph. But death was not the end, as he finds himself in the body of a greyborn bogey named Gherm. Now in a new land, Lev must find a way to survive and—just maybe—thrive.

Ghorza: Gherm's older sister. She and Gherm are greyborns, which makes them slaves according to the bogeys' primitive society. Having lost her parents at a young age, Ghorza cares deeply for her brother, Gherm, and works hard to keep him safe and fed. She's wary of Lev and wonders how much of her brother is left.

Volker: Lev's second-in-command. He is the youngest son from a family of potters. Endlessly loyal to Lev, his honest nature and work ethic shine through despite his timid personality. He's proved himself as a capable leader and combatant who can hold his own in Lev's absence.

Rak: One of the biggest, baddest greyborn around. Even as a child, Rak was always stronger than his peers. Forced to turn to crime to save his mother, his strength, charisma, and loyalty to his men allowed him to take over the mining quarters and southern living quarters in the slums.

Hem/Hemgall: One of the few truly loyal members of Rak's gang. He likes to keep things simple and respects men who can take risks for their ambitions. Besides that, he can hold his liquor.

Vyrga: Considered to be the "Lord of Wretches" and "King of the Immoral", his actions know no bounds. He is no priest nor poet, neither a warrior nor noble. He is a greyborn, but not just any greyborn; a leader with the blood of nobles in his veins. He cares not for the consequences, as long as he gets his way.

Gelmar: Gelmar, the eldest and first child to follow Vyrga, held a unique place in his mentor's heart, serving not only as a son but also as a companion. His arrogance, coupled with his steadfast conviction that he was destined to succeed Ainshard, led to feelings of deep betrayal when Vyrga did not consider him a viable successor. Fueled by resentment, Gelmar hatched a plot to amass followers and instigate a coup. However, his plans were thwarted when Vyrga discovered his treachery and sent him into battle against Lev. Unfortunately, Gelmar met a tragic end. Defeated, he was subsequently slain by his own followers.

Heimo: Serving as one of Vyrga's trusted commanders, he holds the distinction of being the youngest among the protégés raised by Vyrga. His potential surpassed that of his comrades, hinting at a future where he could have reigned supreme. However, his somewhat unnerving demeanour made him inaccessible to others.

Os/Oswald: Serving as one of Vyrga's Commanders, he is also one of the children raised by Vyrga, demonstrating unparalleled loyalty among his peers. Known for his rigid, upright nature, his unwavering devotion has earned him the nickname 'Vyrga's Hound.' Given his steadfast disciplined disposition, he is considered the most probable candidate to succeed Vyrga in the unfortunate event of his passing.

Ludger: One of Vyrga's adopted children and the biological elder brother of Bolo. Despite being obnoxious, quick-tempered, and generally unlikable, he harbours a deep affection for his brother and remains dutifully loyal. His flaws are mitigated to some extent by his exceptional combat skills, particularly his mastery with the spear. He carries a distinct distaste for Heimo and Gelmar.

Bolo: One of Vyrga's adopted children and the younger brother of Ludger. Though his intimidating stature and assertive demeanour may suggest otherwise, he possesses a surprisingly gentle soul. Nevertheless, he won't hesitate to fight when it comes to safeguarding his kin.

Bulgu: As the expedition's leader and the youngest heir of the Jiira chief, he is recognized for his ambition rather than his leadership. His glaring flaws—notably his greed, ineptitude, and lofty aspirations—coupled with an utter disregard for others' lives, render him universally unpopular. He spearheaded the expedition with the objective of procuring a weapon believed to have been once wielded by Ainshard. He held the conviction that such an accomplishment would validate his claim to the Jiira throne.

Rapha: The leader of the harem guard. She is an exile from the Ajiin, a clan renowned for its formidable warriors. Following her father's reckless deeds which resulted in his death, she and her family faced exile from their clan. Her paternal uncle, seeking to make amends for his brother's missteps, joined their exile, only to be killed in a confrontation with a Jiira warband. In the ensuing chaos, she was separated from her mother and sister, ultimately finding herself as part of Bulgu's harem guard. Yet, in spite of these adversities, she clings to her dream of becoming a shieldmaiden one day.

Ruune: An integral part of the harem guard. She stands as Rapha's right-hand woman and closest confidant. Embodying a rowdy and boisterous spirit, she is known for her unfiltered emotional transparency, always wearing her heart on her sleeve.

Gul: A cherished childhood friend of Volker and an established member of Lev's faction. He used his persuasive abilities to coax Volker into joining their ranks, steering him away from a career as a potter. Known for his sharp wit and sarcastic humour, he carries a determined and stubborn disposition.

Molg: One of Lev's followers. He admires Lev and is loyal to a fault.

Jem: Lev's third-in-command; a seasoned, middle-aged Greyborn who has served under various groups, typically shifting allegiances whenever their leaders meet their end. His considerable experience as both a combatant and a leader is commendable, yet he opts to sidestep conflicts and adamantly declines any offers to ascend to leadership upon the death of a group's figurehead.

Shahn: Born to Kafar Ramun, he is a dignified Darg hailing from the thriving state of Edoros. Despite his relative youth, he commands the Dargs under Bulgu's rule. His past is marked by a stint as a gladiator in Brizilum and, earlier still, a seafaring life that mirrored his father's own maritime beginnings.

Varra: One of the Dargs dispatched to participate in Bulgu's expedition. Nursing a soft spot for Volker, she makes a point to safeguard him at all costs. As is typical among mercenary Dargs, she is a proficient warrior, and her combat prowess is further enhanced by the Brizilum-crafted armour and weapons she wields.

Rogga: A member of the Burga who joined the expedition. He displays typical Burga traits: aggression, a lack of sociability, and a somewhat narrow mindset. However, he compensates for these shortcomings with an honour-bound nature, and an unwavering sense of duty. In ordinary circumstances, he would never consider abandoning his comrades.

Gozzag: He is the revered leader of the Deka dispatched to support Bulgu in the expedition. His age and accumulated experiences have shaped him into a wise leader who commands respect from his men.

Ban: Serving as Gozzag's right-hand man and trusted confidant, he blends a firm determination with a congenial and easy-going personality. He's a man of action, never shying away from a confrontation, be it a physical fight or a spirited drinking contest.

Thorst: A gifted green bogey. He transitioned from serving as a guard to supervising greyborn miners and is recognized as Kul's protégé. Generally exhibiting an easy-going demeanour, his attitude shifts when it involves Ghorza, for whom he harbours romantic feelings.

Kathaga: As a Priestess of Zeja, she was sought out by Lev for Zeja's blessing. Unbeknownst to Lev, Kathaga would masquerade as a mere temple servant before revealing her true identity as the priestess. Her knowledge extends beyond Lev's expectations, to the point where even his true name isn't concealed from her. Ultimately, she bestowed Zeja's blessing upon Lev's army in anticipation of their impending clash with Gelmar's forces.

Kul: An old, pale-green bogey overseer. Once considered to be one of the best warriors of the bogey race, he fell from grace after failing to protect a noble's son during a rebellion against the Jiira. He was a good friend of Gat, Gherm, and Ghorza's father, and decided to take care of them in order to repay his debt to him.

Rogg: A bogey herbalist and witchdoctor who is neither skilled enough to treat commoner and noble bogeys, nor kind enough to charge greyborns a fair price for his services.

Maria: Raised along with Lev and Brutus in the orphanage, she's strong-willed and hard-headed. She left Eurasia at the tender age of eighteen.

Eric: A reluctant sergeant and former member of the fourth regiment's reserves in the fifth defence force. Eric was like all NCOs in the Eurasian army, having completed a five-year service term before resigning. His decision to leave wasn't spurred by cowardice, but rather due to necessity, prompted by the physical injuries and mental trauma he sustained on the battlefield. Despite objections from his wife, he felt compelled to return to duty, nurturing the hope that his service would eventually earn his family citizenship. Moreover, should he ascend high enough in rank, he harboured ambitions of enacting beneficial reforms within the military.

Brutus: Lev's childhood best friend. Despite his large size and intimidating, scarred visage, he has a kind heart and can be shy during social gatherings.

Bogeys: A goblinoid race known for being physically weak, but intelligent. The typical lifespan of a bogey is sixty years, and they tend to produce less offspring than other goblinoids. Within the intricate web of bogey society, the roles are colour-marked: green-skinned bogeys are categorised as commoners, blue-skinned ones hold positions akin to nobles, and unfortunately, grey-skinned bogeys are confined to the status of slaves.

Greyborns: Bogeys born with dark grey skin, silver hair, and yellow eyes. The greyborn are slaves among slaves, as the tribe they belonged to was a victim of war between the goblin Jiira and kobold Kur. Although it was once an honour to be greyborn, a failed coup by greyborn elitists centuries ago has long besmirched their reputation.

Goblins: As the most numerous and ancient goblinoid species, they stand a tad taller than most bogeys, boasting robust resilience and adaptability to various environments. Their physical prowess is offset by their limited magical capabilities and relatively short lifespans, typically not exceeding that of bogeys. Due to their distinctive looks, aggressive disposition, and impulsiveness, they often find themselves unfairly stereotyped as violent, unintelligent brutes—a stereotype many male goblins inadvertently perpetuate. Female goblins, on the other hand, tend to display fewer of these perceived negative traits.

Dekas: A species of large red goblinoids, these individuals are distinguished by a single horn protruding from their forehead. Their impressive size, formidable strength, and intimidating appearance make them a terrifying presence on the battlefield. However, what often surprises others is their intelligence and keen logistical skills, which defy common perceptions. Additionally, they demonstrate exceptional horsemanship, with many among their ranks choosing to serve as mercenaries.

Dargs: A fascinating species of purple goblinoids, Dargs are known for their long hair and elongated ears. Despite their graceful appearances, they are formidable warriors and skilled sailors, traits that often surprise those deceived by their elegant exteriors. Primarily residing off the mainland in the prosperous state of Edoros, the Dargs experienced a substantial setback when they lost to Brizilum, subsequently becoming its vassal. This change in status led to many Dargs being subjugated as slaves and gladiators.

Burgas: Belonging to the goblinoid species, the Burgas would bear resemblance to goblins, if not for their increased size, pronounced tails, and more robust jaws. Although they may not possess the intellectual prowess of other goblinoids, they compensate for this with their exceptional senses and superior tracking skills, rendering them ideal scouts and hunters. Renowned for their outstanding honour, Burgas are exceptionally loyal; under normal circumstances, they would scarcely ever forsake their comrades.

Bugbears: A species of large, yellow goblinoids, known for their notable physical strength but less so for their intellectual capacities. Their natural aggression often overshadows their conversational skills, rendering them less appealing partners for dialogue.

Merits: Merits serve as a form of lead-based currency. Intentionally dull in appearance, they are primarily used to compensate greyborns for their work. Enforced by the upper class, this near-valueless medium of exchange was designed to limit the greyborns' access to high-quality resources and equipment.

Chosen Ones: Deemed as the reincarnations of gods or their divine champions, Chosen Ones are distinguished figures within the mortal realm. Not only do they retain their past memories, but they also command powers that exceed natural limitations. These capabilities can span from extraordinary strength to the more profound, reality-altering abilities.

Lost Souls: A reincarnated or transmigrated individual that retains their memory, but unlike a chosen one, doesn't have extraordinary abilities. Most of them die in obscurity but a few, using their past life's knowledge and experience, rise to become legends.

The Expedition: An annual event mandated by the Jiira, the expedition serves to harvest refined haze crystals and excavate treasures hailing from Ainshard's era and the age of the gods. Owing to the unique nature of this expedition, Lev and his men find themselves forced to participate, necessitating a truce with Vyrga. This year's expedition is further distinguished by the unprecedented involvement of Bulgu, a Jiira prince, who brings along with him a cadre of slaves and mercenaries from various goblinoid races. Under the ostensible leadership of Bulgu, the group confronts a relentless struggle as they battle their way to the lower floors, their journey plagued by limited opportunities for rest.

The Cycle: The cyclical process of life and death as understood in bogey mythology. The cycle is represented by four distinct facets: life, death, the afterlife, and reincarnation.

Cyfrac Oil: Cyfracs are a rare family of plants, found on the fifth floor and below, that resemble a red-coloured rye and are easily combustible. Their oil has many uses, from ceremonies to smithing, but is most valued by shamans and witch doctors because its flames spread fast and last a long time.

Bluecatcher Mushrooms: A giant, blue, carnivorous species found on or below the second floor of the monster cavern. The mushroom uses its sticky sap to catch prey before encapsulating it for digestion—the sap also works well as an adhesive for wood, leather, and cloth.

Haze Crystals: A special crystal that can store immense amounts of magical energy. This makes it a great alchemical reagent, and essential for making focus tools for shamans. Before refinement, they are highly corrosive towards creatures with low magical resistance. It is rare to find them outside of the bogey and monster caverns where they naturally grow..

The Ancient Shrines: Mystical constructions originating from the era of Ainshard, if not earlier. These shrines possess the power to teleport small bands of individuals to corresponding shrines elsewhere. Upon the Jiira's first exploration of the caverns, sacred sites above the third floor were demolished, deemed by the Jiira as symbols of heretical worship. The survival of the remaining shrines was a fortunate accident. A pioneering group from an expeditionary force rediscovered their teleportation ability when they were seeking refuge from peril while laden with treasure.

Killigs: An order of great holy warriors who served as Ainshard's elite troops. They were all the same height, about twice that of a goblin, so goblinoids eventually started measuring things relative to their height.

Corpse-eaters: A species of carnivorous, black-scaled lizards with striking emerald eyes. These creatures display a preference for scavenging on carcasses over actively hunting prey, earning them their distinct name. Characterised by their prolific reproduction, they are a ubiquitous presence across the vast expanse of the cavern.

Bogey Caverns: A section of a mysterious cavern abundant in haze crystals, artefacts from the age of the gods, and treacherous beasts. The bogey caverns are situated in the upper regions of the cavern, encompassing the entrance and first floor, which are under bogey control and serve as their living quarters.

Monster Caverns: An alternative designation for the caverns inhabited by the enslaved bogeys. This term references the lower floors, areas not under Bogey dominion. In contrast, the zones under Bogey control are referred to as the Bogey Caverns.

Hivelings: Giant, ant-like creatures that inhabit the monster caverns. They left the bogeys alone to begin with, but years of bogey invasions into hiveling territory turned the hivelings aggressive. They come in various sizes and shapes. The smallest are the workers, with the largest being the warriors.

Spiderlings: Brownish-green spider-like hivelings that dwell on the lower floors of the monster caverns. They're known to favour ambushes over direct confrontations. Their yellow blood has paralysing properties.

Ainshard: Ainshard the Great, also known as The Enlightened One, is believed to have been a goblin who conquered all the people of the forest and established a great kingdom centuries ago. The land under his control encompassed the central and western parts of the continent and was home to hundreds of tribes of bogeys, goblins, kobolds, and various other species. He's worshipped by many goblinoids, and in the eyes of the Jiira and some bogeys, he's the *only* being deserving of worship.

Jom: Revered as the father of all and the world's guardian against creatures of the void, he is a deity familiar to goblin-kind, often credited with the creation of the goblinoid races. Although his popularity has waned among most goblinoids—particularly those who lean towards Ainshard over him and his pantheon—he still commands the faith of certain races, including the bogeys. He fell victim to The Void Walker in a brutal clash, but Zeja, in an act of divine intervention, resurrected him.

Under her leadership and alongside the other gods, he managed to triumph over his nemesis.

Maga: The goddess of love and fertility, she presides over her priests and priestesses who officiate marriage ceremonies and provide stress relief to followers. Naturally, such services require a generous donation.

Zeja: Born from a droplet of Jom's blood, she initially took the form of a young girl characterised by white hair and red eyes. Embarking on a quest to the underworld, she collected fragments of Jom's soul and negotiated with Dorn, the god of death, to reassemble these pieces into a singular soul, thereby resurrecting Jom. Blessed by Jom, she led the pantheon into battle against the entity known as The Void Walker, ultimately repelling it back into the abyss. This victory secured her ascension as the goddess of war.

Jorm: Zeja's son and the god of defensive wars and ranged weaponry, he may be classified as a minor deity by many, yet he enjoys significant popularity among the greyborns.

Dorn: As the god of death, he oversees the souls of the departed in the underworld. He arbitrates whether souls should be reforged for another opportunity—at life or to join the gods' table—or sent into the cycle of reincarnation for rebirth.

Tanach: As the god of slumber and dreams, he is often perceived as indolent, forever asleep. In truth, his sleep is not without purpose. He vigilantly monitors the dreams of others, purging them of any demonic influence.

Mal: The goddess of deception, she commands a following of cultists and is known for dispatching demons to possess individuals during their most vulnerable moments. Once ensnared, these victims are manipulated into committing unthinkable deeds under her influence.

The Void Walker: An enigmatic force that once sought global domination. The Void Walker clashed and overcame Jom, the father of all, and could have vanquished his kin if not for Zeja's intervention. After resurrecting Jom, Zeja marshalled her armies and ultimately brought about the demise of the Void Walker.

The State of Edoros: A once-powerful city-state that remains prosperous, situated on an island to the north-east of the continent, bordering the White Sea. It is the heartland of the Darg and their largest settlement. Despite their fall to the Brizilum, becoming a vassal state in the process, the Darg retain their pride as exceptional seamen, traders, and warriors, continuing to regard themselves as the undisputed masters of the White Sea.

The Jiira Tribe: A goblin tribe founded after Ainshard's empire collapsed. They are aggressive and arrogant, given their heritage, but their cultural and technological advantages among the goblinoids are disappearing at a steady pace.

The Kur Tribe: A tribe of Kobolds that fought with the Jiira for domination over the region. Not much is known about them among the bogeys.

The Brizilum Republic: A great republic situated in the eastern half of the continent. They're expansionists who seek to engulf all their rivals, converting them into vassals.

The Neutral Zone: The only unclaimed zone on Earth with resource-filled, fertile lands. It is the main theatre of war between the Eurasian and Imperial Armies.

The Technocracy of Eurasia: The Technocracy is one of the world's few superstates. The Technocracy and its United Council rule over Eurasia with an iron grip. The Technocracy is the largest continental superstate on Earth, spanning over most parts of Europe and Asia.

The Empire: The oldest nemesis of Eurasia, ruled by the 'Emperor of The West.' The Emperor's realm spans over North and Central America. Unlike Eurasia, they're highly advanced both in civilian and military technology.

CHAPTER I

PRECURSORS

How long has it been since I entered this world? It must have been half a year by now, I'm sure of it.

A few months ago we set off on an expedition to the depths of the monster caverns, in search of the precious minerals and treasures our Jiira masters so greedily longed for.

As we ventured deeper and deeper, though, we invited the wrath of those who dwelled in its depths: hivelings. When I first encountered them, they reminded me of ants—hulking, impenetrable, and vicious. However, they must see *us* as ants—small, fragile, and at best pests to be eradicated. No, they would probably treat even ants better than us goblinoids, who pillage their homes and eviscerate their kin.

And just when I'd thought I'd seen it all, I touched that mask. In the blinding white light, I felt something grab hold of my soul and drag it out of my body—out of Gherm's body. And it was there that I encountered that dreadful, robed figure.

As though my distress were audible in this oppressive silence, it said my name.

"Leonard Erand Vandersteen."

My true name.

The being had an otherworldly feel to it, as if it were from another world, another plane of existence. It smiled at me, white light spilling forth from its mask. And as it towered above me, I felt it scrutinising my very being.

The sheer power the creature held was fascinating, something I'd never experienced in all my years of life. But despite its alien nature, the creature felt almost familiar, as if I'd encountered it before.

Then it dawned on me. Images of countless relics flashed through my mind and I was reminded of the gate before which I had stood mere moments ago.

"Leonard Erand Vandersteen, I've been waiting for you."

* * *

Lev stared in bewilderment at the gigantic robed being as it observed him in return. Its glowing white eyes seemed to read his soul memory by memory, line by line as they pierced through its mask.

The staring contest seemed to take an eternity, long enough to get on Lev's nerves.

He took a deep breath, then spoke. "So you know my name, my true self. Care to explain how?" He continued to stare into the light. "And do tell me what you want from me. What are you and why am I here?"

The creature smiled at him, sending a chill up Lev's spine. As more white light spilled out of the corners of its upturned mouth, Lev felt increasingly unsettled.

Regardless, he persisted. "So, will you answer my questions?"

The robed being chuckled.

I could, but my compatriots always complained that I was too verbose. Instead of telling you, let me show you.

"What do you—"

Before Lev could finish his sentence, the being snapped its fingers, and the void was filled with blinding light once again.

Lev faded in and out of consciousness. When he came to, he found himself floating above a grand hall. Lev's weightless body could observe its surroundings, but seemed formless, incorporeal. Looking around, he saw the white-masked figure from before below him. It glided towards another figure dressed in full regalia, seated atop a golden throne.

In the darkened area behind the throne, Lev could discern a few unmoving, robed figures, who seemed to be listening intently. Although Lev could not see their faces, he could pick out some sharp angles where he imagined those would be.

Lots of masks here, I see, Lev mused.

The white-masked figure halted and kneeled before the throne, which was decorated with various symbols and had a menacing aura to it.

The aged and tired goblinoid figure on the throne shifted as it began speaking, almost too softly for Lev to hear. He made a concerted effort to listen as intently as the other masked figures and found himself able to understand its raspy words.

"How was Kram's latest report? Has he addressed the Korrigal rampaging near our borders? They have been destroying valuable mining sites for months now. Without intervention, our deficit will continue to increase, and—"

Fret not, my master. Kram has foreseen all and has acted accordingly. It's a pity we lost more men than anticipated during the recent elf rebellions, but our great empire will endure. As it always has.

Who's Kram? Lev thought. *What am I looking at? Where am I?* He saw the apparently subordinate creature move closer to the throned figure and bend down, as though to whisper in the throned figure's ear. Lev could not hear the creature's words, but the throned figure visibly relaxed and slumped in its throne.

"I see. Then all has been solved by Kram."

Indeed, my lordship. His armies are dealing with the threat of the tusked ones and their accursed armies in the north as we speak.

The robed figures behind the throne nodded in unison.

"Marvellous!" the throned figure said, its voice regaining some power. It was as if youthful vigour had blessed the figure, if only for a mere moment.

*Armies? Tusked ones? Gherm didn't know about any races capable of *waging large-scale war like that. Surely a civilization that sophisticated would have stumbled across the cavern,* Lev thought, baffled.

Then again, that... masked creature said that he would 'show me,' so maybe this is from the distant past, when 'tusked ones' were still a fearsome foe.

As he came to this realisation, something clicked in Lev's mind. *Wait. I heard about this from the goblins' sermons. After Ainshard rose to prominence, he crushed a civilization of tusked folks, among other things... That's right. They called themselves 'Korrigal.'*

According to the history Gherm had been taught, centuries ago powerful, godlike figures roamed the land. But there were no mentions of robed figures, much less a war against them. Back then, the Korrigal was a loose coalition of small, independent raiding bands, certainly not a society capable of mobilising a unified army.

This must be taking place after the Age of Gods then, Lev concluded.

The white-masked figure un-bent itself and floated towards the door where two equally otherworldly guards were stationed. Their jet-black, horned armour emanated an aura of power and discipline, prepared to ruthlessly strike down their master's enemies with but a single thought. If Lev were in the flesh, he would have taken every pain and more to avoid drawing their ire. He hated to imagine how even the strongest bogey would cower before them.

The masked figure took one last look back at the throned figure. *Ainshard, my lordship. You know when to summon me. I have given you everything needed to advance to the next stage.*

Lev suddenly snapped his head back to the throned figure. *Ainshard!* In goblin folklore, Ainshard had united numerous races under his banner and conquered vast swaths of land. It was not inaccurate to call Ainshard akin to a god. Yet this decrepit shell of a figure, clutching feebly to both the throne and his last days in the world, seemed a mockery of the myth.

Ainshard cleared his throat. "I'm grateful. My time is limited, as you know. Let's hope Kram's wisdom serves us well one last time."

The guards hoisted open the giant obsidian doors. The masked figure left the room, and the figures who had been lurking behind the throne followed in his footsteps. The guards gently closed the doors and returned to their posts.

Lev could hear whispering coming from within his head.

"But why?"

"Why did Kram act so late?"

"Have I gone too far?"

"How much… How much time have I left?"

Lev tried to find cohesion in the thoughts that rapidly assaulted his brain. *Are these Ainshard's thoughts? Why can I hear them? Unless—*

Lev momentarily glanced at Ainshard. The whispering continued, faster and faster, each thought flowing and roiling into a whirlwind of whispers. Just as Lev thought he was losing himself, his vision blurred and his sense of weight returned. He found himself back in the void from before, standing next to the masked being he had seen leaving Ainshard's throne room.

As I told you before, the being began again, *it really is better when I show, not tell.*

"So you were on good terms with Ainshard. Were you his advisor?"

In a sense, yes. I am an ancient. I served as one of the guides and guardians for Ainshard and the kingdom he founded. My goal is to restore the empire to its former prosperity.

"And?"

And for that, I've determined, I need a worthy emperor. The being flew backwards, almost elegantly, to its original position.

Lev staggered under the mental weight and physical pain of the oppressive, reverberating thoughts. In a brief moment of clarity, he willed his gaze skyward.

What a surprise... No stars. His mind quiet at last, he returned his attention to the masked being, which was hovering above him. Lev briefly looked down; the emptiness below him made him wonder whether he was falling without knowing it.

Don't worry, Leonard. Everything in this place is... under my control.

As if that would calm me down, Lev thought as he alighted upon the transparent floor, a barrier perceptible entirely by touch rather than sight. This being could likely remove that safety barrier with a flick of its fingers.

I have been waiting for you, Leonard. In fact, I've been waiting for you for a very long time.

The creature hovered closer and extended a single, long, wrinkly figure at Lev. It chuckled almost benevolently.

How a fragile creature like you could have managed to get this far is... admirable. Its voice seemed to echo off of the floor-like barrier.

"Then why did you summon me? I'm a bogey. Weakest of the weak. I have nothing to offer you."

It's not that, the being said. *You are like him. Ainshard. Your mind is foreign, having devoured the original soul within your body.*

Devoured? Lev thought.

Yes, devoured, the being replied. *Your mind is not constricted by the world you inhabit.*

It was clear from the being's response that it could read his conscious thoughts, and even memories, to a limited extent.

Limited?

Shit! Lev cursed.

The light behind the mask flickered.

I see. Gherm was the original's name, correct?

"Yes."

How peculiar. Your memories are full of one-sided conversations. Your actions have been quite... erratic, as well. The last embers of the previous owner's soul could have put up a fight at first, but it typically takes less than a week for the new soul to devour the original. I may need to examine you more thoroughly.

The light behind the mask flickered again, and Lev felt the figure's gaze as searingly as before. He attempted to shield his memories with all his willpower; this manifested as a thick, opaque barrier through which the being's light could not travel.

Surprised, intrigued, and perhaps frustrated, the being once again pointed its finger at Lev.

"Stop!" Lev yelled.

The being lowered its finger. *Oh my, it seems I may have taken this too far. I mean no disrespect, but I tend to lose myself in my curiosity. My apologies.*

Lev stiffened his immaterial visage, though his true feelings revealed themselves in his tone of voice. "Apology accepted."

The being shrugged. *Your barrier looks cumbersome... Anything for a cordial relationship, I suppose.*

I'm sure, Lev mentally verbalised as hard as he could. The being did not reply. Lev was unsure as to whether his barrier was effective or the being was merely ignoring him.

Lev smiled anyway. "Well, then, it's my turn to ask questions. Who are you? Not your role, but who are you as an individual? What is below the monster cavern floors, and where are the others?"

Too soon... Too soon.

Lev wanted to yell at the mysterious figure. "After all you've put me through, don't I deserve at least these few answers?"

Hmm. You're in the Enlightened One's frontier dungeon, one of the last remaining dungeons of Ainshard.

Lev frowned. "The Enlightened One?" Although Lev understood from Gherm's memories that the "monster cavern" was actually a dungeon, Gherm's memories hadn't associated the dungeon with Ainshard.

Now, now, Leonard. It is my turn to ask a question. What has happened during my absence from Gherm's world?

Lev hesitated. Maybe the being intended to dispose of him after getting the information it wanted—empty promises of power in exchange for intel were common in Eurasia—but if that were the case, it would have shown him Ainshard's empire in its prime. Who would want to inherit a country in decline?

"We were on an expedition…"

Lev described the conditions of the outside world. How the Jiira had oppressed the bogeys and enslaved the greyborn, how he had been made to undertake an expedition more akin to a death march.

The being remained silent long after Lev had finished.

Lev turned impatient. "It's your turn to answer me now. Where are the others? Are they safe? Where even is this place?"

With no warning or additional verbalization, the being turned towards Lev, slightly lifted its mask, and opened its mouth wider than Lev had thought possible. There was nothing within—its mouth revealed an empty pit of nothingness.

Though Lev never saw something similar before, the answer came to his mind. He gasped. "You're hollow, aren't you?"

Yes. If I do not find a successor soon, the hollowing will continue. I feed on the prayers of my believers and direct excess worship to my master and his kin. In the absence of sustenance, I starve, and this place digests me.

So Ainshard had relatives? Interesting. Lev made a mental note.

"Ah, but of course. That's where I come in, I take it."

Correct. The being alighted upon the same surface Lev could feel beneath him, though he could not see its legs. *Now, let me grant you Ainshard's will.*

With a wave of its robed, billowing arm, the being materialised a document that looked like aged parchment.

Lev had heard stories in his previous life about people signing away their souls so that vague figures could grant their deepest wishes. "With all due respect, I don't think I need Ainshard's will."

Do not misunderstand. This is a contract between equals, Leonard. The penalty for breaching this contract is the shattering of the soul, and without a soul, one can neither reincarnate nor transmigrate. In a way to which death cannot compare, one would cease to exist.

"You claim it's a contract between equals, but there's a huge knowledge differential between us. What insurance do I have that there aren't any loopholes you can exploit?"

The being grumbled indistinctly about some unpleasant individuals from its past before answering Lev's question. *Leonard, you flatter me so! Greater powers than I exist, and it just so happens that those greater powers would enforce our contract mercilessly and without bias,* the being chirped excitedly. *Not... that I have personally ever observed any breaches of contract.*

"And what if I refuse?"

Then I will toss you asunder and choose another.

Lev sported a smug smile. "You can't, now can you? You said it yourself, you've waited a long time for me to come here."

I can wait for another.

"True, you could wait for another. But I'm curious—how long would you have to wait for another like me to appear before you?"

Lev waited for the being's reply, but there was no answer. Only silence, as it stared at him with a blank expression.

After seemingly eons of silence, the being caved. *You're right, I don't have that time. But you can't leave my humble abode without my permission, can you?*

"Let's see. All the abilities you've demonstrated involve memories, visions, and thoughts. I know I can project a barrier by pure force of will. I believe as long as I concentrate, I should be able to leave this… mindscape."

The sound of applause filled the area as the being chuckled. *Bravo, you figured it out. Now then, please try and leave.*

Lev frowned. The being was clearly leading him on, but to what purpose, he was unsure of. As he'd done to create a barrier, Lev gathered his willpower and concentrated on leaving the area.

Nothing happened.

Leaving is not as simple as forming a barrier, Leonard. If you wish to leave, you have no choice but to sign the contract. The alternative is to stay here and pray for the others to take care of your body for you. Will they? Perhaps they will for a short while. But as time passes, they'll understand your unconscious body to be the liability it is; will they continue to care for you then? I think not.

"I don't appreciate being blackmailed," Lev growled.

Nobody does, but this isn't blackmail. It's an agreement based on equivalent exchange. With this power, you will be able to grow stronger, gain more followers. And as you grow, so will I. The few tasks I've added will benefit us both.

"Such as?"

Just a few small tasks. Releasing my comrades, exacting vengeance upon my enemies. As you can see, I've been trapped here for a while. I'm not the only one in such a predicament. Before you ask, though, let's leave the tedious details for another time. Just know that these enemies are destined to be yours, regardless of whether you sign this contract.

"I see. So those comrades must be the figures I saw behind Ainshard's throne, right?"

The being paused for a second before answering Lev.

Yes, they were my comrades. I still require their service, and so do you.

Although the being's story did sound odd, Lev had to acknowledge that such powerful beings would definitely be useful to him in achieving his goals. The only concern was that they could betray him in the future.

To that end, Lev would need to find a way to bind them to contracts forcing them to swear their allegiance to him. If breaking such a contract would shatter even the souls of beings like the one standing in front of Lev, then surely, it would work just fine on his comrades.

Look, be honest with yourself. You're too weak for the challenges ahead. I promise you the power to free yourself, and all I ask is that you use that power to bring me my own freedom. If you sign it, I promise to not bring you down the wrong path. You will also be able to complete the tasks at your own discretion. So please, sign it and break both of our chains. The being begged Lev as it handed him the contract.

Lev pondered the being's words as he read his way through the contract a few times. After the tenth read, he finally came to a decision.

"I'll sign it."

After Lev signed the contract, the being shuddered from joy.

Wonderful! You will not regret it, Leonard.

The being's finger closed in and touched Lev's forehead. From the point of contact, a strange, electric sensation sparkled through his being. Immediately after, Lev lost control of his muscles and slumped to the ground.

Slowly retracting its long, spindly fingers, the being floated back a few killigs to observe the fallen bogey.

"What did you do to me?" Lev coughed. "Answer me!"

The being stayed silent and unmoving, simply continuing to observe Lev as he tried to regain his balance and stand up to confront the former.

I just took the first steps to fulfil my part of the deal. All shall be made clear soon, Leonard. And besides, isn't it time for you to unlock your true potential?

Lev's vision blurred as he fell to the ground once more. As the last wisps of his consciousness left him, he saw the being disappear into the darkness.

* * *

"Lev. Lev! Is everything alright?" Rapha shouted.

"What happened? We lost you for a moment there. What happened!?" Hemgall roared.

"Did you see anything?" Rapha asked.

"Don't... touch..."

"What?" Rapha looked at the gate Lev had touched before collapsing. The masks and intricate symbols covering the gate hadn't shown any signs of change.

The gate blocking their route remained unopened.

"Wait, something's off," Hemgall remarked. "The gems, they're glowing!"

Rapha glanced at the five masks. The gems in each of the masks' eyes now softly glowed, and a stream of light escaped through the carefully crafted masks and symbols, lighting up the gate before them. Much to their relief, the gate finally opened.

Rapha soon returned her attention back to Lev, who had started moving about again, if awkwardly.

"Here, let me help you," Rapha said as she stretched her right hand out towards Lev. Rapha pulled Lev up and waited for him to start talking.

"How long was I out for?" Lev asked.

"I guess it must've been—"

"About two hours, if my count isn't off," Vyrga interrupted. "It's remarkable that you didn't stop breathing. After all, this musclehead started accusing me of treason the moment you fell. When did I even have the chance to hurt you?" Vyrga stared daggers at Hemgall.

"It was only natural for me to suspect you, you fancy immoral bastard," Hemgall snarled.

"Oh look, a mangy cur is calling me a bastard. Funny, since you're also a bastard."

"Why, I oughta—"

"Can you two shut up for one minute!" Rapha shouted.

Lev straightened his back. "Rapha, let's return to the cavern. We've made it far enough."

Rapha nodded, relieved that the gates had opened and they could leave the room posthaste.

"You heard him," Hemgall said. "Orva, help Rapha out with Lev so he can keep up. No matter how many hivelings we have to shake off, we cannot lose pace on this climb."

CHAPTER 2
RELICS OF OLD

"What is this place?" Hem muttered as he gazed at his surroundings.

It had been a while since Lev and the others had passed through the gate, and after the long walk, they found a large space filled with ruins covered in vines.

Orva answered him with an excited grin. "It seems to be some kind of temple. Fascinating. How is all of this underground?"

The darg, Shahn, replied. "Sinkholes, maybe. The building's likely been dragged down over time. What I found more fascinating is how there're plants littering the place. We're still at the bottom of the monster cavern, after all. How are they surviving?"

"I believe it's because of that." Lev pointed at a giant blue ball of energy floating in the distance that resembled the one on the sixth floor. "Considering the mostly-intact ruins and the fake sun, I'm inclined to believe everything here was intentionally brought underground."

"Oh, is that a fake sun? Can't believe there's another one of those. Hearing that there was a fake sun on the sixth floor was a shock on its own," Shahn replied.

"Well, at least you're used to there being a big ball of light over your head," remarked Orva.

"True."

Orva took a deep breath, "This source must be similar to the one found back in the sixth. I'm sure of it!" she cheered.

"Keep it down. A light source like this might mean that there's a high concentration of haze nearby, and we all know what that means," Vyrga said, glaring at Orva. If she were any louder, a pack of hiveling scouts could notice their party and alert the rest of the hive. Uncharted grounds and a hiveling army were a deadly combination for sure.

The beauty of the second sun had caused Orva to forget how precarious the group's situation was. Ashamed, Orva gazed down at her feet. "Right. Hivelings."

"Actually," Lev said, "I don't think there'll be any hivelings near this temple. As I recall, hivelings make their nests by digesting and excreting rock and other such materials. The temple would've been destroyed long ago if there were hivelings nearby. Not to mention, there's a distinct lack of tunnels in the area."

Rapha and Shahn stared at Lev with doubt clear in their eyes, but his self-assurance was hard to counter.

"Seems like you know more than us, haha!" Shahn howled.

"Keep it quiet!" Vyrga snarled.

"So what do we do now?" asked Hem as he knelt near the remains of a fallen statue resembling a warrior.

Lev recognized it as one of the armoured giants that guarded Ainshard's hall. A killig, a ghastly sentinel born from the depths of genetic manipulation.

It wouldn't be surprising if the beings and Ainshard made this, Lev thought as he looked at the magnificently intricate designs decorating the few erect pillars in the patches of hardened dirt and stone. Much of the area was overgrown with vines, and the temple ruins seemed to consist of a layered mixture of marble and some form of shining stone, mashed together into a unique hybrid. Lev couldn't remember seeing a nearby vein of the shining stone, and certainly not one of marble.

Seems like these were imported. Looks like Ainshard's realm not only stretched far, but had excellent infrastructure and logistics. Because of the hierarchical nature of goblinoids, Lev couldn't imagine his kind and other goblinoid species working together to achieve such a daunting task.

They continued making their way through the decrepit remains of what was clearly once an illustrious temple towards what seemed like the centre of the ruins.

The centre revealed several destroyed pure marble statues. After taking in the mystical sight of these giant statues, Lev noticed that there were two statues still intact in the centre. They were protected by what looked like a barrier of some sort.

Lev immediately recognised who the statues represented. They were of Ainshard and, behind him, the being he'd encountered at the gate.

Near Ainshard was a smaller feminine statue with writing in a foreign language carved into the platform near its feet. Its head and arms were destroyed, and Ainshard's statue looked to hold one of its severed hands.

"What does it say?" Lev asked.

"How should I know?" Hemgall shrugged.

"Should be ancient Ainshardian. Anyone here studied it?" Orva replied.

The deka chuckled. "Ainshardian? Really? Does everything here have 'Ainshard' in its name?"

Shahn shook his head. "Only the local goblin tribes are obsessed with him, Grasha." He turned to Rapha. "Do you know anything?"

"I'm not from around here. Where I'm from, we have our own heroes, villains, and tales."

Vyrga rubbed his forehead. "Simpletons. It says 'the whore who sold her people for the affection of a monster.'"

An empty platform lay to the left of the three statues. Vyrga read the inscription on its surface aloud. "Our hero. She who cleansed us from the sins of her father." Vyrga felt a tinge of pity, though whether it was for Ainshard alone was a question he couldn't answer.

What... happened? a familiar voice emanated from within Lev. *I felt... your soul... being pulled by something... white hand.*

While Gherm's soul was stabilising, it was still mostly a mess of incoherent thoughts, but Lev could make out what he was asking.

I met him, Gherm. One of Ainshard's most loyal guides.

Guides?

Long story short, powerful beings that supposedly helped Ainshard achieve the success he did.

How... did you escape? Doubt presented itself within Gherm's shattered pattern. It was as if Lev had just told him the impossible.

He wanted something from me and I agreed to give it to him. In return, he gave me something... else.

What? Did you... give?

Nothing, actually. Only that one day I'd gain the power to achieve my goals. And his, too, I guess.

Lev felt Gherm's anger intensifying. He clearly didn't like what he had heard, but Lev felt relieved that the being had been unaware of Gherm's continued existence. Who knows what it would have done to Gherm?

Lev smiled. *I don't know why you're bothered. We can use this to our advantage. As long as he doesn't know that you're still with me, we can deceive him.*

Use us...

He won't. I'll make sure of it.

"What are you thinking about?" Hem asked, bringing Lev back into reality.

Lev felt Gherm fading back into his subconsciousness as he regained his senses. "Nothing important."

"Anyways," Hem continued, "what do you think of this place? It's weird, isn't it? Ruins in the cavern aren't new, but ruins this deep and sophisticated? Now that's something worth investigating. Maybe we'll find something worthwhile."

Lev closed his eyes. "I think we should continue this later, Hem. We need to get out of here first. There may be creatures worse than hivelings waiting for us. Perhaps even worse than that abomination we fought earlier."

Hearing those words, Hem's smile dimmed. "Yeah... better not throw caution to the wind. Though it looks like everyone's already searching for loot. Can't really blame them. Danger or not, we do need to find some supplies, especially spare weapons. Stone weapons tend to chip, and bronze ones are hard to come by. Especially without the expedition's supply lines."

Lev sighed. "Fine. Let's go."

* * *

Lev walked towards the outer ruins, whilst most of the others focused their search efforts around the statues in the centre.

Shortly after reaching the remains of a ruined building, Lev saw a foreign object glimmer from within the shadows.

Intrigued, Lev approached the object and inspected it briefly. A sense of familiarity immediately struck him, and a second later he realised why, as he recognized the crude design of a rudimentary firearm.

A musket? What's it doing in a place like this? It looks similar to a matchlock, but there's no sign of damage caused by blackpowder usage, and it's made from bronze instead of steel... Interesting.

The "matchlock" had a tube extending out of the handle that looked to attach to another nearby item. It looked like a container of some sort.

They must've used another technique to propel the projectile. Interesting.

Upon closer inspection, however, Lev's excitement dwindled. Countless holes were scattered around the matchlock's corroded, green-tinted hinges, as well as across most of the metalwork. The weapon, as it was, was nothing but a health hazard, prone to exploding in his face if he fired it.

Lev decided to regroup with the others and leave the rusted ancient weapon behind. "I found nothing. What about you all?"

Shahn grinned. "I found some gold coins with that bastard Jiira god's head engraved on all of them."

"A greenish bronze sword and three spears," Hemgall replied.

Vyrga raised a corroded bronze sword. "This, along with some gold and silver coins."

Rapha shook her head and shrugged, clearly showing her bandaged left arm. "I kicked some rocks around, but it looks like the coins are the only things worth anything."

Orva laughed while holding onto bundles of weathered leathery books and scrolls. "Maybe for you, but for me this place is a treasure trove. Sigils, ancient runes, books, and scrolls!"

Vyrga glanced at her. "But you can't read the old language."

"But *you* can. Read it for me sometime, will ya? Oh, I also found this awesome staff." Orva whirled around, revealing a golden staff covered in runes. None of the bogeys could ignore the magical power emanating from the artefact.

Lev facepalmed. "With such a relic, you do realise you've made yourself a target, right?"

"Hah, let's see if anyone tries. You all need me for magical support. Can you handle another abomination without me?"

"With torches? Yes," Vyrga replied with a smirk plastered on his face.

Orva shot a fiery glare at him. "Sure. See how you fare with torches. Just know I won't go down easily."

Lev clapped his hands to refocus the conversation. "More importantly, has anyone found an exit yet?"

Vyrga nodded. "I did."

"In that case," Rapha continued, "let's get out of here!"

Lev and the others nodded in agreement as they headed towards the discovered exit.

"There, can you see it?" Vyrga pointed at a gap under a giant banner with Ainshard's insignia on it.

"There's something in there. A way out of here if we're lucky enough."

They made their way through the gap and a metal door became visible in the distance.

Hemgall walked towards the door, trying to force it open. Alas, it didn't give in.

Lev took in his surroundings. "There must be a way to open it. Anyone see a switch? Lever?"

Soon enough they found one, hidden near yet another statue, this one with half of its face missing. It vaguely resembled the being Lev met, a guide of Ainshard, but something was off. It had a different type of mask. An inscription had been carved into the wall near the statue. Lev didn't need Vyrga's help with translating as the name came naturally to his mind. "Kram."

Vyrga leaned closer towards the inscription.

"Kram, wretched player of flesh, bone, and stone," Vyrga translated.

This bastard must've killed thousands, Lev thought as he glanced back at the broken statue, its face resembling a crow's.

After pulling the switch, the door opened a crack before abruptly halting.

"Looks like it's jammed," Shahn said, looking for any debris causing the malfunction.

Hemgall approached the door, using one of his bronze spears to pry it further open. "Looks like my newly acquired gear came in handy after all!"

The door swung open and the group exited the ruins. They found themselves on a path that sloped upwards, headed towards a bright light in the distance. Lev covered his sensitive eyes as the sun glared down upon them with its golden rays.

Lev took a deep breath of fresh air and after his eyes adjusted to the intensity of the light, he lowered his hand and gazed at his surroundings; a clear blue sky, a large valley filled with all kinds of trees and, to his surprise, a giant abandoned city in the centre of the valley.

Orva whistled. "An abandoned temple, and now an abandoned city. Guess our adventure isn't over yet."

"Far from over! Haha, fuck," Hemgall said as he took the first steps towards the city.

"He sure is an avid adventurer," Vyrga remarked, causing Hemgall to growl at his poor attempt at making a joke.

Lev sighed. "What are we gonna do now?"

With the ruins behind them and the other expedition parties scattered around the various floors, the party slowly started making their way towards the city.

CHAPTER 3

KINSLAYER

Inside Heimo's tent, sobs could be heard.

"It shouldn't have been like this," Heimo muttered in grief. "I didn't mean to kill him. Os shouldn't have died," he cried.

"It was an accident," he desperately assured himself. For a brief moment, a maddened blue glow sparked in his red puffy eyes.

"Os. Forgive me."

As he wailed, a plump blue hand patted him on the back.

"Oh, come now. You killed a brother and you're acting as if it's the end of the world. Just ask your mother to bear another one. Ah, you two weren't even related in the first place," the blue bogey jested.

In a fit of rage, Heimo grabbed his short glaive and pointed it at the blue bogey's throat. "This was your fault to begin with, Bodobert! If only you hadn't—"

"If only I hadn't what, Heimo?" Bodobert asked with glee, "Agreed to hear your proposal? Weren't you the one who approached me once you lost favour with your supposed father?"

"You wanted me to!" Heimo hissed. "Don't take me for a fool. Why else would your men treat me and my followers well and aid us on multiple occasions?"

Despite having a blade to his throat, Bodobert chuckled. "Are kindness and decency sins, boy? Many of my peers might deny it, but we're all bogeys. Our ancestors were once one people."

With a frown, Heimo pressed his short glaive even harder against the man's throat. "That's rich coming from a blue-skin, let alone one selling out his people to the goblins.

"You'd have a better chance of me believing you if you treated the others the same, yet I, the fallen son, was the only one you chose to share your *decency* and *kindness* with," Heimo sneered.

"It seems you really do take me for a fool. What makes you think I won't kill you after all this? I know—and deserve—what will happen to me once my brothers know. And I'm sure the news is already spreading like wildfire."

For the first time, Bodobert frowned. To Heimo's surprise, there was no fear in his eyes, only disappointment.

"How naive. I never took you for the type to give up before redeeming your sins."

Heimo grit his teeth. "My sins? You dare say this after all your little tricks and traps to make me join you?"

"Yes, your sins. I did want you to join my side, but I also feared that you'd be discovered by one of your brothers. I won't deny that when Oswald arrived and you two fought, I feared you'd spare him in the end. That would have allowed him to expose us. Yet, you were the one who killed him using the very same weapon you're pointing at my throat."

"It was because of that accursed vial! The one belonging to your goblin masters!" Heimo yelled.

"Which you drank to defeat Oswald!" the blue bogey argued back. "I warned you of the concoction's repercussions! You're the one who lost control, not that I blame you. From what I've heard of Gelmar's fate, I am unsurprised that perhaps you blame your father and brothers for his plight."

Silence filled the tent. Seeing the despondent look on Heimo's face, Bodobert sighed and pushed away Heimo's short glaive. "Deny it as you might. That outcome can no longer be changed. I would give you time to move on, but I have no time to give. With the previous floors cleared, it will not take for us to reach sanctuary. And when we do, my *masters* and I will need your help to save us all. For goblinkind to survive and flourish, Bulgu and his line must die."

For a moment, Heimo was flabbergasted. "What? Not only Bulgu, but his entire line? And how in Ainshard's name do I play a part in this?"

Bodobert chuckled. "Do you think I can keep my promise to set the greyborns free if those tyrants remain? My compatriots are aiming to bring the Jiira under a new order. To do so, the previous must be erased."

"The real tyrants are your kind, Bodobert," Heimo retorted, "All the goblins care about is the haze crystals. You and the rest of the blues are the ones placing us under the heel. At the end of the day, it's just the heroic blues punishing the wretched greyborns for their betrayal."

"That's why once Bulgu's gone, we'll have to get rid of the chief's retainer and his lackeys. To do so we need you, Heimo, to rally the greyborns."

Bodobert grinned as Heimo's eyes widened in shock.

"Once the chaos settles down, we will need to cleanse the filth before committing to change. I admit, it will be a difficult road even with those scoundrels gone, but they would sooner wipe us out than lose even a smidgen of control. Especially the Jiira. They'll wipe us out the same as they did the true founder of the Jiira tribe."

Heimo couldn't believe his ears. "The true founder?" He asked.

"A tragic figure. The great Ajiira, loyal follower of Ainshard, was abandoned by more than just his master. After working himself to the bone to ensure the Jiira's prosperity during the collapse, his people repaid him by assassinating him and his family. Only a few families know of this ill history, and those who know hide that knowledge to protect their own skins. In the end, their skins weren't worth more than a few drinks." Bodobert elucidated with a smile.

But his merriment didn't last long. "We're running out of time, Heimo. The Jiira's corruption isn't the worst of our issues. Don't think I'm supporting one of their factions for no reason. I'd gladly see the fools doom themselves, but we need the might of the Jiira restored to avoid a greater threat. A horrifying calamity known as Brizilum."

Heimo frowned. "I have heard about the republic, but I don't know what this has to do with our peoples' survival. They're busy fighting the other pink-skins. Besides, aren't they on trading terms with the Jiira?"

Bodobert growled. "You don't know the half of it. I may have not seen the republic myself, but during these years I've counted enough spies amongst the Jiira to know much of their neighbours and the outside world.

"Brizilum isn't friendly to anyone. For a time, they'll hire your men as mercenaries, trade with you... and isolate you from the rest of the region. Thankfully, while the Jiira trade with them, few are keen to be mercenaries. The same can't be said of the deka and darg, who will pay dearly for their actions. But once Brizilum is done assimilating their primitive neighbours, who do you think is next on the chopping block?"

A shudder went down Heimo's spine. "The Jiira, then..."

Bodobert nodded. "Then we'll have new masters. Demanding ones who might not be satisfied with just an annual expedition."

Heimo closed his eyes and contemplated the blue bogey's words.

Exhausted from all the standing, Bodobert decided to sit down and waited for Heimo's response. It didn't take long for Heimo to open his eyes.

"To me, these are all conjectures. For all I know, not a word of what you said was true. Whether it be an invasion from the republic or the protection of our people's freedom, there are others more fitting to aid you than I."

"Yet you agreed," Bodobert countered.

Heimo's expression was grim. "Father is gone, the expeditionary force is in shambles, the leaders are incompetent buffoons, and supplies are running low. You're connected to the advisors who swayed their greedy lunatic of an heir to turn back. I did what was best for my men. Now, why did you choose me?"

The blue noble grinned and magnanimously spread his arms. "Bogeykind needs a good ruler, one who's not tied down by echoes of the past and is able to make the right decisions. One who understands the true value of greyborns. Considering your education and accomplishments, you're the one most suitable to lead the greyborns while I take care of the rest of bogey society.

"Once I am in power, even if I am unable to free your people, I can at least improve their place in the social hierarchy. Your magical abilities are wasted on digging for corrosive stones. I am one of the few who understand that."

Heimo scowled. "Then why did you never ask my father? You had previous dealings with him, yet you never offered such a deal."

"I wanted to trust your father, but who can believe in a man willing to sacrifice his son for his own goals? A serpent who skinned his parents and made peace with his son's killers? I, for one, do not. As for his other sons, Bolo isn't leadership material, and Ludger, as you well know, is a fool. That one is better off left playing with his pointy sticks."

"What about Rak?" Heimo inquired. The slight twitch from Bodobert's eye and the look of disgust was the only answer he needed.

"Forget I asked. And Oswald? You could've chosen him. I'm sure that even discussing the matter once would've prevented this tragedy."

Bodobert frowned. "If only he was reasonable. He was too loyal to your father, to a degree that he still believed Vyrga to be alive. How foolish of him to grab onto false hopes. The old man's corpse is probably rotting in the depths by now."

"I'd not insult the dead if I were you," Heimo warned.

Bodobert scoffed. "Don't deny the truth, Heimo. He wasn't in his right mind. Why else would he suspect you of betrayal and attack the moment he saw us together?" I fear that unlike you, he wasn't strong enough to sever his shackles. Out of all the remaining greyborns, only with your help can we change this rotten system.

"We could end the madness, Heimo. No more madness, no more suffering and humiliation by the hands of tyrants—"

"Spare me the drivel." Heimo jeered. "You had a point until you mentioned suffering. What would a blue bogey know about the hell we greyborns live in?"

"You don't need to be a greyborn to know the taste of humiliation," Bodobert replied. His tone was colder than frost, all glimpses of playfulness and joviality gone from his face.

Heimo's eyes widened as he subconsciously took a step back.

"Pain knows no race, species or class. Remember that, boy. This will be my last offer to you. Will you join me?" Bodobert offered.

There was a pause. The two stared at each other, calculating, judging, until finally Heimo answered.

"No more expeditions and we'll live on the surface. You said the talent of greyborns is wasted in the mines, but I'd be a fool to believe that you and the goblins will stop using us as miners. I'll accept that we are best suited to mine haze crystals, but we have the right to be people, not slaves."

Bodobert giddily clasped Heimo's hand and shook it. "Wonderful, Heimo! This will be the start of a friendship that will carve out a new era."

Heimo shook Bodobert's hand away. "I have matters to discuss with my men, so now that we're done, would you kindly leave?" He asked with a frown plastered on his face.

Bodobert nodded. "I believe I've overstayed my welcome then. If you'll excuse me, I'll inform our collaborators."

Heimo didn't reply, but Bodobert didn't mind. With a small spin and a skip to his step, Bodobert walked out of the tent.

Once he was out, Heimo sneered. "Good riddance. I'll play your game for now, blue-skin, but once I have the chance, us greyborns will no longer be your tools."

After Bodobert was away from Heimo's camp, he was approached by his entourage.

"Sir, the thug's brothers found out, and are coming for vengeance," a green bogey informed.

"It's not our issue if the rodents kill each other. It'll be more beneficial if they weaken themselves enough for when the time is right," Bodobert replied.

"More importantly, have someone fetch me a jug of water. I touched something dirty," he told another retainer. "I'd have wiped my hands with my clothes, but the last thing I need is a sobbing fool's filth over my new garments."

If you dislike him that much, why did you meet him?

"Time to inform those weaselly goblins of our agreement. It'll keep them happy enough until they stab themselves in the foot. And smuggle out as many haze crystals as you can... I need to pay the Priestess of Zeja a visit."

"We will, sir."

"Good, very good," Bodobert replied.

Let's hope your predictions were right, Kathaga. For if he survives...

CHAPTER 4

A DARG'S WORTH

Through the uneven terrain of a decrepit tunnel, several greyborn slaves pushed a weathered wooden cart. The sting of the whip kept them motivated enough to keep the cart going onward, to wherever the goblins wanted them to move it.

From the path they'd taken so far, the slaves figured that the expedition force was on its way back to the fourth floor. With every step they took, they felt a certain sense of relief, as they were just that much closer to home.

That sense of relief, however, was muddied with weariness. The disastrous defeat on the fifth floor a week earlier had made it clear to everyone that the expedition was coming to an end. For both slave and master.

Not only had the expedition been a slaughterous travesty, but many leaders and commanders who had maintained the balance of power in bogey society, greyborn or not, had been slain or taken away. As a result, many groups and gangs were now mired in chaos.

Despite this, the stubborn Bulgu had refused to retreat—that was, until his advisors eventually convinced him to return to the bogey caverns. Sure, the expedition hadn't gone as planned, but they had managed to extract some refined haze and other lesser minerals on their way down.

Still, Bulgu wasn't willing to completely turn tail. Instead of heeding his advisors' advice to leave behind the lesser minerals and use the shrines to teleport the haze crystals to higher levels, Bulgu had insisted that every piece they'd gathered be brought back, by foot if necessary.

Combatting his vast greed, however, was Bulgu's ever-increasing sense of paranoia. If they were retreating, he wanted to return to the fourth floor as soon as possible—without losing a single gram of his previous loot.

And so the expedition force found themselves traversing these godforsaken, abandoned hiveling tunnels. It was a risky path to be sure. After all, who knew when the hivelings would return to these tunnels. But thus far it'd proven an efficient, safe shortcut.

Lost in daydreams of home, a slave pulling one of the trailing carts stumbled over a rock, causing the cart to tilt over and fall on its side.

"Halt!" a goblin soldier yelled as a pile of minerals lay scattered next to the cart.

"It isn't his fault! The axle on the front wheel broke!" one of the slaves pleaded.

"Try explaining that to his lordship, trash." The soldier scoffed.

Even Bulgu's goblin ears noticed the commotion behind him.

"What's happened?" Bulgu yelled, his heart racing.

"One of the carts fell over and spilled its cargo," Ruune, the newly-appointed leader of the harem guard, explained.

She glanced at the shivering slaves and sighed deeply. "Their cart's axle broke. They're requesting that we stop so they can fix it."

"What was inside the cart?" Bulgu asked, slumping back in his palanquin.

Before Ruune could answer, Bodobert coughed. "Lesser minerals from the fifth floor. Good men died protecting them during the spiderling ambush. But remember our situation, my lord," he pleaded.

Bodobert's pleas, however, evaporated into thin air. Bulgu directed his attention towards the group of greyborn slaves hastily retrieving the minerals. "Well, looks like the problem is already being solved."

He turned to Ruune. "Have the slaves repair and refill the cart. Assign the last darg to oversee them."

"But my lord, we should keep our most skilled warriors close by our side!" Bodobert protested.

Bulgu glared at Bodobert. "I wasn't talking to you, was I?"

Bodobert let out an audible gulp.

Bulgu stroked his red beard, thinking about his next course of action. The darg girl was indeed one of the few professionally-trained warriors still remaining, aside from his own soldiers, but the thought of the darg informing her people of his disastrous expedition shook him to the core.

She has enough to be grateful for. After all, I've kept her close and safe since the ambush.

He glanced at the darg walking a few paces behind his palanquin. *But I haven't seen a single hiveling since, and we're almost back to the fourth floor. The risk of her mouth blabbering loosely is too great.*

Bulgu grinned. *No matter. Accidents happen often during expeditions.*

He looked around him and found the worried expressions of Bodobert and Ruune staring back at him. "Didn't I tell you to assign her to oversee the slaves?" he finally yelled, breaking the uncomfortable silence.

"Y-yes, my lord," the new harem guard leader answered. Bodobert remained silent.

"Make sure not a single shard goes missing. Not a single shard. Understood?" Bulgu demanded.

"Understood... my lord."

Once out of Bulgu's earshot, Ruune groaned, then turned and made her way towards the darg guarding Bulgu's palanquin procession.

Once she approached Varra, the darg greeted her with a respectful nod.

"What does he want this time?"

"What do you expect from that— our chief... he wants to make it hard on everyone," Ruune grumbled.

Looking at the curious Varra, she sighed and continued, "Well, as you've probably noticed by now, a cart at the back tipped over. We can't lose more valuable men but we also can't trust the greyborn to quietly accept Bulgu's *reasonable* request either. We need you to oversee them and make sure the cart joins up with the expedition force once the task is finished."

Varra glanced at the cart. She recognized the frame of a tall, broad greyborn, accompanied by several other familiar, smaller figures as they assisted others in refilling the cart. She squinted her eyes before recognizing those figures as Rak, Volker, Molg, and Jem.

Sweat formed on her brow at the thought of Volker staying behind in these dodgy tunnels. Even though the greyborn boy hadn't yet returned her feelings for him, she still wanted to protect him.

"Understood," she promptly answered.

Ruune let out a tired sigh. "I've got to admire your strength, Varra. Just losing Rapha killed the soul of the harem guard. I can't even fathom how you're still going strong. Now go help Volker and the others. Not like they need someone to keep an eye on them, but I'm sure they'll be glad that it's you."

Varra didn't comment, but gave a curt nod in response.

Not much later, Varra, Rak, Volker, Molg, Jem, and a few greyborn slaves stood alone in the eerie silence of the empty tunnel. The expedition force, as planned, had moved onward without them.

"Volker, we don't have much time. Can't we just dump the rest and move on? I'm sure Bulgu wouldn't notice," Varra said.

"I'm afraid you're mistaken," Volker said, still focussing on carrying another batch of crystals back to the cart.

"Mistaken? How? Everyone can see that green bastard's a fool. Besides, aren't the haze crystals more valuable anyway?"

"You're right about one thing," Rak said as he inspected the ground in front of the cart.

"About what?"

"The haze crystals are more valuable than the minerals."

"Then what are we waiting for? Let's go," Varra pleaded.

"Let me clarify myself." Rak continued. "The haze crystals are more valuable than the minerals, but both are more valuable than us. Once we're safe, Bulgu will kill us if he even *thinks* that even a single mineral shard has gone missing."

"No one is let off the hook if we piss him off." Molg added.

Jem walked in between Varra and Volker and made eye contact with the former. "That includes you, albeit your punishment would be less severe," Jem said before looking back at the other greyborn.

"Besides." Jem continued. "I've been talking with the craftsmen, and that cart's axle was partly cut. It didn't break on its own."

Rak frowned. "Who would do that?"

"Workers trying to get out of hauling?" Volker chimed in.

"Could be. Or maybe someone wanted us to stay behind," Jem answered.

Rak snapped his fingers. "Must've been one of Vyrga's spawn. Probably that skulking youth, Heimo."

"Either way, Rak," Jem started, "I still question why you didn't bring more of your men to help us."

Rak let out a long overdue sigh. "All I'm saying is, my men have suffered enough already. Give them a break.

"Besides"—Rak pointed towards the general direction of the entrance of the tunnel—"we don't even know if hivelings still use these tunnels. Judging by the cracks on the walls and the seeming lack of recent spitter activity here, even if we encounter any hivelings around here, they'll be scouts at best. This bunch is more than enough to clear out those pests."

"So tell me, darg." Molg lifted another heap of crystals from the ground. "Are those odds worth leaving behind these crystals and facing Bulgu's wrath?"

"I guess not..." Varra replied, defeated. "Then I'll help load them."

"Volker, send a man to guard the entrance of the tunnel. We don't want any nasty surprises." Rak advised.

"On it," Volker answered before motioning to one of the greyborn slaves.

After some more time had passed, the cart was finally back to its maximum capacity. Volker swept off the sweat on his forehead, ready to push the cart with the others. To where home was.

He closed his eyes, trying to collect his thoughts before pushing. *Can't be thinking about Lev right now. I'm sure he made it out alive. I have to focus on the present.*

"Hiveling!" A distant voice from behind echoed throughout the tunnel, breaking Volker's line of thought. His eyes snapped open and he grit his teeth. He recognized the voice to be that of the bogey he assigned to guard the entrance.

"What now," Rak said in a slightly annoyed tone. "Who cares about a single hiveling scout, it won't attack once it sees our numbers."

"Hiveling Warrio—" The voice suddenly cut off. In its place, the screeching of something much larger than a hiveling scout moving about could be heard emanating throughout the tunnel.

"Warrior." Volker completed in a cold, bone-chilling tone.

A giant shadow appeared on the wall around the corner that led back to the tunnel's entrance. The sound of meat and bones being crushed into smaller bits and pieces now filled the tunnel. The crunching pierced everyone's ears.

"What in Mal's name—" Rak started, but stopped as soon as one of the warrior's antennae peeked around the corner.

"This must be some sick joke," Varra said between breaths. She'd never faced a warrior without the support of other dargs, and the times she had faced them could be counted on one hand. "We should run!"

"We can't. It's like Rak said. We're dead either way if we abandon this cargo," Volker placed his hand on her shoulder, brandishing his spear in the other hand. If Volker had seen her now red face, he might have reconsidered touching her so suddenly.

"Besides, we now know how those giants fight. They have terrible eyesight. And it looks like it's alone. Without the support of the smaller hiveling drones or their pheromones to give it commands, it'll have to rely on its instincts. Without a connection with the hive, it'll fight like a dumbfounded larva."

True to what Volker said, Varra observed no additional hivelings around the creature. It also displayed weird, erratic behaviour. Its antennae weren't as focussed as she was used to seeing. They bumped into stalactites and swept every nook and cranny of the tunnel for guidance. The beast was out of its element—they had a chance to beat it.

"Seems like its antennae are all that's left preventing its complete isolation from the outside world," Varra said while looking at Volker, a tinge of hope visible in her eyes.

Volker smirked, much like Lev often had. "Then let's take those away," he said before passing an axe towards Rak.

Rak caught the axe. "Got it. Its movement is much slower than usual, so I might be able to—"

What are they doing? Varra thought as her eyes darted between Volker and Rak. *Don't tell me he's going to throw it.*

In one fluid motion, Rak threw his axe in a near-perfect arc towards the hiveling warrior's antennae, but once it was about to cut the warrior's left antenna, the warrior lowered its head with speed the bogeys and darg hadn't anticipated.

Rak gritted his teeth. "So it can still sense things close by, duly noted."

"Looks like we need to get close and dirty, Volk. Even a disoriented warrior still has tricks in that insectoid head."

What should I do? Varra thought as she saw Volker nodding.

Varra was brought out of her daze as the hiveling let out a deafening screech. Like a blinded veteran it approached, searching for the origin of the axe.

Not one to waste time, Rak grabbed a spear from one of his men and hurled it at one of the hiveling's eyes with incredible speed and precision. This time, the hiveling's senses were too slow for it to respond in time— its right eye erupted in a gory mix of haemolymph and nerves.

The hiveling screeched even louder this time. It'd been injured by a tiny goblinoid. A pest from above. It couldn't allow such a creature to infiltrate its Queen's nest. The hiveling's remaining eye intensified its red glow as it focused on Rak. There was no doubt that the beast wanted Rak dead first.

It lunged forward. One of its legs pierced the ground where Rak had stood, but the bogey had already jumped out of the way. The hiveling clicked its mandibles once more, clearly frustrated.

"I hate to say it Rak, but you need to play bait a bit longer," Volker yelled. "Lead it towards the other stalactites! It might cause a cave-in and trap itself."

Rak simply nodded whilst evading the hiveling's attacks. With each missed attack, the beast grew even angrier.

The insect slammed its body on the ground, hoping to create a shockwave that would make Rak lose his balance. Despite its best efforts, the muscled greyborn still remained upright.

Rak smiled and cockily beckoned for the hiveling to try again.

Even though Rak had been able to evade its attacks so far, he'd done so by the skin of his teeth. With the hiveling's attacks growing wilder and more aggressive by the second, it was only a matter of time before one would strike true.

Knowing this, Rak glanced at Volker with an exhausted look.

Almost, Rak. Hang on a tiny bit more. Volker nodded at Rak.

Just as one of its legs was about to strike Rak, the warrior's head bumped into the roof of the tunnel. Stalactites scraped against its chitin, slowing its movement. Unwilling to have its progress impeded, the beast slammed its head forward multiple times.

With each intensified hit, the roof shook and more stalactites broke off, falling to the ground.

"We need to get it even angrier," Volker yelled as he, Molg and Jem ran towards the creature. They stabbed at one of its front leg's joints with their spears.

More stalactites fell on the ground, closer to where the mineral cart was.

"Move the cart out of the way!" Varra ordered the flabbergasted bogeys. Once out of their daze, they slowly pushed the cart forward, out of harm's way.

I need to help them. I'm supposed to be their superior, after all. Varra grabbed her xiphos and charged at the beast, much to Volker's shock.

Even the creature was taken aback by the tiny purple creature approaching it at breakneck speed.

"Everyone, back off and help move the cart! The stalactites won't stop falling now that it's angry."

Rak, Molg, and Jem didn't waste a moment and retreated towards the cart. Once there, their strength sped up the cart's escape significantly.

"You too, Volker!" she yelled as she sliced at the gaps in the warrior's chitin.

The creature had had enough of the goblinoids' games. If it was going down, it'd bring them with it. It slammed its head with brutal force against the ceiling one last time. Rocks, stalactites and dust fell onto the creature and Varra.

Volker was thrown backwards by the collapsing force. Once the dust cleared, a single antenna was visible, peeking through two large boulders. It twitched one last time before losing strength and collapsing.

Volker's heart dropped. He ran towards the debris and dug through the rocks with his bare hands.

"No, no! Don't die on me, Varra! I've lost enough on this damn expedition!" He cried.

The others rushed forward to help. Despite that stalactites and rocks were still falling from the tunnel ceiling, they continued grabbing at the rubble to find the brave darg.

"Please don't leave me…" Volker muttered wearily. Just as he was about to give up hope, a purple hand emerged from underneath the rocks.

Volker's heart skipped a beat. He turned towards his men and yelled, "Get the healers! Tell them the darg was injured. Do whatever it takes to convince them to come!"

Volker and those remaining cleared out the rubble around Varra. Once there was enough space to, he dragged her out of the pile.

Varra was in bad shape. One of her arms was broken, and the rest of her body was covered with wounds. Not to mention, there was a nasty, bleeding gash on her head. Still, she was alive and conscious, albeit barely.

Volker thought back to Lev's lessons and tried his best to apply first aid to Varra's wounds.

"Thank goodness you're alive," he muttered in relief. Tears streamed down his face.

Despite the pain, Varra tried to fake a smile. "I won't let those bugs wipe us out, Volker."

"Yeah, I know you won't. I won't either."

CHAPTER 5
A BOGEY'S LOSS

In the cold glow of the faux stars and the luminous grass of the fifth floor, the shuffling of feet could be heard.

Actually, it was all Volker's weary ears could hear as the expedition group continued its march towards the bogey caverns. Even though taking that decrepit hiveling tunnel had allowed them to cut through a considerable chunk of the fifth floor, they were still engulfed in shame and despair.

Due to Varra's injuries, she was allowed to take the shrine to the fourth floor. It'd taken much convincing, but Bulgu had agreed to let her stay in the bogey caverns and live with the blue nobles until she was healed. Though, Volker was sure she'd stay in the bogey caverns long after she'd healed. Bulgu wouldn't allow a loose end like her to wander back to her people.

Bulgu had sent a messenger to the next floor alongside Varra, supposedly to order his subordinates outside the cavern to gather more forces. Fearing that the greedy madman was planning another expedition, the remnants of the expedition force were only placated when several of Bulgu's advisors promised that any attempt at another expedition would be stopped in its tracks.

Only one painful fact remained. Lev was gone. He and Vyrga had been among those taken away by the hivelings. Volker didn't know when or if they'd be reunited. Uncertainty haunted his mind.

If not for Hemgall pushing Rak out of harm's way during the spiderling ambush on the fifth floor, things would've been even worse. Hem was the second in command, but that didn't mean that everyone would accept him as Rak's replacement. Without Rak and his strength, who would enforce his contract with Lev?

Volker bit his lip. *If we had chased the Hivelings, we could have found Lev and the rest. But Bulgu's lackeys stopping us from continuing after the ambush likely kept us alive.*

Beyond Volker's personal worries, the expedition force was very much in ruins. Bulgu's greed and poor decisions had irked even his most loyal advisors and soldiers. Desertion was rampant. Even some of the non-Jiira goblins, brought on to support Bulgu and his closest associates, had scattered; splintered off and made their ways toward the teleportation shrine. Aside from a scant remainder of bogeys, only a few bugbears, dekas, and burgas remained.

"Alright," Bulgu snarled at his men, "there's no time for slacking! Pick up the pace!"

The men were exhausted. Considering the need to constantly defend against stray hivelings as they marched, they had every right to be. The lack of supplies didn't help, either. The only remaining food and water was in the hands of the few remaining goblins. As a result, everyone else was furious... and desperate.

"Why can't we just leave our gear and minerals behind?" a green bogey near the rear end of the group shouted.

"We can reach the shrine in a few days if we keep pace without it," another one added.

Volker thought the same. If not for the expedition's heavy equipment and stacked minerals, they could've easily cut their journey time in half. Those shrines were a blessing for expedition scouts when they needed a quick escape upwards. Why couldn't they use them?

If only that greedy prince would let us use the shrines, Volker thought. *If only he understood the gravity of the situation.*

Volker gazed at the green bogey. He knew the bogey was right, but Bulgu wasn't the kind to give into his subordinates, let alone a mere bogey. There was no way for them to convince Bulgu to leave his precious loot, his spoils, behind just to save a few lesser goblinoids. As long as he brought back enough loot, he would return as a true Jiira prince worthy of his title.

But even the goblins didn't care anymore for Bulgu's loot and his promised legacy. They too were starving, searching for a way out of the grass-infested floor.

The earlier bogey looked left and right, making sure he wouldn't be heard by any goblins.

"Fuck this greedy bastard. More than three-fourths of the group has been wiped out and he still wants us to risk our damn lives like we're greyborn trash. I'm a shaman, dammit."

"Orva was a shaman too, but look what happened to her. She's probably larvae food right about now," his partner replied.

Lev's group, along with the other missing goblinoids, had been part of the vanguard. Their task had been to seek out enemies, such as hivelings, that spawned depending on the floor they were on. Their secondary task had been to secure uncharted grounds in advance of the main force. Important tasks, to be sure, but clearly ones for those who were easily replaceable.

Shamans, however, were different. Versatile ranged units, all shamans possessed offensive capabilities. But shamans trained in the healing arts could bring entire armies back from the brink of death. For this reason, a single shaman's worth was beyond that of an entire vanguard squadron.

In desperate times like these, however, everyone was just looking for a way out. Shaman or not, they would all die a dog's death if this pride parade of Bulgu continued as it had for the past few weeks.

"I'm sure she's still alive... what? What's with that look?"

"You're not serious, are you? Gods, you're as dumb as those two groups of greyborn trash and Bulgu's goblin girls."

Suddenly a giant greyborn appeared, towering over and startling the two bogeys. It was Rak.

"I don't appreciate having my intelligence questioned," he snarled as he placed his hands on their shoulders.

Their breaths ran cold as their egos crumbled under the grey giant's piercing gaze.

"I didn't say anything," the youngest of the two squealed.

Rak grinned, his teeth gleaming white from the light reflected off the glowing grass.

"So, calling us greyborn trash isn't saying anything, huh? Interesting."

"You can't kill us... Bulgu will have your head! And it's not like I'm lying. You're all crazy for thinking that those kidnapped by the hivelings are still alive! You saw the puddles of blood on the sixth floor!" the older one shouted.

"Can't kill you, huh? The way I see it, everyone's too tired to do their damn job. Maybe we should see who's right." Rak yanked their foci amulets from their necks and lifted the shamans by their shirt collars.

"Don't... Please don't," the young one pleaded.

An audible sigh could be heard as another figure approached.

"Let's end this nonsense. Using two numbskulls to vent your anger won't solve anything."

It was Volker, followed by Gul, Jem, and Molg.

Rak growled and squeezed the necks of the two bogeys before turning to the weary youth.

"You think you can order me around?" Rak said, still holding on to the bogeys.

"I'm not ordering you around, Rak. Just stating facts. We need to organise our men and stabilise the situation before doing anything else."

Rak laughed. "You already took over Lev's gang? I thought you idolised him."

Volker glared at Rak. "I didn't take over. I'm just making sure he has a gang to return to, and he *will* return."

"What makes you so sure? I hate to admit it, but snot-skin over here is right. They're likely dead, and if they're not, they will be soon. I've never heard of anyone escaping a hiveling's nest alive. Lev won't return. Not him, not... Hem."

A crowd began to form around the two. Grey and green bogeys alike stood by to watch the desperate greyborn leaders converse.

Volker sighed. "Dead or not, Lev isn't just another bogey. Even you have to admit that. And as long as we get back home safely, it doesn't matter if he returns. It's our responsibility to maintain order."

Out of the corner of his eye, Volker spotted some goblins joining the gathering crowd.

He turned to Rak. "Besides, it's not the time to mourn anyone. That will have to wait until we're in the clear. And let those two go. Goblins are starting to take notice."

Rak hesitated, but after seeing the approaching goblins, let the two bogeys go. They fell unceremoniously to the ground, coughing loudly as they massaged their necks.

"You'll pay for th—"

"Shut up." The younger shaman immediately shut his friend's mouth before he could worsen the situation.

"Good choice," Gul said with a nod.

"Now move along," Jem added.

The two shamans hastily grabbed their foci amulets from the ground and ran back towards the others, leaving Rak, Volker and the others behind.

Rak was audibly peeved. "You didn't just come here to make sure I didn't kill those two, now, did you?"

"No," Volker replied.

"Vyrga's lackeys?"

Volker nodded.

Rak scratched his chin. "Depending on who ends up leading them in Vyrga's place, we could have a problem."

"I heard it'll be either Oswald or Heimo. Is that right?"

"It had better not be Heimo, for your sake."

"Why?"

"Gelmar, that's why."

"He's still not over what happened!?" Volker exclaimed. "Gelmar was the one who started it. This isn't the time for pettiness."

Rak shook his head. "You just don't get it. He was like a brother to Heimo. Heimo's not going to ever forgive Lev, you, or anyone else who was involved."

"Forgive us? It was a battle! If Gelmar didn't want to die, he shouldn't have attacked us."

"And that's why Heimo had a grudge against Vyrga afterwards. From what my men gathered, their relations had run rather cold during the expedition."

"And what about Oswald?"

"He's been busy licking his wounds and replenishing his men's numbers. That guy is too... stale."

"Stale?"

"Cold and boring. He's too orderly, rigid, and disciplined for his own good."

"Can't see why Vyrga would've chosen him."

"He's loyal, smart, and his men are well-trained. He also knows when to pick his battles, and against who. He would've been the captain of the overseers if he wasn't greyborn."

"So he won't pick a fight with us anytime soon? Where is he anyway?"

"Scouting ahead of the expedition. And yes, he won't. He'll most likely—"

"Boss!" a thin greyborn with a short beard yelled as he ran towards Rak. After slowing to a half, he tiptoed to whisper into Rak's ear; Rak's expression turned grim.

"This doesn't look good," Molg mumbled.

"Definitely not," Volker groaned.

Rak's words confirmed their suspicions. "Oswald is dead. Butchered by Heimo himself."

"...Shit."

CHAPTER 6

STELLAR ESSENCE

Hemgall arrived first at the city's gates.

Old, decrepit buildings stood tall, reaching towards the sky. Hemgall sighed at the view.

How could anyone have built such behemothian constructions? He wondered.

Sharp black edges littered the scenery. They were made out of an unknown hybrid of obsidian and precious minerals. Its glossy surface reflected the light of the morning sun, gazing down upon the city, almost blinding Hemgall with its magnificent rays.

"Hem! Dammit, why did you run so far ahead?" Orva said exhaustedly as she and the others caught up to him.

Hemgall didn't respond. He was still taking in the spectacular view ahead, of the surrounding wonders and monuments. Many included depictions of goblinoids riding insectoid, almost hiveling-like creatures. Based on the cryptic runes they had found earlier, the symbolic legend of hivelings and bogeykind fighting side-by-side may have had some truth to it after all.

"Orva, do you know anything about these constructions? I've never seen this kind of architecture before. I know there are a lot of ancient relics scattered around the various floors of the monster cavern, but this... this is different."

"No, I don't. But the place does give off a familiar scent. I don't know how to put it into words, but it's like I've been here before."

Orva had noticed it as well. Not only were the buildings incredibly impressive for something presumably constructed by goblinoids and monsters of yore, but the buildings also emitted a low vibration that rattled their bodies.

Vyrga ran his fingers through the city's pavement. "Static background? Interesting. To think something is still active, even after all this time."

Lev slowly nodded as he took in the surroundings, which bared a vague resemblance to his old world.

After catching up with Hem and Orva, the group entered the jet-black labyrinth, seeking the source of the vibrations.

Along the way, a variety of runic symbols could be seen on short black walls that stood between taller constructions. Unfortunately, Lev couldn't make out what they meant or why they'd been put there in the first place.

Why was this city built here? What the hell do these runes mean? Lev wondered, among other things. *Judging from the cavern's resources and the shrines and relics within it, the only possible explanations are that it was built as a frontier mining city or research outpost.*

There were countless monoliths constructed of precious minerals positioned in intervals across the city. Pure haze, bronze, gold, and other unknown minerals appeared in flecks. Strangely, the monoliths glowed a fascinating rainbow-like hue that constantly travelled from the top of the monoliths to the bottom, then into the ground.

"If only we could take some of these materials with us. It's a shame to waste them like this," Hemgall said whilst observing the monoliths' glow.

"Who said anything about them being wasted here?" Vyrga asked.

"What do you mean?" Hemgall grunted, still staring at one of the larger monoliths.

"I mean, what makes you so sure that they're worthless? They were clearly placed here for a reason. They likely serve some unseen purpose"

"I have to agree with Vyrga here, or why would they have runes on them?" Orva concluded.

Lev took a look at the strange engravings covering the monoliths and couldn't help but agree with the two. "Too many, at that. I'm not an expert in ancient runesmithing, but these look like it took them plenty of time and effort to engrave. I'm sure they didn't put them in a city near an entrance to a cavern full of haze just to look pretty."

"Fine!" Hem conceded, "They're not worthless, but don't you at least wish we could take a few of them with us?"

"I do," Vyrga concurred, "but we need to find the source of the vibration first. Hopefully it'll explain why this city was constructed this close to the cavern."

"I guess you're right. Though it may also be dangerous and kill us."

Vyrga rolled his eyes. "Just like everything else we've encountered during the expedition. Don't worry, we'll be fine as long as no one with your level of intelligence touches anything."

Hem sneered. "Har har, very funny. If we were in a different place, I would've beaten your ass and ripped you a new one."

Lev felt uneasy as the group approached the centre of the city. Something was off, but he wasn't sure what.

After a lengthy stroll, the group reached a plaza positioned in the centre of the city. In the plaza centre sat a black floating orb surrounded by strange black particles.

Given that the orb was translucent, Lev and the others were able to see other materials floating within the orb. They were flowing around in an unidentifiable liquid. Whenever the runes on the monoliths glowed, so did the liquid.

Vyrga halted. "This must be the source."

Lev walked closer towards the anomaly, making sure not to touch any of the floating black particles that spawned near the orb.

I've felt this before, from when I was transported to the Being's world.

It was as if the black orb was calling to Lev, and had always been calling for him. Waiting for someone to touch it… to feel it and be absorbed by its essence.

No! Lev broke from the orb entrancement, only to see Hem approaching him.

Hem passed Lev, still caught in the orb's pace.

"Hem, what are you doing!" Orva yelled, but it was already too late. Hemgall was already absorbed by the beauty of dancing mineral fragments and ingenuity of the orb.

Thankfully, Hem suddenly snapped out of his trance and turned back toward the others. "I… I don't know what came over me."

"This thing isn't safe," Lev muttered.

"It's obviously a trap. We would have to be as dumb as ground birds to fall for this," Rapha added, catching Lev's attention.

"What did you say?" Lev asked.

"It's obviously a trap?"

"The other part."

"We would have to be as dumb as ground birds to fall for this."

That's why. Lev realised why he'd felt uneasy… there were no signs of life. His ears twitched as he heard creaking from above.

"Everyone, watch out!" he yelled as he rolled away from his previous position. A rusted bronze spear resembling a crudely sharpened pole pierced the ground where Lev had been just moments ago.

From where the spear had been thrown, he could make out over a dozen robed figures wearing wooden masks resembling crows' heads. They were a head shorter than greyborns, and they were close, standing on a rooftop of a nearby building.

"Dìon ulaidh Kram!" one of the figures screamed, only to be pierced in the throat by a rusty bronze spear. It struggled in a pool of its own blood as its body melted away, only leaving its mask behind. Seeing this, the strange creature's brethren screeched before lunging forward.

Hem groaned as he grabbed his axe. "Can't we go a single day without having to fight some newfound horror? I'm getting sick of this shit."

"You and me both," Lev replied as he grabbed his spear.

"Make that three." Vyrga deftly reached for his bow.

"We're all sick of this shit. Rapha, stay behind us," Orva raised her staff, prepared for combat.

Lev sighed. *Things will get pretty bloody.*

The creatures charged at them with fury. One hurled another spear at Lev.

Lev jumped away, the spear missing him by mere inches. In a fluid motion, he grabbed the flying spear the creature had thrown and tossed it back, piercing the creature's chest.

As the creature fell on its knees, Lev smirked. "Good aim, but not good enough."

The creature cried out to the others and five of them gathered around Lev, leaving no room to escape.

Despite being surrounded, Lev remained cool, taking stock of his enemies' positions and stances.

Only five of them surround me. I can do this.

The creatures were clearly intelligent, capable of reacting to their adversaries' moves in a fight. However, their language was foreign to Lev's ears. It wasn't Ainshardian, and certainly not any dialect he knew, from this world or his last.

Lev studied the approaching creatures. They looked frail, but appearances could be deceiving—the spears they threw seemed too heavy for their physiques. After all, the tallest among them was a full head shorter than Lev himself!

They can't be underestimated, Lev thought as one of the creatures — a juvenile judging by its size and demeanour — slowly and apprehensively approached with spear in hand. Interestingly, the approaching juvenile had a blue mask opposed to the others' red ones. The others raised their spears but didn't interfere.

Lev chuckled. *Using me as a training dummy? This is beyond stupidity. Maybe it's someone special, judging by the mask.*

The creature jabbed its rusty spear in his direction, but Lev managed to deflect all of its futile attacks with his spear. This displeased the creature.

Lev thrust his spear towards his enemy's chest, switching targets to its shoulder at the last second. The creature didn't fall for Lev's feint and managed to block the blow.

It counter-attacked, but Lev easily parried.

The two exchanged blow after blow. Impatient, the creature thrust forward just slightly too far. Lev immediately dodged and closed the distance between him and his enemy. With a swift kick to the guts, Lev knocked the creature to the ground.

It dry heaved as it tried to get up.

"Sorry. I know that I should take this seriously, but I'm getting bored of playing with you."

Though it couldn't understand Lev's words, the juvenile clearly understood the meaning behind them, and was furious. It was supposed to be the victor of the fight. Not the abandoner. Not the one who had dared trespass on its sacred grounds.

"Marbh e! Cuir às do na h-uile a thrèig Kram!" the juvenile creature shouted. The others now stepped closer, raising their weapons.

They halted, glaring at Lev with red eyes ablaze from behind their masks.

"These bastards don't know when to stop," Lev grumbled as he prepared his stance for their attacks. Playtime was over.

His opponents crouched in unison, holding their spears in an iron grip with their right hand. They placed their left hand on the ground and focused their strength into their legs, growling in anger all the while.

Suddenly, a bright orb exploded overhead. The creatures, all but one, howled in pain as they were engulfed in flames and fell to the ground, rolling to rid themselves of the fires. Two figures leaped forward, one grey and one red, and slashed at the necks of the creatures with axes. Their targets' heads flew into the air before dissipating into dust. A brief moment later, only their masks remained.

"Dr... Draoidheachd... ciamar as urrainn do Kram leigeil le luchd-brathaidh draoidheachd a chleachdadh...?" the blue masked juvenile muttered in pain after ridding himself of the flames.

Seeing its brethren turning to dust, the last standing figure broke out of its stupor and tried to run away, leaving the juvenile to fend for himself. For its efforts, it received an arrow to the back of the head before dissipating as well.

Lev grinned. "Took you all long enough."

Hemgall swept the dust off his face. "I had to deal with the others first. What even are these things?"

Although Lev didn't know anything about their language, he had clearly heard a familiar name.

"Kram. I think they were followers of Kram the Wise, isn't that right?" He smiled at the juvenile.

"Now, I think we need to have a little discussion, don't we?"

The creature tried to stand up, only to receive a kick in the side.

"Ouch..." Lev hissed as he rubbed his foot. The juvenile's body was harder than it looked. "I really need to get some boots," he grumbled.

Ignoring the snickers from some of his companions, especially Hem, Lev grabbed the creature by the neck, turning its head so it could face him.

"Na cuir fios thugam! Fàg mi mar a tha mi!" the juvenile yelled.

"I don't get what you're saying, but I can guess. You're not getting away anytime soon, so just stay quiet. Let's see what's behind that mask of yours."

"Leig leam falbh!" The juvenile struggled until Hem and Shahn restrained it further.

Lev nodded in gratitude to the two before turning back to the figure. He reached out, fraught with anticipation.

An arrow pierced the juvenile, turning it to dust before Lev could even touch the mask.

"Fuck!" Hemgall cursed.

Vyrga was the first to turn the direction the arrow had flown from and fired his own, barely missing the retreating figure.

Shahn sighed. "Well, that's just great."

"I know," Lev grumbled.

"At least no one died," Rapha said.

"Thank the gods there are no serious injuries," Grasha muttered before slapping Hem on the back, almost knocking him over.

"Yeah, yeah. Thank them," Orva said as she studied the juvenile's blue mask.

Lev took a knee next to the fallen masks and scattered dust.

So there are still followers of that ancient being.

"I think we should set camp near the outer edges of the city," Rapha frowned as she spotted the setting sun.

"Bad idea. This is their territory. We should go back to the cavern. It's the safest place we've found so far," Orva replied.

"That's also not a good idea. There could be more of those aberrations we fought inside the caverns coming our way," Vyrga said.

Rapha sighed. "Well, we still shouldn't stay here any longer. Who knows what other creatures hide in the shadows?"

As the group argued about where to rest, Lev clapped his hands to grab their attention. "Guess there's no choice. We'll secure a building far away from this orb and barricade it before it gets too dark. We'll have a night watch set up for any attacks.

"Seems like those creatures are protective of this thing—it's best to stay away from it. A building near the outskirts will also allow us an easier escape, if need be. Any opposition?"

No one replied.

"Good. We don't have too much time before it gets dark, so let's get going."

Having agreed to the plan, the group set off to pick a building and set up camp with the scarce resources that had survived their fall.

Hopefully, the next day will be better for us, Lev thought with a chuckle.

Heh, I doubt it.

CHAPTER 7
DINNER FOR THE WICKED

"Hey…"

"Lev…"

"Hey, Lev. Wake up."

Lev groaned.

"I'm up, I'm up," he muttered to Rapha as he got off the hard ground. He sighed as he massaged his aching back. The previous night, they had traipsed through ancient alleyways, from house to house looking for a basement suitable for camp. They'd then installed as many traps and alarm systems as possible to protect themselves from Kram's cultists.

"Thanks for waking me up."

Rapha beamed a gentle smile. "No problem. Breakfast is ready by the way."

"Let's go, then."

They climbed up the stairs and walked towards the kitchen to see Hem cooking. Orva was still sleeping on her rug, while Vyrga and Shahn were keeping watch through the openings of the barricaded windows.

"Ah, the lovebirds have arrived," Vyrga announced without turning around.

"Shut it, Vyrga," Rapha growled.

With his back still turned, Vyrga grinned at Rapha's retort.

Lev whistled as he stared at Hem stirring the pot under the chimney. "I didn't know you could cook."

"Everyone has their hobbies," Hem replied with a smile.

"I'm sure it will be delightful," Vyrga mocked whilst rolling his eyes.

"More delightful than your little lonely songs. Those are crap. You should really find another hobby. Oh, and don't bother focusing on wood carving."

"Wood carving?" Rapha asked.

"Hem, shut up," Vyrga muttered in an agitated tone.

Hem grinned. "Nope. Other than playing terrible music, this guy also likes to carve little figures all alone in a small roo— Arrrrghhh!" Hemgall roared as he rubbed his head, while the clattering of a copper plate could be heard on the floor.

"I'll deal with you once we're safe."

"Yeah, keep barking that, you son of a—"

"Hey. Don't want to interrupt the drama, but you guys had to interrupt my sleep, didn't you?" Orva sneered as she slowly stood up. Lighting crackled from her staff.

"It's too early for this sh— oh shit," Grasha said as he emerged from the basement.

"Calm down, she won't do anything," Hem told Grasha while turning back towards the pot.

Orva glared at his back. "Wanna bet?"

Hem stood silent for a while before turning towards her, clearly exasperated. "You wanna lose your best fighter *and* cook? Be my guest. We all know you can't cook to save your life."

"How did—"

"Fourth floor, after a hiveling attack. We set up camp and put you on cooking duty, even though your acquaintances told the goblins it was a bad idea. Bet on whether you could boil water."

Orva shifted uncomfortably. "What did you bet on?"

"I lost three haze crystals. Guess."

Orva looked down at her feet, and the lightning around her staff died down.

"Every bone in my body and ounce of experience I had told me you'd fail, but I wanted to have faith in you. I won't make that mistake again."

"Oh..." she muttered.

"It was my fault. Anyway, looks like the meal's ready. Help yourselves."

Everyone grabbed a copper plate from a battered metallic closet, wiped them clean, and sat around the table to have a warm meal for the first time in a long time.

Lev studied the plate's contents. It was a stew of turnips, onions, and some chunks of meat. "Where did you get the meat and the fresh vegetables?" Lev asked.

"Shahn found some kind of big brown rat with really long ears."

"A rat with long ears?" Lev inquired.

"Yeah, long ears with black tips. Oh, and long hind legs. I think I've heard of them before. Either way, they live outside the cavern and nobles love to hunt them in their spare time."

"A hare?" Rapha asked.

"I'm sure they're called rabbits," Orva wondered aloud.

"Rabbits are different. They're smaller and have shorter ears than hares," Rapha replied.

"Well, I didn't see the thing's head, so we can't be sure now, can we?" Orva argued.

"We can't, but I'm sure it was a hare."

"Whatever."

"And the vegetables?" Lev inquired.

Hem grinned. "I had guard duty before this. Got a little restless, got lucky. Found them in some kind of square area surrounded by a broken fence."

Grasha almost spat his food back into his plate before coughing uncontrollably for a few seconds.

He continued to cough uncontrollably before clutching his throat.

"Gods, someone give him some water!"

"Here." Shahn handed the deka a waterskin.

Grasha grabbed the skin and drank a few mouthfuls. Once he could breathe again, he sighed in relief.

"Thanks," he said before giving back the waterskin.

"Welcome. Be careful next time."

"It just took me by surprise that they don't know what a farm is," Grasha replied.

Looking at his current compatriots, Lev sighed in relief. *Good thing I found myself with reliable company. Playing nice with the others and maintaining my men's discipline paid off in the end.*

During the expedition, squads were made up of various goblinoid races, typically a mixture of bogeys, goblins, dekas, and others. Friends, family, and factions were usually split amongst the squads to lessen the likelihood of riots and insurrection. With some exceptions.

The strongest bogeys and other races were put in the same group and served as the expedition's vanguard, its advance guard. The weaker ones were put at the rear sections or in the back, serving as support for the vanguard and central section.

As for why Lev had been placed with others he was familiar with, this was likely the decision of one of the expedition leaders. The nobles, after all, were aware of Lev's accomplishments.

Grasha coughed loudly, grabbing everyone's attention. "Not to be rude, but I want—no, I need—to ask a question to the bogeys here. Do you guys really not know what a farm is, or is this guy here, just, ah... how to say... lacking in intelligence?"

Hem sneered. "Hey! Who are you calling an idiot? I know what a fucking farm is! We grow mushrooms, dammit!"

"Growing mushrooms in logs and caves is different from planting seeds in the dirt," Grasha retorted.

Hem growled at Grasha as he stood up.

"He's right, though," Vyrga interrupted.

"That we're incompetent idiots?" Hem said with a glare.

"No, that only a few of us know about farming. The Jiira just keep us under their thumbs. I mean, only a few greyborn have ever been granted the privilege of hunting aboveground. The rest of us practically beg for provisions, and hoard what we can from our starving greyborn kin."

Vyrga softly chuckled with a pained expression as he continued, "What's even more laughable is that they take most of what we manage to hunt as taxes."

"How unjust." Grasha lamented.

"Exactly. I heard it's a punishment for a revolution that happened three decades ago. They tightened the chain around our necks because they're afraid we'll revolt again. As it is, the situation is tense enough that a single mistake could send us over the edge. Fortunately, I believe that mistake has been made already."

"What mistake?"

"Bulgu. He's prideful, selfish, cowardly, quick to anger, and extremely shortsighted. Not to mention stubborn. He'll definitely cause a riot when he calls for another expedition. When the riot happens, how do you think he'll deal with it?"

Rapha muttered, "He'll use brute force to quell the riots."

"Exactly. Intimidation might tamp the rioters for a moment, but tension is bound to overflow."

Shahn stared at Vyrga with a worried look before asking, "Your leaders wouldn't allow that, right? Wouldn't you just lose again? Can you bogeys even survive another war?"

Vyrga chortled heartily. "The Jiira are getting weaker by the day. I know from my sources that ten years ago, due to countless foolish decisions and aggressive actions by their previous leader, they finally alienated the last of their neighbours, and now they're at war with just about everyone. They could have handled it, but many other enslaved tribes have begun to riot. The Jiira are stretched thin, and attrition is on our side."

Thinking back on recent events, the group couldn't help but silently agree with what Vyrga had told them.

Vyrga then looked towards Lev and the other bogeys, " Haven't you noticed that the price of food has been skyrocketing? Food prices were at an all-time high when we left on the expedition."

Lev snapped his fingers. "Turns out feeding your labourers to hivelings for your own protection means no one can tend to the farms. Have the Jiira also been losing land?"

"Barely. Not enough to shift their focus away from their continued expeditions"

Lev sighed. "Their nonchalance will be their doom."

"Indeed, but we need to get back safely first."

Hem nodded. "You want to organise your men and establish yourself to our people. Knowing you, you're aiming for something high."

Vyrga displayed a savage grin. "I want to be the new chief. Not a merc retainer for the Jiira, but the proper chief of the bogeys."

Everyone but Lev and Hemgall gasped.

"You're as crazy as I've heard. Aren't you afraid now that you have exposed your grand plan to everyone here?" Shahn grumbled.

"Hah, no. Most of you mercenaries don't care about internal strife as long as you get paid. Am I right?"

Shahn narrowed his eyes. "True, our only job is to assist Bulgu in this expedition, but we'd have much to gain from warning him of a potential coup."

Vyrga scoffed. "Oh, please. Don't act like you hate him any less than the rest of us."

"I don't know what you're talking about," Shahn replied, deadpan.

Vyrga nodded. "Of course not. Just know that you'd do a huge favour to all of bogeykind by keeping quiet about me."

He then reached for a bag and unceremoniously dumped it on the table between him and Shahn. "After all, we're friends, aren't we?"

Shahn grabbed the bag and opened it before shielding his eyes from the glow of the haze crystals inside. He smiled as he emptied half the bag before throwing it to Grasha. "Guess we are, right?"

Grasha toothily grinned as he tucked the bag away. "The best of friends."

"What about us? What can you offer?" Orva asked.

"Other than freedom? All the magical records of the chief's retainer and the nobles."

Orva shrugged. "Good enough for me."

Hem frowned. "You do realise neither I nor Rak would serve you, right? You've too much blood on your hands, Vyrga."

"I know. Just don't interfere. For now, we need each other."

"For now. Can't promise you much on not interfering down the road," Hem growled.

"When the time is right, I'm sure you'll change your minds. Now for Lev."

"Let's see what you'll offer, shall we?" Lev said with a smile.

"I honestly don't know what to offer you. Throughout the expedition till now, you've proven yourself a strategist, a fighter, and a leader. I don't know what to offer you, but your ambition is plain to see. Do you also want to be chief?"

Lev chuckled. "No. My target lies much higher."

Vyrga frowned. "So is mine, Lev. Becoming the chief of our tribe is just the beginning. A foundation for what's to come."

Lev narrowed his eyes. "What? A king?"

Vyrga smirked, his orange pupils seemed to glow with ambitions too tall for a greyborn. "No, an emperor. The ruler of an empire that rivals Ainshard's."

"Ainshard!?" Hem bitterly roared. "Have you lost your mind, trying to become another Ainshard? Isn't that kind of thinking what brought Gelmar down!?" Hem jeered.

"Please don't remind me," Vyrga replied with a tinge of sorrow laced in his voice.

Lev shook his head. "I'm surprised you'd even negotiate with me after what happened."

"If it wasn't you, it would've been someone else. My failure as a mentor and father is what brought him down the wrong path. Other than his training, I should've made sure he stayed away from Ainshard's dogs."

"Then why are you following the same path?" Hemgall inquired.

Vyrga chuckled. "You seem to be mistaken, Hemgall. My purpose isn't to merely imitate Ainshard but to surpass him. To right his wrongs. Now, what do you want, Lev?"

Lev smiled. "To change the world. There have been many great kingdoms and empires throughout history, Vyrga, and there are more to come. But eventually, they all collapse. Mine will endure far longer than any other."

"So what is it you want, immortality?" Vyrga chuckled.

"Not physical immortality, no. I wish for a legacy that will last until the end of time."

Vyrga frowned. "Don't exaggerate."

"You'll see."

Silence filled the room as the two figures stared at each other.

After a long pause, Vyrga looked to the side and chuckled. "Interesting... Guess I'll leave my offer open then."

Lev grinned. "We'll see. But that's enough talk about the future. We should focus on what's in front of us. There are still masked cultists lurking in the shadows, and who knows what else beyond."

"Agreed. So what should we do?"

Hem banged on the table, startling everyone. "Let's eat breakfast first. The two of you droned on so long the food's gone cold. You've completely wasted my efforts!"

Lev nodded. "Sorry, Hem. Good idea. We'll continue our discussions after eating."

CHAPTER 8

GHORZA

A girl twisted and turned in her sleep, screaming as her mind was ravaged with terrors and nightmares. Scenes of her parents' corpses, desecrated by hivelings digging through their bowels to feast on their entrails. She sat there stunned, just as powerless as she'd been on the day it'd happened.

She wanted to cry for help, cry for someone she should have known but could not remember. Someone who was special to her, whom she'd vowed to protect. Someone whose name she could not recall, until...

The corpses turned towards her and asked, "Where's your brother, dear? Where's—"

Ghorza snapped awake, heaving heavy breaths, her back drenched in sweat. It took her several moments to realise that the nightmare was over, and several moments longer for her ragged breath to return to a normal cadence.

Ghorza looked at the empty, raggedy mat that belonged to her brother.

Ghorza sighed and rubbed her forehead. She'd never thought that she'd suffer from such dreams again after all this time. It'd taken a year after the event for her to sleep normally, and her recovery had been in large part due to Gherm's presence by her side.

"Gherm..."

It had been months since the beginning of the expedition, and Ghorza had been waiting all this time for her brother's return.

She sighed again, got off her mat, and prepared herself for another hard day of work.

Ghorza brushed her hair with her mother's old, wooden comb, had breakfast by herself, and proceeded out the door to find Thorst standing nearby.

"Hey," he greeted.

"Hi."

"You look even wearier than ever. Wouldn't it be better if you took a day off?"

"You know I can't. They've increased both our work hours and penalties."

"I know. Thankfully you haven't been transferred to mining duty."

Ghorza shook her head. "I can't help but feel sorry for those who were."

Ghorza vividly remembered the sight of the crying girls as they'd been forced into the mining area. As Bulgu had called for an ever-larger expeditionary force at the last moment, most of the men had been pulled along for the expedition. In turn, many women and girls had been assigned to hard labour in the mines. Work that had normally been left for the men.

Thorst shrugged. "We all do. For now, until the men come back, let's do our jobs."

Ghorza immediately looked at him with wide hopeful eyes. "Is the expeditionary group on its way back?"

Thorst immediately placed his hands over her mouth. "Quiet! Don't spread any false rumours!"

"So... there's no news?"

"None."

"Then what do you mean by 'until the men come back'?"

"I'm sure it won't be long until they do."

"But what if... what if they got wiped out? What if Gherm's in danger or worse... gone?" Tears filled Ghorza's eyes as she spoke. She couldn't imagine life without her brother, the only family she had left.

"Don't worry, I'm sure he's fine. He's a tough one. Much tougher than I recall, at least."

Lev's the tough one, not Gherm, Ghorza argued in her head with words she couldn't say. The higher-ups wouldn't spare a greyborn lost soul, even if he wasn't a chosen one.

"He'll be fine," Thorst reassured Ghorza. In return, he received a hug and a peck on the cheek.

A peculiar shade of red covered his face, and he began muttering like an idiot. "I-I—"

Ghorza giggled. "Sorry, I need to go. I'm late for work. See you later, Thorst!" She proceeded on her way to the mushroom farms, leaving Thorst dazed in the middle of the street.

* * *

"My arms are killing me," Ghorza moaned as she rubbed her tired wrists. The day had been quite hectic. Despite having worked for hours, this was her first break of the day, and possibly her last.

After massaging her wrists, Ghorza stretched her back, popping several vertebrae back into place. She didn't have long to relax, though, as she immediately made her way over to the quartermaster for her daily meal. After waiting in line, Ghorza was delighted to receive two slightly stale loaves of circular flatbread, a pinch of mouse meat, and a rare treat: a slice of cheese and a cup of mushroom ale.

In normal times, only commoners and those of higher rank had access to such luxuries. It was only during expeditions could greyborns have cheese or mushroom ale. The former for energy, and the latter for morale.

Speaking of morale, Ghorza hadn't witnessed any floggings or other harsh punishments since the expedition force had departed; she suspected the higher-ups were wary of a potential revolt. Shaking her head to clear her mind, Ghorza reminded herself to forget such thoughts and focused on enjoying her meal.

Ghorza hummed a tune her mother had often hummed for her as a child as she wrapped the meat and cheese in the flatbread. Ghorza had learned this peculiar habit from her father, as he had quite enjoyed mixing the flavours in his meals.

Other greyborn bogey women arrived in the area, gossiping as they ate their meals.

In the past Ghorza would have ignored their chatter, as it wasn't her business to snoop around. Lately, however, she had developed the habit of keeping her ear out for any news regarding the expedition force.

She noticed three with brightly-coloured hair conversing out of the corner of her eye. *How did I not notice them before? The dye must've cost a fortune.*

"Have you heard what happened?" a girl with short black hair asked her two friends.

"Heard what?" the blonde one replied before stuffing a piece of bread into her mouth.

"Something about the expedition?" the youngest looking of three, a girl with long brown hair, asked.

"What? No. It's about—"

Ghorza sighed as she lost interest, until she heard the brunette girl's reply.

"Hear it? I saw it. My home is near the common area, in case you forgot. Three commoners jumped on a goblin!"

What!? Ghorza thought before returning her focus to the conversation. This was a serious issue.

"The bastard tried to force himself on a small greyborn girl, but he got what he deserved. Everyone's sick of the goblins."

"No shit. For as far as I remember, they've been making our lives hell. They kill whoever they want, steal from whoever they want, and play with whoever they want. Can't we ever have a damn break!"

"Shh! Calm down!" the black-haired bogey hushed her friend in a panic.

The blonde snorted. "'Calm down'? Oh, please, like being calm would change anything. Must be nice not to have anyone you care about in danger!"

"I'm sorry. I forgot about your brother."

"My *youngest* brother, mind you. I thought he was a nervous wimp, but turns out he was just too proud to continue the family business. So he joined a gang instead!"

"Look, I'm sorry I said that, but can you pipe down? People are looking."

"Oh, they'll lose interest. Well, except for the short girl who's been eavesdropping this whole time," the blonde answered before glaring her intense, yellowish-orange eyes pointedly at Ghorza.

"U-Um... Sorry. I thought you'd know something about the expedition... My brother's on the expedition as well. I've been worried sick."

The blonde lightened up. "Oh, you too? It's okay then. Can't blame you. Now come on over. The more the merrier, anyway."

"Didn't you just basically call her a creep?" the brunette girl interjected.

"Meh, minor details."

Ghorza hesitated for a second before grabbing her stuff and sliding into a seat amongst the group. As she fidgeted, the black-haired bogey coughed, grabbing her attention. "Well, then. Seems like introductions are in order. My name's Lore, the little girl's name is Reeza. Our wonderfully brutish and vulgar friend over here is Abelarda. Waste of such a classy name, if you ask me."

"Not as much of a waste as your face."

"See what I mean? A pity, that personality with her face."

"Not as much of a pity as your lack of a chest."

The brunette laughed while Lore glared at the now-smug and, as Ghorza just now realised, ample-chested blonde girl.

Ghorza couldn't help but laugh along. She hadn't truly laughed for months, ever since the beginning of the expedition.

"See? She gets it," giggled the short brunette, Reeza.

"Just shut up."

"Welcome to the club. We're always in need of new members."

Ghorza smiled. "Thanks."

* * *

After her short break with the greyborn girls, Ghorza returned to the farms. She worked tirelessly, harvesting mushrooms and edible plants and piling them inside heavy crates.

Eventually it came time to return home. Ghorza's normal path was a straight walk home since most bogeys, including greyborns, lived close to their respective work areas. Today, however, she took a loop around, closer to the edge of the cramped slums she called home.

After passing by the various workplaces that surrounded the slave quarters, she saw a familiar face. It was Kul, a former overseer and good friend of her late father, Gat.

"If it isn't Ghorza passing by. It's rare to see you this close to the outer edges. Are you looking for anyone?"

"No, I'm just passing by."

Ghorza took another look at the workplace in front of her. It was a run-down wood workshop, used to shape logs into crude furniture to be used in the homes of countless bogeys.

"Yeah, I know. It's a mess. Ever since they went on the expedition with that oaf of a prince, I've been having trouble finding good artisans for the workshop."

Kul was an old green bogey who'd originally been made to work in the southwestern slave quarters as an overseer after failing to protect a noble's son several years ago. Since Ghorza and Gherm's house was near the overseers', it wasn't a surprise for her to run into him every now and then.

But things had changed for Kul recently. After gaining experience as an overseer, he'd been instructed to help the taskmasters and leave the area he supervised to Thorst. Despite the change in scenery, however, Kul wasn't dissatisfied with his new taskmaster work schedule.

He'd been a warrior, after all, so changing jobs was nothing new to him. He would do as he was told.

Ghorza couldn't wait any longer. "Kul, do you know anything about the expedition? Everyone's worried sick."

The old bogey nodded. "Hmm. I might know something, but I don't know if it'll help you. I heard that a messenger arrived at the gates this morning."

Ghorza looked up at Kul, eyes wide, eager to consume any information he would give her.

"Although I don't know the exact state of the expedition force, I did overhear one of the overseers at the northern slave quarters talking about how the main force had been attacked and scattered. It seems that the expedition force is fighting its way back in a state of disarray."

Despite the many emotions swelling up within her, Ghorza kept a straight face. After all, she didn't want to bother Kul with any of her problems. Despite Kul's calm facade, Ghorza knew that the old bogey had many fears of his own.

"Thanks. I'll leave you be now," Ghorza said whilst gazing at her feet.

"Sure. Let me know if you need anything."

"Of course!" Ghorza said with a smile, trying to hide her fear as she left the old, green bogey behind her.

After a while, she passed by a couple of older looking greyborn who'd come from the mining area. Ghorza didn't bother paying attention to their conversation, as the elderly workers only ever talked about booze, women, or how shitty the overseers had been to them.

But on this day, their chatter wormed its way into Ghorza's ears.

One of the old bogeys chuckled, "Yeah, the expedition. I knew it wasn't gonna end well this time around, not with Bulgu and his underlings leading the main force."

"Especially with such bad blood running through his veins! Haha, you know what the goblins say about their royal family. Bulgu's blood is as rotten as any in their lineage!"

The others laughed, continuing their mockery of Bulgu and his pitiful attempt at organising an expedition.

"Oh, and by the way, I've heard that one of his messengers arrived at the lower gates this morning."

Ghorza stood still, frozen in anticipation. Was it her brother they'd sent? Or was it someone else bearing news she would regret overhearing?

It can't be. Gherm... Lev would never give up that easily, she told herself, trying to divert her attention to the chatter of the old greyborns.

"He told one of the guards that they lost a good portion of the vanguard. The damned insects ambushed them and took a big chunk out of the main force. A decent chunk of the vanguard force collapsed and went missing. They're likely hiding out across the various floors."

One of the greyborn frowned. "How's that even possible? Isn't the vanguard supposed to wait for the main force at each of the floor's shrines?"

"Well, apparently that incompetent prince had ordered the vanguard to stay close to the main force on the fifth floor. They didn't scout the area properly, and got ambushed for it. He's gone mad for sure! At least the previous expedition leaders weren't stupid enough to break formation."

One lit up a crude pipe. "Anyway, it's no use talking about it. A failure like Bulgu is expected to mess up at some point. If not for the nobles trying to curry favour with him, he likely wouldn't even have known of the shrines."

Their chatter soon devolved into the usual banter between old bogeys after a hard day in the copper mines. After waiting to see if the topic of conversation would return to the expedition, Ghorza decided to walk away.

After arriving home, questions both answered and unanswered kept her awake throughout the night. She couldn't help but replay the old bogeys' conversation over and over in her mind. Had it just been chit-chat? Exaggerated tales and rumours?

She quickly made up her mind. *No, they could have been speaking the truth. Thorst needs to oversee the lower gate tomorrow. I'll decide after hearing from him.* She finally fell into a deep slumber, leaving the hardships of the day behind her.

* * *

Aside from waiting for Thorst and distracting herself with her newfound lunchtime company, the new day seemed as normal as the days before, at least in the beginning.

As she was sawing the stem of a giant mushroom, she heard a commotion in the distance. Before she could head over to see what was going on, Reeza approached her.

"What happened?" Ghorza asked.

"One of the overseers was looking for you. Did you do something?"

"An overseer? What did he look like?"

Reeza replied with a raised left eyebrow. "Lazy eyes. Slim, good-looking face. Short black hair."

"Thorst!" Ghorza almost yelled. "Do you know where he is?"

"You know him? He's asking the farm taskmaster if he can borrow you for the day. You might want to intervene before he gets a blue eye due to a misunderstanding. Taskmasters don't take kindly to stalkers."

"Thanks!" Ghorza exclaimed before running towards the taskmaster's post. There, she found the taskmaster panting and covered in sweat. The taskmaster moved forward, trying to punch Thorst. The latter nonchalantly dodged to the side, easily avoiding the blow.

"Damn you! Stay still for a second!"

"Yeah, no. I don't feel like getting punched."

The taskmaster gasped for breath before glaring at Thorst. "Go fuck yourself. I know your kind too well. I won't stand by, not this time."

The taskmaster charged towards Thorst, looking to tackle him to the ground.

Thorst frowned and grumbled, "Looks like talking won't work."

To Ghorza's horror, Thorst sidestepped the taskmaster, rotated him by the arm and shoulder, and slammed him onto the ground.

The taskmaster screamed from the pain. As he strained to get up, Thorst stomped him on the chest and held him down.

The two struggled with each other for a moment before Ghorza broke from her stupor and screamed, "Thorst! What are you doing!"

Thorst snapped towards her and tried to explain. "I-It's not what you think!"

"You mean you *didn't* get into a fight with Hilger!? You overdid it again!"

"I wasn't the one that started it this time! It was— wait, wasn't Bruna your area's taskmaster?"

"She was transferred to wood gathering," Hilger growled. "Now remove your foot before I cut it off."

Thorst looked down at the taskmaster. "You gonna try to punch me again?"

"Lift it and let's see."

After a few seconds, Thorst removed his foot and backed away from the furious taskmaster. "You're not going to attack me? I expected at least another punch."

"You've done enough damage to my image. Besides, it looks like she knows you after all. Right, missy?"

"Yes. I'm so sorry! He's usually not like this."

"It's not your fault. It's ours."

"You mean yours," Thorst interjected, only to receive a glare in return.

"I mean ours. You didn't even try to explain yourself."

"You didn't give me a chance to."

"With that arrogant tone earlier and that punchable face of yours, nobody would!"

Thorst took a deep breath to calm himself down. He looked at Ghorza and reminded himself of his original purpose.

"I'm sorry, alright? I'm used to fighting my way out of stuff. It's how we do it in the mining area."

Hilger's eyes widened. "Ah, that place... No wonder. But don't forget where you are now. Violence doesn't solve everything."

"Don't you mean 'anything'?" Ghorza interjected.

"I'll keep that in mind," Thorst replied. "Well, may I borrow some of her time? I've news for her."

"Oh. I'll leave you two alone, then. We'll talk about how you'll cover my medical treatment later."

"Fine."

After that, Hilger left, leaving Thorst and Ghorza alone. Ghorza stole a look at Thorst's expression, then hesitated as her fears gripped her heart. In the end, she forced herself to ask. "What did you find out?"

Thorst sighed before grabbing a piece of cloth from his pocket. "Looks like you already guessed," he said as he wiped the tears from her eyes.

"Gherm's gone…"

"The hivelings kidnapped him, along with many others. The expedition force searched for survivors, but… " Thorst looked away, his pain evident in his voice. "I don't want to say this, and I really want to say that there's hope, but—"

"The hivelings took him… Gherm!" Ghorza broke down crying as Thorst held her in his arms and gently patted her on the back.

CHAPTER 9
KRAM'S ENIGMA

"Is there a reason we're still exploring these damn ruins?" Grasha asked. He pushed aside another stone from the doorway before them. The door led to a tall, circular building with a spike protruding from the centre.

Shahn had noticed the strange, decrepit building two hours ago. The building was more or less intact, unlike the rest of the city, but it had also clearly been made with longevity in mind. Steel poles and quality timber could be seen poking out from the holes in the wall. The building was also highly decorated; it clearly served some special purpose.

"We need to get out of here and back to the hideout," Lev replied.

"Do we really need to go back? And if we're going back, why are we searching these damn buildings?"

"Well, you can stay here, fighting for your life in enemy territory, if you want," Lev whispered, pointing at three masks which had belonged to a party of the city's inhabitants. They'd managed to ambush the patrolling creatures and take them down before they could cry for help.

Lev continued. "But many of us have our own goals. Besides, don't you want to join your fellow dekas?"

"Nope. Other than Gozzag and Ban, I hate most of the others. As it is, I don't really have any good memories of our clan."

"What about a family? A spouse? Kids?"

Grasha groaned. "You had to remind me... Again, no. I'd almost bagged one, but when I heard that I was joining Bulgu's party, I rushed home to tell my bride-to-be. Imagine my surprise when I found her trading spit with one of the guards. A well-known ass to boot."

Everyone stopped what they were doing and turned towards him.

"Don't give me that kind of look. I got my revenge in the end."

"What did you do?" Orva inquired.

Grasha grinned savagely. "Let's just say he can't have kids anymore."

"Ouch," Hem muttered.

"W-What about your parents?" Orva asked.

Grasha laughed. "Don't know 'em. Threw me away right when I was born. I was raised by a mean old man who wanted a personal army of pickpockets. That's how I lived until I was old enough to become a fighter."

Something twinged Lev's heart, and it wasn't Gherm this time. Hem's face expressed a rare pity; Vyrga was uncharacteristically silent.

Silence filled the distance between them until Rapha steered the conversation elsewhere.

"Let's continue work, shall we?" Rapha offered. "It's already almost noon."

* * *

"Almost there. Finally!" Hem yelled after pushing what appeared to be a large, fallen monolith out of the doorway, allowing enough room for the group to enter.

"Be careful. Don't know what we'll find in there."

As they entered the building, they were stunned.

Lev shook his head. "What a waste of resources."

Despite the obvious signs of decay and disrepair, thick carpets of dust, and a broken item here and there, the place still was very much intact. Albeit, a little messy. Luxurious faded purple carpets adorned the floor, almost giving Shahn a heart attack. According to him, his people had a monopoly on the manufacturing method of that particular colour.

The walls were embedded with statues and figures, many of them still intact. Fountains and vibrant waterways decorated the building.

"I find it quite classy," Vyrga mused.

"Of all the people in the world, the last person I want to agree with is this ratface, but this place actually does look nice. It really feels— Aghhh! My foot!" Hem yelled as Vyrga "accidentally" dropped a brick on his foot. "I'll pay you back double, you miserable fuck!"

Vyrga snorted. "Try me."

"I sure as hell will!"

Vyrga shrugged. "Sure, whatever you say."

As the duo continued to argue, as they usually did, the team approached the building's centre, where a giant obelisk pierced through the roof.

Lev inspected the ceiling. "This must be the spike we saw on the outside."

"Seems like it, and can someone tell me what these lines are?" Shahn pointed toward some lines running along the side of the obelisk.

"They look like connectors. Those are lines engraved to connect various runes together to perform certain functions. There should be a rune over here."

Orva looked up and down the obelisk until she spotted something. "Ah, found it." Orva approached the centre of the obelisk and wiped away the dust covering the rune, activating it by accident.

"I didn't use any mana. It shouldn't have activated!"

"It sure looks active!" Hem replied, axe ready in hand, as purple light flowed through the connectors. The waterways lit up with a purple light, and several statues' eyes glowed, brightening the room.

A sonorous voice filled the area. "Welcome."

What's that aura? And why is it so familiar? Lev thought.

A glowing purple figure with a crow mask coalesced into being, towering over Lev and the others. Its appearance reminded Lev of plague doctors from a long forgotten time back in his old world.

Bolts and various mechanical parts jutted out from the mask's glossy and detailed metallic surface. Two hollow, purple eyes shined from the mask's sockets, looking down upon the group.

The figure's robe was decorated with various symbols, the most prominent of which was made of two tangled snakes leaning over a chalice.

Kram! It was him, Kram the Wise.

Kram was easily recognizable to Lev, given recent events. After all, Lev had seen Kram's half-destroyed statue in the underground temple, and fought off the creatures that called out his name and wore masks in his image. Kram even had an aura similar to the white figure's.

"Welcome to the city of Pàrras, one of the newest frontier cities established by the great Ainshard and his followers, dedicated to Kram. Please tell me how I can be of assistance."

Dedicated to Kram. Does that mean that this isn't the real Kram?

"Who are you?"

The creature let out a mechanical sound as it processed Lev's question. It floated, staying perfectly still mid-air.

"I am this city's artificial manager, made in Kram's image. K-35. My task is to keep the nexus running until Kram's return."

So he's like an AI then, Lev concluded. In Lev's world, AI had been outlawed in the Technocracy after the continental declaration a few centuries ago. An understandable decision, given the cruel acts AI had committed against humanity in the forbidden history textbooks Lev had read.

On the other hand, they were an essential part of the Empire and its foundations. Instead of being deterred by past setbacks, the empire used the power of AI to expedite their technological progress, widening the gap between them and the technocracy's ability in that area even further.

The glow around the creature changed from a deep purple to a dark blue, and a few visual glitches could be seen reappearing on its artificial surface in set intervals.

Lev looked behind him, at his companions. They were frozen, entranced in how otherworldly the creature looked. They had never seen the likes of it before, even in this supposedly magical world.

"W-What is that thing? Does anyone know what it is? Lev!" Rapha yelped as she snapped back to reality. The creature's emotionless eyes followed her, tracing her every move as she fell on her back and crawled backwards to avoid its gaze.

The creature croaked yet again, "Fear me not. I can do no harm to beings of flesh and bone. I was instructed not to. I exist only to serve the city and my master."

Lev explained the situation for Rapha, who hadn't heard or didn't understand the artificial manager's first words. "It's not actually Kram. I don't think it'll harm us. Not for now."

"That is correct. Citizen. I do not know your name, as it is not in my records. Please. State your name," the creature declared haltingly.

"Lev. My name is Lev."

The creature returned Lev's gaze, leaving the scared goblin girl alone.

"That is correct, citizen Lev."

Citizen? This AI must've gone haywire a long time ago.

Vyrga stood up. "So, you're this city's chief?"

"That is correct."

Vyrga sighed. "The name's Vyrga."

"Citizen Vyrga."

Vyrga took another good look at the creature, walking around it. As Vyrga moved, the creature kept its gaze focused on him.

Vyrga stopped, sitting back down. "Or would you prefer to be called its king?"

The creature's motions halted as it processed Vyrga's words.

"If 'chief' or 'king' is to be defined as the leader of this city, then that is incorrect. I am merely the city's manager."

"I think he would be the equivalent of the head taskmaster," Lev interrupted.

"That would be correct, citizen Lev. Now, I assume you have no further questions and do not require my assistance. I have much work to do, much to accomplish for my creator. Moreover, as an administrator with *his* key, you should require no further information."

"Wait!" Lev shouted.

Despite Lev's shout, the creature turned and slowly vanished into thin air, leaving behind blue hexagonal particles as it did so.

A door in front of them slowly opened, revealing another section of the building.

"Hey, at least it was kind enough to open the door for us. A weird one, isn't he?" Hem said as he walked to the door.

Vyrga grinned. "That's a mouthful, coming from you. When that thing appeared, you were stone-cold frozen with fear, weren't you? At least you didn't wet yourself this time."

Despite Vyrga's words, Hem didn't look to be in the mood to retort. After glancing at Hem, Vyrga set his gaze upon Lev for a moment before turning his attention elsewhere.

Most of the group still hadn't spoken since the appearance of the city manager. While they understood the title and the purpose of the thing's existence, they'd never heard of such a thing as a city manager before. And they'd certainly never seen an artificial being before.

What scared them the most was that despite the being's ability to converse in a natural manner, it was most certainly rather... uncanny.

"Maybe we should go back," Orva stated.

"Aren't you the one who usually jumps headfirst into anything involving magic?" Hem asked.

"Yes, but this feels off. Horrible. I have a feeling that if we do something wrong, activate the wrong rune, we'll get dragged straight into the abyss."

"Looks like we don't have a choice! Enemies incoming!" Grasha yelled and everyone turned towards the door. Sixty or so masked figures were approaching from the outside.

"Block the exit!" Hem shouted before attempting to push a large, brittle-looking obelisk towards the door. Seeing what Hem was trying to do, everyone joined in and managed to topple it over. The obelisk cracked in half upon colliding with the wall, and the two halves fell in front of the entrance, effectively blocking the enemies from entering.

Lev sighed. Even he was exhausted by the constant presence of danger. "Looks like we have no choice. We better find another way out before they find one in."

"Wonderful. Just wonderful." Orva groaned.

The group proceeded through the door that led further into the building and inspected the room. Everything inside was coated in a deep shade of dark blue. It was hard to see anything.

Lev instinctively searched for a switch, tracing the walls with his hands. Then he felt it, an elevation on the wall's surface. After probing a bit more, he made contact with a bronze lever, and pulled it down.

The room came to life as a few light sources flickered on, revealing the true worth of the room they were in, stuffed as it was with relics and ancient weapons.

As the others spread out around the room in search of useful weapons and tools, a weapon near Lev caught his eye. It was a glaive, embedded in pure haze with a steel tip instead of the usual bronze, with a decorative dragon sculpted onto its socket-shaft.

Lev carefully observed the room before returning to the glaive. *This must've been the city's armoury, or what's left of it. This glaive looks... expensive. Gaudy and impractical.*

As he touched the glaive's handle, the steel tip lit up, revealing countless pure haze crystals that were intertwined within the steel blade itself.

Lev felt his senses change dramatically. It was as if time had slowed down. He felt a concentration building up within him, his senses heightening. As he looked back at the others, who were still inspecting or toying with the stuff they had found, Lev felt that something had changed.

He had gotten stronger somehow, more in tune with the world. But how? He then suddenly heard a chilling female voice in his head.

New Master... I shall obey.

Lev dropped the glaive back on the ground, stumbling backwards as he fell. As he lost contact with the glaive, he felt his heightened strength and senses fade away. *What even is this thing?*

"Hey, are you alright?" Rapha rushed to Lev's side, inspecting him for injuries.

Hem chuckled. "Must've been too heavy for ya!" he said as he toyed with a haze-imbued axe.

Vyrga walked towards the back of the room where smaller relics were gathered.

What would they've used these for? They look utterly useless.

Vyrga examined a few small relics that looked like compasses and took one out of curiosity .Orva was the one who knew the most about these relics. After all, foci amulets and staffs were based on an ancient relic design they'd found in the cavern decades ago during the earliest expeditions. He could ask her about them later.

"I think we should go," Orva said softly as she felt the air grow colder. "These things have been abandoned for a reason. We should go now."

Despite her words, no one moved. "Let's go—"

And as she was about to repeat herself for the third time, Lev's glaive twitched before blinding everyone with brilliant golden rays of light.

CHAPTER 10
WEAPON OF GOD

"What's that light?" Rapha shouted, alarmed.

"I can't see a damn thing!" Hem roared.

"By the gods! Someone stop it!" Grasha screamed.

After a while, the light faded considerably, and everyone turned away from Lev and the glowing glaive. Only once its light dimmed did they turn to face him.

"Finally," Vyrga grumbled while rubbing his eyes. "Would you kindly explain what just happened?"

Lev groaned and stumbled about, disoriented. As he'd been the closest to the glaive, he'd been hit the worst by the sudden explosion of light. Once his sight cleared up, he turned towards Vyrga.

"I don't know. The glaive decided to turn into a miniature sun on its own."

"But why would it do something like that?" Orva asked as she approached to study the peculiar weapon. She marvelled at the way the haze crystals were embedded into the metal and how the light reflected off their surfaces. She wondered how the haze crystals blended so well with the metal. It was something goblinoids of today would never dream of crafting.

"I wonder why as well," Lev replied as he grabbed the glaive once again. Weird voices or not, the high quality of the glaive and remarkable design meant it'd be a waste to abandon it. Despite the bizarre nature of the voice, he didn't feel any ill will from it.

Enemies approach. Failed, abominable experiments, they worship a traitor's feet. They must be purged, the glaive whispered, this time clearer than before.

Not liking this... said a voice Lev hadn't heard ever since he left the cavern—Gherm.

Strange presence. Shall it be purged? The glaive asked.

Maybe it's better to get rid of her, Gherm suggested. Lev could also hear Gherm's voice more clearly than before.

You're saying the glaive's a girl? Lev asked him.

Yes. There's a girl's soul in that thing, but it's wrong. She feels completely wrong.

A hindrance. Trying to weaken the new master.

Lev... It's wrong. She feels twisted. She's broken.

Lies. This one is whole. Ready to rid the world of its sins for the glory of Ainshard. For the glory of the empire.

See? This isn't normal. Get rid of the glaive.

Rid yourself of this weakling instead. He hinders you.

Who talks like that?

He must be terminated.

She's crazy, Lev!

He's useless.

Get rid of her!

Get rid of him!

Quiet! I've had enough of you two yelling and yelling in my head! Either communicate directly, or shut up! Stop giving me a goddamn migraine! Lev roared in his mind, silencing the two "guests."

"Hey, kid. What's pissing you off?" Hem asked with a worried look on his face.

"Nothing. I was thinking about something quite... unpleasant."

"Okay. You do you then. Now check this new axe I got! Can't believe that the legend of Ainshard making iron stronger than bronze was real. Well, it wasn't iron. What was it called again?"

"Steel. Just like the pillars we saw earlier, your axe is made of steel," Vyrga replied in Lev's place.

"Yeah, yeah. Steel. To be honest, it's beyond what I expected it to be! I really need to find some armour to match it. At least a helmet would— wait, do you hear something?"

They're here, the glaive growled in Lev's head.

The sound of footsteps and hoarse screams filled the previous room. Everyone prepared themselves for battle, drawing the weapons and tools they'd found from the previous room.

"Bàs do nàimhdean Kram!" screamed one of the masked creatures as it entered the room, only to receive an arrow right in the forehead.

Others of its kind poured into the room, charging towards Lev and the others.

Three rushed towards Lev in a cone formation, one holding a sword in the centre while the two others wielding spears covered the sides.

As his enemies approached, Lev felt his concentration heighten again. His opponents' movements seemed to slow as his own quickened. Taking advantage, Lev rushed to the right and lunged at the sword-wielding creature with his glaive, piercing its brain in the process. He then swung his glaive to the left, chopping off the spear wielder's right arm before it could block with its spear.

It screeched in pain, but it wasn't the loudest. The loudest screamer was the axe-wielder rolling on the ground, desperately trying to put out Orva's flames. It was about to succeed when it was engulfed by fire once more. The poor creature released one last cry before turning to ashes.

The second spear-wielder was momentarily distracted by the commotion. Using this momentary lapse in concentration, Lev swung his glaive at its now crying comrade's head, embedding it halfway through the elbow.

The remaining spear-wielder was flabbergasted as it saw Lev nonchalantly remove the glaive from its comrade's elbow. Upon meeting Lev's cold gaze, the creature lost all desire to fight. Its three claws let go of the spear, and it turned tail. As it attempted to flee, Lev swung at its feet with the glaive, cutting off the creature's left foot. It held its screams as it tried to crawl away, but Lev ended its misery by embedding his glaive in its chest.

Lev normalised his breath, gradually exiting his enhanced state. "That's all of them."

Were these creatures summoned by K-35 or did they come of their own volition? Lev looked at the piles of ash the creatures had left behind after their swift demise. He was sure that they'd covered their tracks while approaching the building, and it hadn't been long enough since they'd entered for their enemies to have noticed their missing allies.

Vyrga sat near one of the piles, blowing the dust away. He then turned towards the others. "I believe our shaman friend had the right idea. We should get out of here."

Grasha approached the exit before stepping back. "I can hear more of them ahead. Argh, looks like we'll have to find another way. I think I saw some holes in the northern wall. Let's try to pry our way through."

Hemgall smiled as he hefted his new axe. He proceeded towards the northern wall and smashed the broken stones with his axe, cracking the wall open.

"That should do it," Hem said with a satisfied grin. "My buddy here sure has some smashing force to it! Rak will be jealous."

Vyrga looked back at Hem, who was still gushing over his new toy. "Just don't break it too soon. We still have to make it back to the cavern, remember?"

"Right."

They made their way through the opening Hem had created for them and found themselves in yet another room. This time, though, the room looked decrepit and old, with nothing of value. Rocks pierced the walls, allowing rays of light to peek through.

Hem was disappointed, as he'd been hoping for more trophies to add to his growing collection.

Orva quickly scanned the room for any relic mana frequencies, just to ensure there was nothing of note.

Lev focused his thoughts on the glaive.

Are there enemies of Ainshard nearby? Miss... glaive?

The glaive didn't respond.

I guess not then. Maybe it deactivated after the fight, or maybe it needs some time to recharge, Lev concluded.

It didn't take long for the glaive to prove him wrong.

Attention, a large concentration of the failed ones are approaching from the south. Please go to the nearest teleportation device. The glaive finally responded after the initial delay.

I'm guessing that the way we came from was south. Now where's the nearest shrine? Lev asked.

A moment. Searching for the nearest teleportation gateway—it's north of here. Hurry and enter the gateway. The enemy numbers too many for us to handle.

Will do. Can't these creatures leave us alone? How many must we kill before they learn? Do they even care if they die? They do seem to have a divine duty to kill us.

They are nothing but the creator's failed experiments, abandoned and left to their own devices. Extinguishing them is an act of mercy.

What about K-35? Do you know him? Something tells me he's more important than a manager.

The creator himself ordered K-35 to allow only highly qualified individuals into the armoury. K-35 was also the sole observer of the creator's last grand experiment.

I see. And what did that grand experiment entail?

The female voice paused, supposedly forming an answer Lev would be able to understand.

Finding a way to elevate the citizens without using the creator's power. It was so that Ainshard's children, mainly his eldest son, could have a way to empower servants.

Lev reflected on what had just been told to him. *So the creator had the ability to elevate other creatures. Could it have been Ainshard himself?*

No records of Ainshard found during the final experiment. Now that I have answered your questions, please do as I advise. Find the nearest teleportation gateway north of here.

Lev turned towards the others. "We need to get out of here," he shouted. "They're getting closer."

"How are you so sure?" Vyrga asked.

"My glaive seems to be able to detect enemies. That's why it glowed so brightly earlier. The closer and more numerous the enemy is, the greater the glow." To demonstrate, Lev pointed his glaive south. Its glow intensified. Then he pointed it north. The glow dulled.

Vyrga grimaced. "A favourable ability, but terrible if we need to hide from enemies."

Lev agreed with Vyrga. If he couldn't control the glaive's glow, it would likely prove to be a hindrance in the future. Still, he had a simple way of knowing if he could control the glaive's glow.

He asked the glaive. *Is it possible to deactivate the glow when needed?*

As you wish. Either of us can deactivate it. You only need to concentrate on sealing the ability to detect enemies.

Lev did as she instructed. After a moment of struggle, the glow faded. "I've figured it out. Now let's go."

"Lead the way. I just hope you don't get us killed."

Lev ignored Vyrga as they exited the building, preoccupied with locating the shrine and escaping as soon as possible. A handful of the crow-beaked creatures would be a nuisance at best, but a horde could prove to be beyond their capabilities, even with their new equipment.

Lev was sure that Kram, as any other with relics and treasures in their possession, would have left some sort of automatic defence system, perhaps in the form of traps or sentinels... but they hadn't come across any so far.

Perhaps he was just being paranoid.

"There!" Lev shouted as he spotted the teleportation shrine. Even through the rubble, he could clearly make out the distinct pillars that surrounded the shrine's pad. They were identical to the ones spread throughout the cavern.

An orb could be seen in the distance, just a few killigs beyond the shrine. Every time it glowed, the runes in the shrine's walls followed.

What is this? Seems as if the orb connects to this shrine. Could the shrines in the cavern be connected to orbs as well, and I just didn't see them? Maybe someone stole the orbs around the time when the shrines in the upper floors were broken, but if so, where could they be?

Lev could make out a moving black mass on one of the mountains surrounding the city.

"Everyone, get on the platform!" he yelled.

"Why isn't it working!" Hem yelled as he climbed up the platform.

Orva found a strange cylindrical hole in the middle of the platform similar in shape to the end of her staff. After a brief moment of contemplation, she planted her staff into the hole, activating the device.

"How did you— nevermind. How long will it take to get us out of here!?" Hem asked as he kept his focus on the mass of bodies approaching with obscene bloodthirst.

"Give me a minute. This shrine is different. I can sense multiple shrines and its current destination is currently somewhere further inside the cavern."

"What does that mean!" Grasha yelled.

"It means I need to change the destination shrine."

"Does that mean we'll get teleported closer to the cavern? On one of the top floors?" Vyrga asked. He, like Hem, was concentrating on the mass of approaching enemies. He knocked an arrow and raised his bow, prepared to fight to the death if needed.

Orva activated the haze crystal in her staff. "Who cares? We just need to get away from them!"

"They're almost here!" Vyrga shot his arrow at one of the creatures. Even from a distance, he could tell that the frontmost beast, one wearing a purple mask with four eyes, was stronger and larger than the others.

"Incredible," Vyrga muttered as his arrow glanced off the beast's shoulder, not even breaking its stride.

"It's fast!" Hem cried.

The creature quickly cleared the distance to the shrine and tried to grab Hem's axe.

"No, you don't!" Hem shouted, punching the creature in the face with the hilt of his axe. The creature barely flinched, but it let go of the axe regardless.

The shrine quickly lit up, and the group was teleported away.

The large creature's head and arms, but evidently nothing more, teleported with them as well. As they appeared in the new space, the creature's head fell to the ground, its eyes locked on Hem until they lost their purple glow. The creature's twitching fingers settled down, and finally the remains turned to dust.

"Tch. Thieves everywhere. Even those things tried to steal my loot," Hem said as he caressed his axe like a newborn baby.

Lev straightened his back and looked around, trying to determine their position in the cavern.

"We're on the fourth floor," Orva spoke in a quiet voice.

"You sure? The fourth floor should be littered with lesser hivelings. I remember killing a dozen of them when we cleared this floor for the main force," Hem said.

Hem looked further ahead, where Orva had just been looking. His eyes reddened once he processed what he saw.

"All those bodies… they were slaughtered. Lesser hivelings couldn't have caused this much damage."

"Must've been spiderlings," Lev added. "Look at this yellow goo on the ground. Many in the expedition force must've been injured before arriving at the fourth floor. I think the hivelings followed the main force back up here as they retreated."

Hemgall sadly grinned as he recognized Bulgu's family crest on one of the fallen bugbear guards. "Well at least it looks like Bulgu got his ass kicked by the bugs."

CHAPTER II
GATHERING STORM

A few days passed as Lev's squad looked for survivors, but as they had already suspected, none survived the vile carnage.

Hivelings weren't known for leaving survivors behind, especially when their territory had been invaded and their nests burned down. Hivelings were better known for being ruthless, merciless insects that only cared for the hive and its prosperity. Still, they weren't above holding grudges.

During the first expeditions, the bogeys had tried establishing outposts on progressively lower and lower floors at the expense of the hivelings' territory and population. Once the bogeys expanded down to the third floor and slain hundreds of hivelings, however, the hivelings' patience ran dry. They began retaliating en masse, reclaiming their territories up to the second floor at the cost of exhausting their numbers. The floor above was something the bogeys wouldn't let them recover.

Culling the hivelings' numbers was a secondary objective for the expedition. It would be troublesome for more than just bogeys if the hivelings were able to swarm the first floor, breach the outer gate, and spill into bogey living quarters.

Even the goblins feared the possibility of a hiveling horde swarming from the caverns. Both societal stability and countless haze trade routes hinged on the existence of the bogey settlement as a buffer; without it, civil war was inevitable.

Lev sighed. *Sadly, killing a hundred bugs a day won't stop a species that lays eggs in the thousands. The safest option would be to get as far away from the hivelings as possible.*

"I found some water sacks, stone spearheads, four stone axes, two copper knives and a bronze axe," Orva said as she lay down her spoils in a pile.

The group had spent the last while scavenging leftover food, water and weapons from the corpses. After doing so they rested, recollecting their thoughts. It was possible that they'd find their closest allies and friends' corpses as they climbed up the floors.

"So, what's the plan?" Orva asked Lev, who was taking stock of the food.

"We follow the carnage," Lev said. "It should be the fastest route through the floors and will lead us to the others. We may be able to save some if we arrive on time."

"Lev, there's a matter we need to discuss in private," Vyrga said while gazing at Lev's new glaive.

Before Lev could reply, Hem stood in Vyrga's way with a suspicious glare in his eyes. "What do you want to talk to him about?"

"You wouldn't understand."

"Try me," Hem growled.

Vyrga frowned. "You really shouldn't get on my nerves, boy. If you must know, I need to make sure Lev and his cronies aren't going to stab me in the back as soon as we reach safety and meet up with the main force."

Hem, along with everyone else in earshot, stared at Vyrga for a moment. Then Hem shrugged and moved out of the way.

"Don't do anything you'll regret."

Vyrga gave Hem a bemused glance. "I won't." He faced Lev. "Now, would you kindly join me for a discussion?"

Lev stopped counting and turned towards Vyrga. "I would."

"Great. Now let's go."

They walked a bit further away from the group and stood behind a large stalagmite.

"This isn't just about the future of our factions, is it?" Lev asked.

"No. Guess."

Lev retrieved his glaive from his back. "It's about my glaive, right? This, and the key that K-35 mentioned."

"It's more about the key than the artefact. No, actually it's more about the key's owner than the key itself. Why did the glaive respond to you so... strongly? What are you, Lev?"

"I know your past. As Gherm. How did you, a timid, worthless member of society, suddenly change so drastically? You changed your name, rallied forces... became a deadly fighter. I'm not stupid, Lev. There's only one possible explanation—you are a chosen one."

"What are you talking about?"

"*Don't take me as daft*!" Despite Vyrga's hushed tones, the sheer aggressiveness of his words carried his voice far enough for the others to hear. "You introduced new weaponry and tools, moulded useless, timid miners into a disciplined military, and used that band of misfits to steal victory from one of my most feared followers. And don't get me started on your political moves. Your politicking is clearly beyond that of any of our kin. There's only one thing I don't understand."

"Hm?"

"You've never used any abilities, even passive ones, either in or outside battle. I can understand a chosen one hiding their abilities, but your— *our* lives have been in constant danger. I don't get it."

Lev rolled his eyes and shrugged. "Maybe I'm not a chosen one."

Vyrga grinned savagely and raised his arms while stretching his back. "That could be true, but I've come to the conclusion that if you're not a chosen one, then you're a lost soul."

Lev frowned. "A lost soul? Really? Considering all the things you said earlier about my achievements, why would you call me a lost soul? Not to sound cocky, but you know that the gods wouldn't let someone as impressive as I go free. They'd choose me in a heartbeat."

This time it was Vyrga's turn to frown. "They shouldn't, but they could. The gods are blind, spiteful, and incompetent fools. They have responsibilities to govern this world and its peoples. Yet, what do they do when their creations are in danger and their followers cry for help? They've never lifted a single aetherial finger. They simply leave the world in its suffering as they ponder how to best entertain themselves next."

Lev arched his left eyebrow. "Are you sure you want to say that? Even if there aren't any priests around, won't the gods smite you?"

He was surprised when Vyrga growled and uncharacteristically spat on the ground, something Lev would have expected from Rak or Hem, but not from Vyrga.

Vyrga sneered. "Bah. Let them do their worst, if they even exist, that is. Over the years, I've come to the conclusion that there are only two possibilities: they don't care, or they don't exist. I believe the latter, that 'gods' are nothing more than a false tale made by people to explain the unexplainable."

Vyrga snorted in derision. "Or perhaps the so-called 'chosen ones' invented 'gods' to elevate themselves above their peers."

"You take this issue quite seriously," Lev chuckled.

"I do. Is it wrong to hate being controlled? Is it wrong to hate incompetents? Is it wrong to break free of chains made of lies? What's the worst they can do? Hurt me? Kill me? Damn me? I say, so what? I'm living my own truth, not theirs."

Lev's eyes turned sharp. "Don't take this the wrong way—I really do agree with you—but what if your 'truth' proves bad for you? What if your desires and emotions trick you into destroying yourself? What if you do things you later come to regret? How can you be so sure in your 'truth'?"

"What 'truth' is depends on the individual, it depends on their intelligence and convictions. In my case, if my belief was false, all I could say is that it would be my own damn fault for not thinking things through. In fact, let's return to you, Lev. How can you be so sure what your 'truth' is?"

"I believe I've given it enough thought," Lev answered.

Vyrga grinned. "Changing the world and building a legacy, yes? Pretty vague if you ask me."

"I would be a fool to share the specifics with strangers."

"Fair enough. Even so, there are two things I want to know."

"And they are?"

"I'm not going to beat around the bush. There's no denying that you had a past life, a life before you became Gherm—"

"I'm not a chosen one, Vyrga. Nor am I a lost soul. Even if I were, that still wouldn't explain many of my changes," Lev interrupted.

"So you admit that you had a past life, a life Lev would remember yet Gherm would not. Did you fall short of your goals back then? Did you lose hope and give up? Are you going to give up here, too, if things don't go your way?"

Lev closed his eyes and contemplated for a brief moment. Then, he opened them and looked Vyrga in the eyes. "Never did. Never will."

Vyrga smiled. "Good answer. So here's what I really wanted to talk to you about. It's the matter of cooperation after we return to the tribe. I told you I'd wait and see if you were worth cooperating with. I can't deny you would be a worthwhile ally..."

Then he frowned. "But outside interference changes things. What's the key, Lev, and how did you get it?"

Lev groaned. "That would be a long story, Vyrga. One I really don't want to talk about."

"How can I trust an ally I don't understand?"

"The key is nothing but a relic from a dead city inhabited by failed experiments and worn out magical devices, including our new relic weapons and K-35. The only reason the experiments are still kicking, according to Orva, is some form of self-repair rune that can maintain simple artefacts and devices," Lev recalled as he glanced at the new sword tied to Vyrga's side.

It was a steel leaf sword, with a haze crystal pommel carved in the form of a wolf and a blade covered in runes.

It's not alive, master. It's incomplete. It has the same abilities as I, but its smaller crystal cannot compete with me.

Well, that's reassuring, Lev thought before returning his gaze to Vyrga.

Vyrga contemplated his choices for a moment before shrugging. "Let's have a truce then. A real one. Threatening you would only make things worse between us and we need to cooperate to settle the upcoming chaos."

Lev smiled. "It's a good thing we didn't have to resort to violence. We need to maintain our numbers if we wish to return."

"Agreed. And if negotiations had broken down and one of us had died, the other would be under suspicion."

"I'd be under suspicion, but I'd be able to talk my way out of it. You'd be dead," Lev corrected, earning a scowl from Vyrga.

"Let's go back already. I bet you an arm that Rak's fool thinks I'm trying to kill you right now."

"Agreed."

Their companions peppered them with questions upon their return. Both answered what they could before declaring that they should set up camp for the night on the third floor.

A week later, as the party neared the entrance to the first floor, disaster struck.

CHAPTER 12
CYCLONE

Shrills of delight could be heard. It was a joyous occasion, for a feast for the ages had arrived. A feast so splendid, so full of variety, so full of unique flavours, that none could have expected it. Today was a day where not a single one of the lizard-like creatures would go hungry.

The corpse-eaters had been feasting since yesterday; gobbling mouthfuls of flesh, slurping hiveling and goblinoid blood when thirsty, and picking their teeth on broken chunks of chitin all the while.

One of them shrieked in joy, for it had found a young one. Two dozen corpse-eaters rushed at the corpse of a boy and shrieked loudly. They liked it when the bodies were young and tender.

One began by tearing off the left ear while another bit off the nose. Six corpse eaters began playfully fighting to see who got to eat an eye, while two dragged the tongue out of the bogey boy's mouth and ripped it off.

They continued to play with their meal until they heard shrieks of alarm. Danger was near.

The corpse-eaters turned their heads and saw a group of bogeys charging towards them. One was holding a burning stick and pointing it at them. Fearing death by bogey-fire, this was reason enough for the corpse-eaters to flee.

"What happened here?" Hem asked as he bent down and closed the boy's eyelids. He growled upon seeing that one of the corpse eaters had snatched the boy's other eye before escaping.

The area was riddled with the corpses of bogeys. Of men, women, children, and the elderly. The majority were greyborns, but there were also many green bogeys. Even three blue bogeys lay there, half-eaten.

"They were all civilians," Rapha muttered with a pale face. "There are also women and children over here! I-I think I'm gonna—"

"I don't blame you," Grasha said. He patted his comrade's back as he too turned away from the carnage. Unfortunately, Rapha still hunched over and emptied her insides.

"W-What's he doing?" Grasha asked as he saw Lev searching among the corpses. "Don't tell me he's looting them!"

"Don't be stupid, Grasha," Rapha replied. "It's obvious that he's searching for someone."

"He cares about someone that much?"

"What's wrong with that?"

Grasha hummed. "Don't you think there's something off about him? Something abnormal?"

Rapha shrugged. "Everyone's abnormal in this group."

"True." Grasha admitted. "Maybe it's just my imagination. But Lev, he... just doesn't seem the kind of guy to care about anyone else."

"It'd be better for you two to shut up." Hem growled as he approached the two.

"I'm just stating my opinion. What does it matter to you?" Grasha replied.

"It's because you don't know anything about him."

"Doesn't the same go for you? I heard you 'befriended' him only weeks before the expedition," Grasha argued.

"And over that time I've found that he cares for his men. Besides, I think I know who he's looking for."

"Who?" Rapha asked.

Hemgall sighed and looked at Lev as he began searching through a small pile of bodies. "His sister. It's unlikely she's here, though. With the exception of those assigned to the mining quarters, there shouldn't be any civilians beyond the walls on the first floor."

"The corpses say otherwise," Grasha replied.

"That's what I can't make sense of, but I'm guessing either the goblins or blues forced them to mine outside of safe territory. Probably to please Bulgu enough to avoid a second expedition. If you'll excuse me, I'm going to help. Maybe I'll find some of my men, too."

The two watched Hem leave before exchanging looks.

"I know what you're going to say," Grasha spoke first.

"So?"

"I'll go help them out while you keep a lookout for the bugs. Hopefully we don't find anyone familiar... but maybe we will."

Rapha nodded. "Me too."

Grasha then joined the rest of the search party while Rapha stood guard a few killigs ahead.

As Lev frantically searched for Ghorza, doing his best to ignore the overwhelming miasma of decomposition, he heard a scream.

It was Orva.

She fell to the ground clutching her bleeding right shoulder, stunned. A figure wearing wooden armour had emerged from the corpses and was pointing his spear at her.

Is that—

Lev rushed towards the figure to confirm his suspicions. "Halt!" Lev ordered.

The figure froze before turning towards him.

"Sir! You're ali— Aghhhh!" he screamed as Orva kicked him in the groin. As the figure tried to get up, she swung her staff into his head, knocking him back down to the ground. She raised her staff high for another blow, but Hem stopped her before she could strike again.

"Calm down!" he yelled.

"He could've killed me!" she roared back.

"But he didn't!"

"And that makes it okay?!"

"No! Dammit, just look!" Hem pointed to where the bogey had been hiding. There were four children, two women, and an old man.

"It... It was an accident. I thought she was an enemy," the man groaned in pain.

"What do you mean by an enemy, Gul?" Lev asked as he approached. The figure was Volker's friend and fellow soldier, Gul. Lev remembered the guy mostly as Volker's helper. Volker had once told him that the two were childhood friends and that he'd been the reason Volker joined Lev in the first place.

"Sir... I can't believe you're still alive," Gul cried out. "It's a miracle!"

"We can talk about that later. What do you mean by 'enemy'? The way you attacked Orva, you're not just on the lookout for hivelings, are you?"

"Of course he doesn't mean just hivelings. The goblins attacked! They punished us for that greedy nutjob, Bulgu's, death," said the old man behind Gul. He was a yellowish-green bogey with an ugly pus-filled crooked nose and glowing yellow eyes. It was the old herbalist himself, Rogg.

Lev was surprised. "I never expected to see you outside of your hut."

"And I never expected to hide between dead bodies covered in faeces, but here I am," the old man spat.

"So why did the goblins blame you for Bulgu's death?" Vyrga asked.

"You're with them?" Gul yelled, flabbergasted.

"We were in a dangerous place and needed to make a truce," Vyrga replied.

"Where have you guys been all this time?" Gul asked.

"Pay attention, boy. Tell them what happened," Rogg interjected.

"Huh, first time you didn't immediately call someone a wretch," Hem remarked.

"He saved my life, so he deserves at least that much, you large buffoon!"

Gul coughed. "It all started when we returned to the bogey caverns."

Gul recounted how sustaining massive casualties during and after the spiderling ambush, the expedition force had been forced to retreat despite Bulgu's insistence on advancing further into the caverns. When they'd finally returned to safe lands, much to everyone's outrage, Bulgu had announced that there would be another expedition. They would have but three weeks to prepare themselves.

The higher-ups and Bulgu's aides had pleaded with him to change his mind. It hadn't worked. Even when the people began protesting, his greed and stubbornness knew no bounds. In the end, he was found dead in his residence, a chalice on the ground beside him.

His aides had blamed the bogeys, even though no bogeys had access to Bulgu's food and drink. The aides had then tried to make an example by ordering the death of the firstborn of every house of the blue bogeys, but this had only resulted in a riot. In the chaos, the aides had been killed by the blue nobles' guards, and the goblins' garrison outside was overrun and burned to the ground.

After this, the blues had commanded an all-inclusive conscription to protect themselves. In response, Volker, Rak, and a few other friendly gangs had agreed to prepare hideouts around the bogey caverns to protect their fellow greyborns from the conscription.

They'd planned to make an outpost on the second floor in case the Jiira invaded the city, but the blues had somehow learnt of the escaping greyborns and had sent a force to capture them. The greyborns had resisted until hivelings, which had likely been following the trail of corpses from the first expedition, descended upon the outpost.

"Why were you hiding among the corpses?" Grasha interrupted, receiving a sneer from Rogg.

"I'm sorry, did the boy finish?"

"No—"

"Then be a good oaf and shut up!" Rogg snapped. "Now go on, kid."

Gul hastily nodded. "Yes, we had to fend off both nobles and hivelings. It was a slaughter... They just kept coming."

Rogg took a swig from a clay water bottle he had stowed in his rucksack. "To answer your earlier question, deka, the few of us left here survived that last wave of reinforcements only by burying ourselves among the corpses. We heard some footsteps, followed by screams, orders, battle cries, and screeches. Then you showed up and now here we are."

Hem nodded. "It's a good thing you managed to survive."

Rogg nodded. "Aye, it's a miracle if I say so. There was a safer location to hide in, with some old connections of mine, but worthless apprentice or not, I offered it to my son. Hermit must survive so that our kin doesn't die out."

Lev nodded and turned towards Gul. "Is Ghorza safe?"

Gul averted his gaze.

"Gul? My sister is safe, right?" Lev stiffly spoke.

"She is, sir."

"Then why did you hesitate? Did something happen?" Lev asked, a sense of worry lingering in his voice. He could also feel Gherm stirring inside of him, panicking.

"We couldn't hide everyone. Thorst refused to hide, and Ghorza would have followed him if he hadn't stopped her."

"Thorst? What does this have to do with Thorst? Did he finally confess?" Lev asked.

"Thorst? That easy-going overseer?" Hem asked.

"He's always had a thing for Ghorza."

"Huh."

Lev sighed as he calmed down and felt Gherm calm down along with him. "I guess we need to hurry."

"You're going there? It's hell! I bet it's even safer in the monster caverns at this point!" Rogg yelled.

"I doubt that," Shahn remarked.

"We need to lead our men," Lev replied matter of factly.

Hem nodded. "I can't leave Rak by himself now, can I?"

"I also need to regroup with my men." Vyrga explained.

"What about everyone else?" Gul asked, glancing at each of the members of their ragtag expedition survival group.

"Well, I think I'm gonna stay. Don't want to know if my people joined the war against you guys," Grasha replied.

Shahn nodded. "I will stay as well. Although I made a deal with Vyrga and the Jiira have not been kind to my people, this is not my fight. I wish you the best of luck."

Rapha showed her bandaged left arm. "I can't fight like this, so I'm staying. I'm sorry Lev."

Orva nodded. "Someone needs to take care of her, and I didn't get out of that mess just to dive right in another."

Lev revealed a grin. "Don't worry, we'll pick everyone up once the dust has settled."

"Aren't you worried about hivelings?" Hem asked those who decided to stay.

Grasha grinned. "Look at all these dead hivelings! Besides, with our new weapons and tools, I'm sure we'll be able to handle any that wander up here."

"We could use your help in convincing your people."

Grasha awkwardly coughed. "I-I'd rather not. Trust me when I say that depending on who's in charge, I might make matters worse. More importantly, I advise you to think of a way to avoid your nobles' dogs. Hivelings can't confiscate your weapons and send you on suicide missions, but the blue bastards can. "

"Hmm, good point. Our weapons and tools will be an issue," Hem mumbled. He didn't want the nobles to confiscate his axe, and their little band of fighters wouldn't be able to fight against either army

"We just need to smuggle them. And I'm sure he can do that quite easily." Lev turned to Vyrga.

Hem stared at Lev as if he had just grown another head. "You trust that sly bastard with our stuff?"

Vyrga frowned. "Seems we're back to the usual, aren't we?"

Hem shrugged. "Insults and past grievances aside, can you blame me? Our factions are rivals."

"But our collective survival is at stake here. We'll need to put our grievances aside for the time being."

"For the time being," Hem grumbled.

"So let's go."

"Wait, wait! What about me?" Gul yelled. As everyone turned to him, he realised just how loudly he'd spoken. "Um, sorry sir. But really, what about me?"

Lev patted him on the shoulder. "You've done well keeping yourself and the others alive."

"Thank you, sir."

Lev smiled. "No problem. For now, your new order is to stay here and help Grasha and Shahn establish a safe house. Unless you want to join the fight."

"No, sir," Gul muttered.

"Very well then. We need to go."

"Please take care of Volker. He's like a brother to me."

"You didn't have to ask. I've taken quite a liking to the kid."

The kid? Gul paused. *But isn't Lev only a year or so older? At least he looks that way.*

"Thank you. Really, thank you," Gul added as he broke out of his confusion.

"That's my job," Lev replied before turning towards Hem and Vyrga. "Let's go."

CHAPTER 13
GREEN MENACE

Goblin cries filled the air as lead bullets rained from above. All the goblins needed to reclaim the outpost and regain access to the cavern was to beat some poorly armed bogeys. With the recent losses during and after the expedition, the bogeys struggled to rearm themselves properly.

Greyborn, with the exception of those belonging to the more prosperous gangs, only had stone and wood to arm themselves with. Some of the richer greens and most of the blues still had bronze weapons stashed away, but they didn't have enough fighting experience to handle them properly.

For the goblins, it should have been an easy job.

Many greyborns, as the grunts of the expedition, had been killed or injured. It was mostly inexperienced greens and a heavily weakened blue nobility who stood in their way. So how were these lower goblinoids fending off their advances?

The answer was simple—terrain, training, discipline, and numbers. If a full Jiira army had descended upon the bogey settlement, the battle would have ended the same day it began. But the Jiira had only sent a token force of goblins, sourced from nearby villages.

Worse yet, this ragtag crew of goblins had to siege a position far above them.

If the bogeys were to have the time to buttress their position, even the Jiira's main force would have a hard time sieging it. So when the goblins had arrived at the battlegrounds, they'd immediately sent a messenger to the clan for reinforcements. They'd also decided to regularly attack the bogey encampments and push them back so that their enemies would be unable to stay at a single outpost and properly reinforce it.

The battle was an orchestra of madness, with the two sides trading blows for days on end. The Jiira continuously, viciously, charged at their enemy's defences. The bogeys did their best to defend the few outposts they had managed to secure beforehand.

The blue nobles had forcefully conscripted Rak and Volker, stationing them at the outpost near the southwestern entrances of the cavern. Here, the two greyborn had finally encountered the glowing ball of light, which was called the sun. It was perched in the endless blue expanse, which they'd only peeked at through the scant skyholes in the cavern.

Rak, Volker, and their men were amazed by the natural beauty of the woodlands outside of the cavern and the mountain in which it was nestled. Comparatively, even though it was heavily praised by the best greyborn storytellers, the forest on the sixth floor seemed like a cheap imitation. No wonder their ancestors had worshipped the outside world before the goblins had taken power. The ancient tales of pre-cavern bogeys, about nature gods influencing the world around them, finally made a tad more sense.

"How many heads can you make out?" Rak asked as he and his men sharpened crude wooden stakes. They needed them to reinforce the barricades around their outposts.

"About forty-five goblins," Volker replied.

Rak rubbed his chin. "Not much, if you ask me. We have about sixty men with us. Forty of mine, twenty yours."

Volker sighed. "You had to remind me, didn't you? I wish I could've convinced the others to stay."

Shortly before Bulgu had declared what would turn out to be his final announcement, many of Lev's surviving followers had abandoned the faction. Only twenty from that original group had stuck with Volker.

"Don't blame yourself. They only joined because of Lev, so it's no wonder they left when they did. Think about it this way. Now you know who's loyal to you."

"Not to be rude, but it's weird that you're being this nice to us."

Rak smiled. "Well, you and your men have proven yourselves on multiple occasions, especially against the hivelings. It's nice having you and your men here to watch my back. It'll be even better if you all join me after this mess passes."

Volker groaned and side-eyed the gigantic greyborn. "I really don't want to repeat myself. I'm not joining you, Rak. I'm waiting for Lev's return."

Rak sighed. "He's dead, Volker. As is Hem."

"We don't know for certain yet. They're not the type to die easily."

Rak rubbed his forehead. "Hold onto that hope, kid. Wish I could do the same. For now, let's beat back these green knobs."

"Won't be easy."

"Hah. I've worked with them before, so trust me. It will be easy. We outnumber them three to two, their forces are spread out trying to breach multiple entrances, they haven't bothered bringing in any decent ranged units, and most are just charging in like idiots. More importantly, we can count to twenty without resorting to our fingers and toes."

Volker suppressed a chuckle. "Dumb as they are, they're far better armed than us. Those blue bastards kept all the good weapons for themselves. While it's a miracle they spared us some bronze and copper weapons, the goblins down there are plated in full bronze."

He turned back to the goblins. Their lustrous bronze weapons, shields, and helmets reflected the light of the blaze that progressively engulfed outpost after outpost, mirroring their advance towards Rak and Volker.

Volker sighed. "Rak, make sure your guys use their stakes to build a barricade. Those glorified sticks are going to be useless in battle. Wish those bastards at least gave us enough to build proper traps."

Rak frowned. "I'll make sure they do but what did you expect for our equipment? It's common sense for the blues to ensure the ones they can trust the most are best-armed. They could care less about commoners, nevermind greyborn like us."

"Moreover." Rak added. "It's in their best interest to give us just enough of their scraps so they can take us out along with the Jiira. To them, we're just pests."

"What do you mean?" Volker asked, still too occupied with the sight of the frenzied goblins approaching their outpost, slaughtering anyone on their path.

"We're angry, and they know it. After this battle, what are the chances the green commoners and greyborns don't turn their backs on the blues?" Rak grabbed a bronze-headed pike and firmly clenched it in his left hand. "The last thing they need is for us to have the equipment to bring the fight to them. It's in their best interest to give us... these."

"Then why bother giving us bronze weapons?" Volker cut in, only half paying attention to Rak's rant.

"We're a small exception. We're gang leaders. We hold our men's loyalty in our hands. But even these weapons are a double-edged sword for them."

Volker suppressed another chuckle. "Clever. I certainly wish we had swords."

"Hey, I'm serious here. Remember that greyborn who became a commoner after he performed valiantly in battle?"

"Yeah. He moved to the commoners' area, became a guard, suddenly had the money to feed and clothe his entire family. Not merits, mind you. I remember he left his old friends in the dirt... didn't they find his body in an alley a few streets away from the mining quarters?"

Rak sighed. "It's all a trick to keep us where they want us. Both on expeditions and here, right now, against the Jiira." Rak turned back to the approaching goblins. "But we'll crush them. Their equipment may be better, but they're still a sloppy mess of undisciplined numbskulls. Besides, there's nothing stopping us from snatching some of that fancy equipment off their corpses."

"You know we've been doing well because they sent one of their weakest forces here, right? The other entrances are under siege too," Volker said.

"Like I said earlier, the numbskulls spread themselves too thin. At the very least, this is proof that their commanders are foolish. If I were them, I would have tested each of the entrances to find which was the worst-defended, then forced my way in from there. Attacking all of the entrances at once and hoping for the best is incredibly stupid."

Volker pointed behind him. "Look at the cave entrance we're guarding. It's too small for a large force to fight efficiently in. And each entrance leads to a chokepoint that connects to five other entrances, three minor and two major. Not to mention, all the entrances are pretty well guarded."

Rak hummed. "Guess you're right. In that case, I'd need to occupy at least one major and two minor entrances. I'd use my main force to keep the enemy in the major entrance at bay and send two smaller forces to use the minor entrances to harass the enemy."

Volker interrupted Rak's thoughts with a poke. "Well, think of your strategies later. They're getting a bit too close now."

Rak grinned viciously at the sight of the approaching goblins. "Are your men ready?" he asked with a toothy grin.

Volker nodded.

"Barrels!" Volker barked at his soldiers. Five men toward the back of their defensive formation set aside their slings and prepared to deploy the barrels. Down the barrels went, down the slope and over the edge, arcing gracefully before breaking and splashing dark, viscous liquid all over the advancing Jiira.

This one's for you, sir, wherever you are, Volker thought.

Next came the torches. As the Jiira front line collapsed, Volker wondered briefly how many of the Jiira guards had ever encountered cyfrac oil.

The front line of the Jiira screamed and wailed as they were cooked alive. Those fortunate to have avoided the oil and flames backed off, fearful.

For good reason, too.

"Say hello to Bulgu for me!" Rak spat towards the dying men. Cocky with triumph, he turned to Volker. "Told you it would be easy. They lost six men in an instant. Ah, actually, it seems that they've six new friends…"

Rak and Volker examined the newcomers from their defensive post. Although they didn't say it, the two were rather dismayed. If goblins continued to arrive, it would be damn near impossible to continuously defend their outpost.

The six new goblins had creeped out of the nearby forest, wielding unusually shaped, large, bow-like staves, complete with stocks and a sizable stand.

Even from a distance, the duo could tell that the mysterious weapons were made using multiple components, mainly wood, bone, and bronze.

"What are they up to?" Volker asked.

They watched as the goblins fiddled with the bronze parts of the weapons. They extended the middle section, pointed the weapon towards the ground, then pressed their weight on it.

Volker realised quickly what the weapons were for. "They're archers! Take them out!"

Rak, however, remained silent as he watched the six goblins attach strings to their strange weapons.

Lead bullets flew from the bogeys' slings towards the goblins, killing two. The remaining three enemy archers managed to run and hide behind nearby rocks.

Volker hummed. "Guess that's over with. They'll have to redraw their bow—"

A large object whizzed past him. Two more slammed into their men's shields, knocking them down in the process.

What just happened! Volker spun, wide-eyed, toward one of the shieldbearers who'd been hit. The shieldbearer wasn't injured, but had been knocked out from the impact force of the projectile. Two men in the back of the formation dragged him away to safety. Volker dashed after them to examine his fallen ally.

There were cracks in his wooden armour slightly above the navel with his supposedly sturdy shield was pierced by a large, almost javelin-like arrow.

The goblins cheered, having penetrated their enemy's shield wall. After a brief moment to enjoy their success, the goblins formed up for another charge.

"This doesn't look good," Volker muttered.

Rak stepped forward, weapon and shield at the ready. "Guess you were right. It won't be so easy after all. Men, it's time to make them bleed!"

"Raaaaaaghhh!" his men cried back in unison.

Volker grabbed his own spear and prepared himself for combat. "Men, keep throwing those barrels! Don't stop until they're within thirty killigs!"

We won't go down easily...

No, we'll win!

The real battle had finally begun.

CHAPTER 14
TURNING TIDES

Warcries filled the area as the sun hung over the cavern. Goblin swords and axes hammered against bogey shields, loud thuds filling the air. The ranged units weren't free either as greyborn slingers flung their lead projectiles towards the rear of the goblins' formation and towards the goblin archers wielding the large, complex, bow-like weapons that shot giant arrows.

During the battle so far, the bogeys had lost six men while the Jiira goblins had lost fourteen, mostly thanks to the barrels, torches, and the resulting fire fields.

However, the giant arrows were proving troublesome. As another twang sounded through the battlefield, another greyborn shieldbearer fell.

"We need to get those archers!" Volker shouted.

"What do you want me to do, charge them?" Rak yelled as he thrust his pike through a goblin's eye, piercing his brain.

He wanted to use his axe, but he had to do his part in the battle. As much as he would have loved to jump over the shield wall and get into a brawl with the goblins, he knew he needed to stay safe and command his men. Volker may have earned Rak's respect, but the boy had yet to earn the respect and obeisance of his men.

"We need to get to those archers and kill them already! Our slings can't get close enough to shoot them anymore!" Volker yelled.

The goblin archers learned from the greyborn's initial volley of lead bullets, and with the help of their comrades, dragged their heavy bows and hid them under the protection of the trees.

"What the hell am I supposed to do about it!" Rak roared in rage as another one of his men fell victim to the enemies' bows.

"Just hold out until our reinforcements come! I sent a guy to call for help!" Volker shouted over the din of battle while stabbing a goblin in its left arm.

"Well where the fuck is your guy!?"

"Hell if I know!"

The goblin force pressed forward with all their might. To think that they'd fallen prey to the bogeys' cheap tricks not once, but twice—razing the entire bogey army was the only acceptable path to revenge.

Given the close proximity of the fighting, the bogeys were unable to throw any more cyfrac oil barrels, and even their ranged units were hard-pressed to find clean shots through the woods where the archers had moved their strange bows. In the messy fighting, five more greyborn fell, while only two Jiira goblins passed onto the next life.

Rak and Volker stood their ground, hoping to keep morale high despite their defence struggling to hold back the goblin tide. If reinforcements didn't come soon, they wouldn't be able to hold on much longer.

"I hate these damn goblins!" Rak roared as he thrust his spear into a goblin's heart.

Volker groaned. "You and me both."

So this is how it ends, Volker thought as he looked at his and Rak's men. Exhausted and bleeding, they were truly on their last legs.

Another arrow pierced through a shield, but fortunately only wounded the shieldbearer's arm. Volker ordered him to back away, taking his place. With a swift lunge forward, Volker's spear pushed back a goblin and dented his armour.

The goblin tried to grab Volker's spear, only to be dragged and slammed into the shield wall.

Two goblins took down three more of Rak's men and surged towards Rak. As Rak had broken his new pike, he took the opportunity to christen the bronze axe he'd looted from Gelmar. He chopped straight through the first goblin's skull with a powerful slice, snatched his bronze spear, and chucked it at the second goblin, lodging it in his nose.

The second goblin twitched on the ground before Rak finished him off the same way he had the first.

Covered in goblin blood, Rak took a moment to gather himself. His once-fresh bronze axe slipped out of his hand and fell to the gently-vegetated ground with a thud.

"Rak, get back here!" Volker shouted in the distance. With Volker's shout, Rak suddenly realised that he'd accidentally moved away from the rest of the greyborn formation. Rak surveyed the battlefield with a quick glance. As the battle raged on and the bogeys were pushed back, the goblin archers moved their siege engines forward to keep the bogeys in their reach. Rak saw two more archers had made their way out of the trees and were readying their weapons.

Though the Jiira archers had hid behind trees and giant stones as cover from slingshot fire, they'd arranged themselves in clusters. Rak had an idea. A risky one, but it was a risk he needed to take.

Fuck it. Safety be damned. Drastic times call for drastic measures.

Rak pillaged two bronze shields from two fallen goblins and ran uphill towards the cavern entrance, pushing any wayward obstacles and goblins out of his path.

Rotating himself with a short hop, he then bounded down the slope towards the goblin archers. With every step, or leap as it were, he picked up speed and ploughed over the unfortunate obstacles in his path.

The archers tried to stop him. Two arrows whizzed past his head as he neared the panicking archers. Another ricocheted off the edge of Rak's shield, while the last missed entirely. Rak crashed into the nearest archer, knocked him head over heels with a powerful shield bash, and smoothly finished him off with a stomp to the jugular.

"It's payback time, you green bastards!"

The other goblin archers froze in fear as Rak grabbed a handful of arrows from the fallen archer.

They panicked as they needed time to reload their weapons. Their fingers fumbled over their weapons' bronze mechanisms as their trembling hands struggled to fit the large arrows into their places.

Rak did not panic. He sprinted, bloodlust palpable, towards the nearest goblin, and stabbed him in the stomach with an arrow. The goblin looked at his wound in a daze, perhaps wondering what an arrow with the trademark Jiira plumes was in his stomach.

Rak hurled the now-unconscious goblin into a third archer and dashed forward. Before the archer could get out from under his dying ally, Rak stabbed him in the neck and lower abdomen with swift successive motions. He then hoisted the goblin up as a meat shield against the other archers' shots. .

Seeing him furious and unscathed, the goblin archers turned tail and ran towards their allies.

Noticing the chaos behind enemy lines, Volker grinned. He took advantage of Rak's bloody work to step back from the frontline of the bogey formation and assess the situation.

"Slingers, their archers are gone! Focus fire on the goblin back line with all you got!" Volker barked. "Fighters, set ranks! Hold on a while longer, reinforcements will be here!"

"Yes, sir!" his slingers replied. Even Rak's men took note of Volker's commands.

Volker regarded the goblin front line, who had clearly heard Volkers words. They couldn't turn around and check if the greyborn's words were true, but if they'd lost their ranged support...

As if on cue, Volker heard a shout from behind. He turned to see his messenger hurrying towards him, tens of greyborns in tow.

"He's back! Sir, they're all back!" the messenger cried joyfully.

Back? Wait, is that Hem? And—

"Sir!" Volker cried with a salute.

"It's Lev!"

"And Hem's back!"

"Wait, is that Jem? What is that bastard doing here?"

"Who cares right now? Focus on the damn goblins!" yelled a shieldbearer, pushing back a goblin with his tattered shield.

Only a third of the goblins remained, and they were visibly exhausted. The enemies' timing of reinforcements had been almost too convenient, and the rampaging, oversized greyborn had killed off their archers and was running towards them to wreak havoc in their backline. It was more than they could bear.

"Scatter and retreat!" cried a goblin. Likely a commander, he wore a lightly decorated helmet featuring two straight horns, as well as a shiny ornate bronze chestplate.

The goblins complied and swiftly turned tail, making sure to give the charging Rak a wide berth.

The bogeys were stunned by the instant, unorganised retreat, but Volker reacted first. "Don't let them get away! Avenge our comrades!" he cried with his spear raised high.

Took them long enough. I killed enough goblins to fill an entire outpost. Rak told himself as he inspected the field littered with goblin corpses.

In his haste, he'd killed one of the last two goblin archers, but settled for knocking the other one. As Rak turned around to locate this archer, he noticed that the goblin had regained consciousness and was trying to shakily crawl away.

Rak slowly walked up to the unfortunate goblin. "Where do you think you're going?" Rak growled. "Once we clean up your friends, I need you to answer some questions."

As the bogeys chased the retreating goblins, the goblin commander tripped and fell—Lev stepped on the goblin's back and let the commander's neck feel the cold tip of his blade.

"Hello there, my friend. I need to have a word with you."

"I-I'd never say anything to you fil— Agggggghhhh!" the commander cried as Volker's spear pierced through his hand.

Volker sneered. "If you want to live, shut up. I'm just a moment away from killing you right here."

The goblin commander meekly nodded.

Volker then turned to Lev, grinning from ear to ear. "Thank the gods you're back, sir!"

Lev returned the grin and placed his hand on Volker's shoulder. "It's good to be back. Looks like you've done well."

Volker brightly smiled before glaring at Jem, who was chasing another goblin in the distance. "I do have some questions, though."

Lev turned and saw who Volker was glaring at. "Got it. Ask me later."

The commander whimpered, redrawing Lev and Volker's attention.

"Right. We need to ask our friend here some questions. Volker, could you get me some pliers? I may need them to help persuade him to cooperate."

"W-What are you going to do?" the scared goblin asked.

Lev's smile became more sinister. "Depends on how you answer my questions."

A few hours later, the skirmishing across the cavern entrances ended. Battles were won and lost by both sides, mostly by narrow margins. But at an outpost, on the other side of the cave entrance from where Volker and Rak had been defending, the bogeys had apparently achieved an overwhelming victory.

And with that news of victory came a second piece of news: Vyrga had returned.

Under the nobles' orders, the goblin corpses were decapitated, the heads impaled on stakes near the restored entrance outposts. After all the work was done, and only then, did the bogeys finally allow themselves to celebrate.

And celebrate they did.

Sitting far above the cavern entrance, a lone bogey silently observed those partying beneath him.

He took a gander at the spikes and sighed. *Classical but impractical. There are better ways to waste time and manpower. Well, at least we kept our prisoners.*

This isn't the end. The real fight against the Jiira has yet to begin. Lev thought as he looked at the cheering bogeys, still engulfed in the ecstasy of their victory.

Still, it's nice to let them celebrate for now.

CHAPTER 15
TORTURE AND REUNION

Inside a dark and dreary room with but a single skyhole providing a ray of light, the captured goblin commander screamed in agony and struggled against his bindings as Lev slowly gathered valuable information regarding the Jiira's status, resources, forces, and chain of command.

"Can't you see it's pointless?" Lev said as he attached the plier to yet another fingernail.

"I won't! You may try to— Aaarrgh!" Another nail dropped to the ground as the unfortunate goblin commander screamed, almost hoarse from all the... fun he was experiencing.

The other captive goblins looked on in horror at the sight of their commander being tortured by a small, frail-looking greyborn.

This grey bastard, we should've killed his tribe long ago! We took them under our wing, showed them the light of Ainshard, and this is how they repay us? One of the goblin soldiers thought as he cursed himself and his situation. It wouldn't take long for the commander to pass out from pain and exhaustion, and then it'd be their turn.

Lev leaned in and whispered into the commander's ear. "You only have four nails left. Do you really want us to start pulling your teeth?"

"I-I won't g-give u— aahhh!" The goblins shut their eyes as another nail softly clattered upon the ground.

"How about now?"

"F-Fuck you..."

Lev slowly shook his head. "Believe me or not, I've always hated torture. Received plenty of it, but was never good at it. Looks like I need to use tougher measures."

"Tougher measures?" the commander cried.

"Tougher measures. Wait here till I get back with some much-needed tools."

"T-Tools?" one of the soldiers squealed, causing him to receive scowls from his peers. Nobody wanted to know, let alone see, what this mad greyborn had in mind.

"Nothing much. Splinters, spikes. A small hammer. Just the basics. Now, if you'll excuse me."

"W-Wait!" a goblin cried, followed by the rest of his comrades.

"That's evil!"

"He's had enough!"

"Monster! Vermin!"

Lev took a deep breath before he left the room to get his tools. It was going to be a long day.

Better find someone to play the role of the nice guy and earn their trust. Plain torture rarely, if ever, gets accurate results.

* * *

Volker propped his head against the side of his tent, conflicted by the events of the day. Even though Volker was glad that Lev was back, Volker was unsure what to make of Jem. After Lev was abducted during the expedition, Volker had struggled to keep Lev's forces united. Despite his best efforts, only a small number of greyborn from Lev's original faction had remained under Volker's wing. And one of the factions that had left... was Jem's.

In the very same outpost encampment, another bogey was deep in thought. Jem knew that Lev had ambitions beyond ensuring stability for himself and his kin. He, like Volker, had always supported Lev, and still intended to establish himself as Lev's second-in-command.

A position like that shouldn't be left in the hands of a kid. Especially a runt who's never experienced starvation. Jem grumbled to himself. *What Lev really needs are experienced, tough men who've survived against all odds time and time again.*

To Jem, Volker was still too much of a greenhorn, incapable of leadership. Volker's unquestioning loyalty to Lev meant that the kid was a good underling, but a second-in-command needed to be able to advise, to stand up to the leader's decisions when needed.

Volker wasn't fit to be Lev's right hand man.

* * *

Lev looked around from his perch near the outpost Volker and Rak had defended. Bodies lay about, some piled atop one another. There was a foul stench in the air, the smell of rotting and disease. A few bogeys strolled around the cavern entrances, stripping the beheaded goblins of their armour and weapons before dragging their bodies into piles for burning.

The strange bows the goblins had used and left behind looked familiar to Lev. They looked like large, crude crossbows, much like Roman scorpios, made from materials such as wood, bone, tendons, and leather, held together by a mixture of ropes and bronze plates. Unfortunately, the crossbows had sustained such heavy use in the battle that every single one Lev tried to test-fire broke.

"Rak, collect as many crossbows as possible. I think we can still use them."

Rak looked dumbfounded. "Crossbows? You mean those weird bows the Jiira archers used?"

"Precisely. Have your men collect all they can find. I don't care if they're destroyed; we'll still be able to use the scraps to make a variant."

Rak paused again.

"A variant, huh? Seems like you know more about these weapons than we do."

You have no idea. Lev chuckled at the thought of arming his men with field artillery.

This siege engine, although similar to a bow, could shoot powerful javelin-like projectiles towards their enemies with enough propulsion to pierce their shields. They would prove valuable in the coming battles, and although Lev wasn't certain how to manufacture them, he knew a few bogey artisans who could figure that out.

After all, battles were won through superior firepower, intel, and logistics. These crossbows would prove invaluable for buying time for the bogeys. Soon they would be able to strengthen their ranks again. With enough time perhaps they could even organise a force to bring the battle to the Jiira themselves.

"What about your men, Lev? What are you going to do about them?"

Lev sighed. "Rak, as much as I'd like for Jem's group to stick around, I can't force them to."

"So you're letting them leave, just like that?"

Rak and Lev now stood face to face, and after a few seconds passed, Rak erupted into laughter. His eyes teared while Lev retained his composed expression.

"That's correct. Keeping a faction in my forces that doesn't want to be there would only hurt me over time. A willing army is a unified one."

"You sure know how to talk big, boy," Rak wiped tears from his eyes as he regained his composure.

The two then parted. Rak helped his men collect the goblins' crossbows, while Lev returned to Jem and Volker.

Meanwhile, in a room assigned to Lev and his men, Volker approached Jem. The latter was wiping his newly acquired bronze short sword down—it was time to hide their better weapons from the blues.

"You shouldn't be here," Volker growled at Jem as the latter was just about to finish sharpening the sword's blade.

"And yet here I am," Jem retorted while keeping his eyes on the bronze blade.

"So that's it? You abandoned us and now you think you can just come back?"

Jem glanced at Volker, disgruntled. "Someone's overreacting. We all thought he was dead."

"You didn't even give him a chance to return!"

"We call that a miracle, Volker. Folks don't normally come back after getting kidnapped by the hivelings. Usually you can't even find their bones."

"Well—"

Jem raised his hand. "Before you spout some crap about loyalty, fellowship, and ideology, let me remind you. None of those put food on the table. None of those could have kept my family alive all this while."

Volker stared wide-eyed. "You have a family?"

Jem shrugged. "Most of us do. Sure, some join gangs and get into fights for fun, but the rest of us are just trying to provide, even if it gets our hands dirty."

"But then if you die..."

"That's why I chose Lev."

"Didn't you choose him because he reminded you of your old boss, Dagga?"

Jem closed his eyes and bowed his head. "I was young and idealistic, much like you are now. I was ready to be martyred to end the suffering of our folk. Dagga was everything I wanted in a leader. A great warrior with a wizened tongue. He was daring but not reckless, ambitious but not manipulative. At least not with us." Jem's expression hardened. "Lev is similar in all but one of those ways."

"Lev isn't—"

Jem scoffed. "Stop being touchy whenever I talk about Lev. I know you idolise him, but you're his second-in-command, not his wife!" He then continued calmly. "Dagga treated us like men. Lev treats us like fodder, and you know it."

"Why don't you just go back to Rak then?"

"Tch. Rak doesn't hold a candle to either of them. When I joined Rak's gang, I'd just had my second child, a precious little girl, and I couldn't bear the thought that she might end up poor and fatherless. At first there was plenty of work to be done, plenty of merits to be earned." Jem set down his sword. "But then Veit betrayed Rak, and since then...well. Him strangling me was the last straw."

Volker rolled his eyes. "That's Rak for you. A good leader, and a good guy when he's got his anger issues bottled up."

Jem chuckled. "That's the best description I've heard so far."

"Anyway, if Lev's not Dagga, why haven't you quit?"

"Lev pays well, has potential, and even though we're just pieces in some grand game only he understands, he still treats folks like us well enough. That's good enough for me."

Volker was incredulous. "'Well enough'? You just said you have kids! You could get by without risking your life day in and day out."

Jem stood up and walked right up to Volker. "Volker."

"What?"

Jem took a step closer. "You're from a potter's family, right?"

"Yes?"

Jem took another step closer. He was close enough that Volker could feel Jem's breath tickling his nose. "Then here's some advice. Never say that again, to anyone. Most of us here have never had the opportunity to make a peaceful living like you have."

Volker panicked. "I-I'm sorry. I didn't mean it like that!"

Jem stepped back and tucked his sword into the group's shared cache. "It's fine. I do what's best for me. But keep talking like that, and you'll make a lot of enemies. You're a good kid, so I'd rather not sour our relationship further. Don't think less of me or the others for wanting to survive and provide."

Volker thought for a second before responding. "I don't."

"Great. Now hide your loot before those blue bastards confiscate it all"

Volker nodded and began stashing away his group's items. As he laboured, he couldn't help thinking back to Jem's words.

Volker grimaced. Hopefully they would never have to cross spears.

CHAPTER 16
WEAPON CRAFTING

Lev had just placed one of the scavenged Jiira crossbows onto the table.

"This won't work!" protested a green bogey artisan.

"You're crazy! How are we supposed to create a prototype without any plans or experience? We know nothing of the Jiira's designs!" said another artisan. He was older, with a thin beard and wearing a raggedy bandana.

They were apprentices of one of Volker's acquaintances.

"We're merely greyborns and outcasts, dammit! How could we even—"

Another artisan silenced him before he could finish. Their mentor was glaring at him.

Gorran was the name the old, green bogey blacksmith went by these days, having cast aside his original name long ago after angering the nobles. He huffed once his youngest apprentice shut up and turned to Lev.

"Sorry, kid. Looks like even after everything I've taught them, all they can do is disappoint us. Making a regular goblin weapon would be easy for me, aside from sourcing the bronze, but developing a working 'crossbow' based on a broken one? I'm not sure I'd be able to do it in a couple of days, let alone months."

Lev slammed his palm on the worktable, startling the artisans.

To their surprise, however, Lev didn't tear into them.

Lev regarded each of the artisans. Although their workshop looked like a shabby mess of tools and crafting materials, the calluses and scars on their hands betrayed years of tutelage under a master blacksmith.

"I have the schematics with me," Lev finally said, breaking the tension between the artisans and him.

"Schematics?" the old bogey asked.

"Plans on how to build my crossbows."

"Wait, w-what!" the youngest bogey yelled. "How did you get the goblins' schematics? Every blacksmith knows that— Ow!" The bogey nursed his face as a fresh palm print magically appeared on it.

"Stay silent, Pol! I told you to shut your mouth and listen! You may be able to learn something here!" Gorran protested.

"That's enough," Lev said. He took a rolled-up piece of leather out of his rucksack.

The elder's face quickly lit up after examining the scroll. To start, his expression was scrunched as he struggled to understand the drawing, but after a few moments, his face lit up. "How? This is... amazing!"

The other artisans gathered around the elder, trying their best to understand Lev's altered crossbow design.

"This design looks so foreign, yet it still looks to have most of the elements and mechanics of the original Jiira version. In a smaller package, to boot."

After exchanging looks, the blacksmiths scrambled together their awls, styluses, and measurement lints. Having prepared their equipment, they feverishly sketched wood and clay moulds. A few hours later, they sent Pol away to retrieve Lev, who had left long ago to oversee the burning of Jiira corpses.

After any other battle, Lev would have disposed of the bodies quietly to keep the enemy in the dark about the outcome.

However, this situation was different. The Jiira were trying to both reestablish control over the bogeys and repel the steadfastly invading Kur, a tribe of kobolds, on the opposite border of their realm. Lev's adversaries were in a tight spot logistics-, resource-, and personnel-wise.

As a result, Lev felt like flexing his muscles against the Jiira, who considered cremation sacrilege. He sought both to insult and disorient his opponents, who had underestimated him grossly enough to send a barely-trained force out against him.

Lev's knowledge of medieval crossbow designs proved to be invaluable. During his past life, he had spent considerable time in the library, immersing himself in the study of historical weaponry. This passion had not only stayed with him, but also endowed him with the ability to recall intricate details, such as the schematic for this particular crossbow. It was no mere coincidence; it was a testament to his dedication and his keen interest in the subject matter.

Lev smiled as he recounted his past, which seemed so far away now. *If only I could go back to fetch more books about medieval weaponry.*

After a while, Pol escorted him back inside to face the artisans, who bombarded Lev with questions about how he had gotten his hands on the schematic, and then how he had *drafted* the schematic.

Gorran laughed. "Really, kid, how in the world did you make this? You've got talent, more than I've ever seen before. I could teach you to be a craftsman as great as I am!"

Lev smiled. "Not now. Maybe after this war is over."

Lev's version of the crossbow wasn't a siege engine like the former. It was a crossbow optimised for better firing rate as a counter to the Jiira's focus on penetrative force. The relative lack of decoration, smaller size, and simplicity of Lev's design also made his crossbows both easier to repair and produce.

The first hurdle Lev's prototyping team had to overcome was the length of the wooden stock. Ideally, the stock would have been a length comfortable for the short arms of any bogey, but the only wood available in large enough pieces was knotty and dry, and the artisans' tools turned out to be less precise than Lev had expected, hacking off more material than he would have preferred. Nevertheless, Lev was ready to take what he could get.

After having shortened the wood, the team moved on to carving out the trigger cavity and grooves, one to hold twine and the other to guide an arrow. Pol was the first to volunteer his chisel for this task, but with a single hit, the rusty chisel snapped in two.

"Pol! You've been slacking on maintenance again!" Gorran admonished. "Guess I'll have to break out my own secret weapons."

Gorran stepped out of the workshop for a bit, then returned with a tool set he had managed to smuggle out during his escape. "Pol. These are your master's most prized possessions. Use these carefully."

"Y-Y-Yes, sir!" Pol sheepishly replied. A round of glue from bluecatcher mushrooms later, the stock was ready.

Next, the metal parts were to be cast. Lev's men supplied a handful of bronze spearheads collected from the earlier battle, and Lev observed with vague interest as the master blacksmith and his most senior apprentices fired up a furnace. One that looked clean, too clean, as though it had been waiting to be used for a long time. Lev watched the bronze liquefy, fill the prepared moulds, pop out in solid form, and be ground into shape.

In short order and with frequent references to the schematic, the artisans assembled Lev's prototype, then handed it to Lev, who twanged the twine a few times before tightening it. The artisans looked on in excitement.

He cocked an arrow, aimed at a target a distance away, and depressed the trigger. It nearly hit the centre of the target. He placed the prototype back on the table and secured the bow in place at the front.

Lev grinned. "This should do."

The artisans quickly started crafting more crossbows the way Lev had shown them, their deft hands carving, melting, and grinding in near-unison.

This will most certainly do, Lev told himself as he prepared to leave the workshop.

"What should we do after this? Make armour?" an apprentice asked his senior.

Hearing the apprentice's words, Lev realised that he had his own question for the elder. He turned around and approached the master blacksmith. "May I have a bit of your time?"

"Is it something important?"

"We need armour. Proper armour."

The old bogey grinned. "Of course you do. I've seen the usual wooden armour you wear. Can't imagine moving in those, nevermind fighting Jiira. What do you have in mind?"

"We're already short on time, right?"

Gorran nodded.

"I want to refit the goblins' armour."

"Hm, makes sense. We'll be busy as is with the crossbows, but I'm sure we can make quick work of their gear. So how many men are we looking to outfit? Five? Ten?"

"Forty-five."

"Yes, yes. Forty-five... Wait, forty-five! How were they able to make so many?"

"Jiira society hasn't forgotten the efficiency of mass production," Lev explained.

"Mass production? Isn't that what we do already?" Gorran asked.

"Not quite," Lev replied. "Multiple artisans make partially complete components, and less-trained workers assemble them to make the final products."

"Is this what you wanted, boss?" a greyborn with a yellow armband interrupted. Gorran quickly threw a piece of cloth over the schematics.

"It's fine, Gorran, he's one of my men," Lev remarked as he pointed at the armband. The symbol of Zeja allowed Gorran to sigh in relief.

"I should've known by now, can't be too careful."

Lev gestured, and the greyborn placed several pieces of Jiira armour on the table before leaving the workshop.

"As you can see, the Jiira make several standard sizes and then mass produces them."

Gorran examined the Jiira armour. It was crudely made and lacking in quality.

He then looked at Lev with disappointment. "Crude trash. Are you sure this will help us?"

"It's better than wooden armour, so I'm sure it will." Lev assured the proud artisan. "Now if you'll excuse me, there are some people I have to meet."

"Well, good luck then. Stay safe, Lev."

"You too, Gorran."

Volker contained himself until he and Lev were alone. "We found them. They set an encampment together outside the cavern and they're willing to listen to our offer, sir," Volker said.

"Great. Let's go make some new friends."

CHAPTER 17

REMNANTS

"What happened here?" Volker asked, flabbergasted, as he gazed upon the decapitated heads of a dozen goblins neatly placed on a row of spikes pointing to the east—where, from what they had heard, the centre of the Jiira's territory lay.

"Don't know for sure, but I think our negotiations might go better than expected," Lev replied with a smirk.

"I hope so. The last thing I want is to fight those I consider friends."

Lev glanced at Volker. "I'm sure it won't come to that."

The duo, followed by ten of their men, proceeded to the deka camp. They'd heard reports of a camp outside the bogey caverns, mostly inhabited by deka, that had united after the failed expedition, and under the cover of night, slaughtered goblins in their sleep.

As he stepped into the camp, Lev saw the remnants of the expedition force, whether they be dekas, burgas, bugbears, or even the female goblins who were formerly Bulgu's harem guards. All races that had participated in the expedition, except dargs, were represented.

He saw Bulgu's former hired muscle hurrying about, setting up tents, cooking meals, maintaining their weapons and armour, and tending to the dekas' livestock and mounts.

Looks like the dekas stole some horses, Lev thought as he saw the noble beasts getting fed and brushed inside a makeshift pen. Though the horses were large, they looked quite agile.

Did their former owners breed them for war?

Lev's party observed the grooming process until a boisterous voice interrupted them.

"So are you gonna keep gawking at our new rides or are you gonna greet your buddy over here!"

"Ban!" Volker said with a grin before both locked their arms together. According to what Lev had heard, it was a common way of greeting friends in deka culture.

"Welcome to the encampment, where you can find all the vengeful souls of this campaign," Ban said.

"Vengeful souls?" one of Lev's men asked.

"Well, the camp consists of expedition survivors and some of our people. Those who don't belong in the bogey caverns find refuge here. In exchange, they fight with us until the last of them Jiira heads roll. Well, except for Rogga. He's still recovering from his injuries. He almost died in the caverns when Bulgu left him for dead after the last hiveling attack. Good thing we owed that nose of his some crimson ale."

"Good thinking. It's not safe for survivors to linger around the bogey caverns right now," Lev said as he looked behind him, towards the mountain range that housed the bogey caverns. He could still see the black smoke of recently burnt corpses lingering in the air.

"So what brings you here, pal? If you came for those fucking Jiira, too bad. We already gave them the rumbling they deserved."

Lev replied. "We were wondering how you dealt with the goblins, and also came to ask something of Gozzag. We sent a messenger earlier and he said that Gozzag's currently acting as the leader. We wanted to—"

"Yeah, yeah. Join forces and beat back the Jiira. You reminded me of that," Ban interrupted. He looked at Lev and continued. "I thought it was your nobles who wanted our help, though. No offence, but can you afford it? You're slaves in your society after all."

"We can talk about coin in private. The name's Lev, by the way." Lev extended his right hand.

"The pinkskin's greeting, eh? Name's Ban. I've heard a lot about you from both Gozzag and Volker over here. Weird we haven't met before considering I'm second in command here. Well, no matter. You better like mead! After this meeting, we'll have to see if you can enjoy a drink!" The deka laughed.

Lev nodded with a grin. "You'll know soon enough."

What's mead? Gherm asked.

An alcoholic drink, Gherm.

Alcohol? Oh, beer. I've never had that in my life. You should know that.

Lev paused and checked Gherm's memories and wanted to curse. *Well, let's hope your body can handle it or we'll be embarrassing ourselves. It's not like I can refuse.*

Even you can blunder, huh?

Lev was reminded of the countless drinking parties he'd stomached during his time in one of the closest circles of the Imperial elite. There were times when he'd been forced to drink gallons of exotic cocktails and expensive wine...

His old body had grown used to it, but at what cost?

The master's first. Even he makes mistakes, the glaive interjected.

I guess, Gherm muttered.

Let's end this discussion so I can focus on the negotiations, shall we? Lev instructed the two. He felt their connections fade away into the depths of his mind.

"Is something wrong?" Ban asked, confusion written on his face. To him and the others, Lev had suddenly turned silent.

"Oh, it's nothing. I've just remembered something quite important."

I really need to find a better way to communicate with those two. Lev thought to himself.

"Assuming the negotiations go well, I have some interesting things to show you and your craftsmen. I'm sure they'll be intrigued."

Ban nodded. "I see. Well, now that the pleasantries are over, I'll ask again. Are you really sure you can afford our services? Just a word of warning, the last buyer that tried to leave without paying…" He vaguely waved toward the spiked goblin heads.

"They refused to pay?" Lev asked with a frown.

Ban sneered. "Hah! I wish it was only that. The bastards not only refused to pay us, they even insulted our work! They said it was our fault that Bulgu died since we didn't check for poisons! That wasn't even our job!"

Ban was shouting at this point. "Ours was to protect him during the expedition. And that damn trip's over, so we should've been paid, not ridiculed! Heck, it'll be sky devil season soon, so we should've gotten a bonus! Yet the bastards demanded that we compensate them by fighting you bogeys and threatened to wipe out our homeland if we refused! Can you believe that? I oughta shove a sword up their dirty green asses and—"

"An' we'reh, hic, doin' justh that," another Deka slurred, swaying as he cheered. "Off wit' their heads! Hic! Ev'ry, hic, last one of 'em, hic, wobble-headed lot of 'em."

Lev tuned out the fuming Ban and drunk Deka as they ranted about the Jiira and made a mental note to not ever screw with the dekas. Even though his relationship with Gozzag was cordial, Lev was sure Gozzag would hoist his head on a pike the moment he tried any funny business with them.

Ban continued to rant until Lev loudly coughed, interrupting him

"My apologies, but it would be quite rude to leave Gozzag waiting for us."

"Hm. You're right. Heck, we better not spoil our mood by talking about those ugly green shits, right?"

"Um… aren't there goblins here?" Volker asked.

"The old harem guards? They're alright. Goblins are a weird bunch. They have the ugliest men, yet their women weren't hit by the ugly stick. You'd even think they belong to an entirely different race," Ban replied.

Volker looked at one of the decapitated male goblin heads. If goblin women could launch a thousand ships, then goblin men could too, but in the opposite direction.

"I guess you're right," Volker said, comparing the head with those of the former harem guards.

Ban grinned. "Of course I'm right. Anyway, let's go. We have already wasted enough time. Besides, you're still gonna get a drink with us after the meeting, aren't ya?" he said with his booming voice engulfed in hospitality.

They approached Lev nodded and the group continued onwards to a large tent in the centre of the encampment.

Once they neared, Ban raised his hand. "Sorry guys, but no weapons inside. And even then, only Lev, Volker, and I are allowed inside. It's tradition."

"You can't be serious!"

"You think we'd agree to that!"

"Sorry, but we can't allow the possibility for our leaders to be harmed."

"What if something goes wrong?"

"Enough!" Volker roared, silencing the men and surprising Lev and Ban.

Seems the kid grew up, the two thought as they saw the stern look he gave the men.

Lev turned back to Ban. "My apologies. My men meant no offence."

Ban shook his head. "No problem. If they fear for your safety that much, that means they're good by me. Loyalty's worth more than gold."

Lev nodded and handed Ban his glaive.

But master, the glaive whimpered.

It's just for a while. I promise I'll take you back.

Understood. I'll awa...it yo...ur... return... the glaive replied as its voice faded away.

Don't worry, I'll be back.

"I agree. Now, shall we proceed?"

Lev and Volker entered the tent. The insides could be considered spartan. On the left was an open curtain that led to a makeshift bed inside what seemed to be a chest. The chest was filled with furs covering moss and leaves. On the right was a washing basin, a small altar containing a silver figurine vaguely representative of a two-horned deka, and a table with a set of armour, an axe, and a short sword on it. Finally, there were a dozen crates stacked against the far wall.

"So? What do you think of the place?"

Lev and Volker saw a short-bearded deka sitting on one of four chairs surrounding a large square table. The tip of his curved horn was slightly cracked. From what Lev had heard, it had been damaged towards the end of the expedition, when Gozzag and his fighters had been attacked by a warrior and spitter. Unlike many others, he'd been lucky enough to survive a hit from the warrior relatively unharmed.

"Modest and practical. I like it," Lev replied honestly.

"I don't like to puff myself for no reason. I left the gaudy garbage of my predecessor in another tent," Gozzag replied.

"Don't remind me of that guy," Ban grumbled.

Gozzag grimaced. "Well, I have to ask if he's alright. He and another of our comrades were dragged away by the spiderlings. Do you know if they're alive or did the hivelings separate you?"

"Drogg and Grasha?"

Gozzag nodded. "Are they still alive?"

"Drogg isn't."

"Well, at least Grasha's alive." Gozzag smiled land then eyed Lev. "Where is he?"

"He decided to stay with my companions for the time being."

Ban heartily laughed. "Typical Grasha. Still, better to have the weirdo than that pompous fool."

"Ban!" Gozzag smashed his fist on the table.

"What? I'm telling the truth. Even the damn chief didn't want that violent, obnoxious, arrogant asshole of a son."

Gozzag groaned and rubbed his forehead. "I'm trying to have a formal discussion over here."

"You're being too stiff. If you keep talking like this, we'll be here forever. We all know Lev and Volker want our help in exchange for some loot, so let's finish this up and go drink some mead. Leave complex negotiation for the dargs. It's not our thing. And next time, start with a greeting first like a normal person."

If looks could kill, Ban would've earned two holes in the head right then and there. Gozzag slumped in his seat.

"Why did I let you in?" he muttered before he stood up, walked around the table, and approached Lev. "Glad you're back, Lev. I'm sure you went through hell, but we can talk about that once we're done here."

"Agreed. I believe our messenger told you why I'm here?"

Gozzag nodded. "So what can you offer us for our aid? We want as much revenge as the next greyborn but we need to wait until we can contact the Dragma and prepare a raid party large enough to make them regret the day they were born."

"The Dragma?" Lev asked.

"The home of all Deka, or at least what's left of our people. It lies east of Jiira territory."

"Noted. As for your question, we want the same thing you want, to protect ourselves from a threat," Lev replied.

"We told you, we can make easy work of the Jiira. They're not as powerful as they want you to think. Not anymore. Terrible leadership, lack of progress in military technology, and constant border clashes with the Kur have stretched them thin. Even without our help, they'll die out in the coming decades. Only their nobles have weapons and armour worthy of note."

Gozzag went to one of the crates, grabbed two pairs of armour and placed them on the table next to each other.

The one on the left was a bronzescale mail armour. It consisted of a sturdy tunic that covered the shoulders and reached down below the belt. The rows of scales were strapped by lacing to the tunic and layered over each other, leaving only a few spots unguarded, such as the armpits and the head. It was much more refined of an armour than the ones Lev had scavenged from the fallen Jiira.

Lev examined the armour. *Looks like it'd offer good protection. But it's quite rigid.*

"Only four of them were wearing this outdated thing," Gozzag grumbled.

"Outdated?" Volker asked in surprise.

Gozzag nodded and motioned towards the other armour.

After examining the second armour for a moment, Lev almost jumped in surprise. *Is that steel?*

"This is called chainmail. It's made from small interconnected metal rings made out of a form of refined iron," Gozzag explained.

"Isn't iron supposed to be soft?" Volker asked the dekas.

Gozzag was about to answer, but Ban interjected. "We're mercenaries, not blacksmiths. All we know is that this form of iron is tougher and lighter than bronze."

"So bronze is outdated now," Volker muttered, receiving a laugh from the two dekas.

"No, you idiot. If it was, why's everyone still using it? Iron is easier to get and better if you know how to treat it in this special manner, but smiths who know how are rare and far between, especially outside of Brizilum. What's outdated is how armour is made. Scale mail is too rigid compared to chainmail. It's too heavy and can't cover your entire body."

Volker carefully examined the steel mesh. "This looks hard to make."

Ban slammed another set of armour on the table. "That's why we wear this. It's more popular in the southeast and they call it 'lamellar.' It's good, tougher than chainmail and scale armour, but isn't very flexible. It's not cheap either, but we can afford it."

"Hey, that's my armour!" Gozzag yelled.

"Ah, right. Forgot that."

"Never mind. Anyway, back to our discussion. The Jiira aren't a threat to us."

"I never mentioned the Jiira," Lev told Gozzag.

"Then who?"

Lev smiled. "Who's conquering the east? Who's trying to assimilate everyone in their path?"

"You don't mean—" Ban muttered.

"The Brizilum Republic."

Everyone stood there stunned, staring at Lev.

Gozzag, the first to recover, furrowed his brow and pinched his nose. "I see. And you think you can stop them? Do you even know how powerful they are?"

"They have a large, well-organised, and highly trained dedicated army, despite their use of mercenaries."

"Yes."

"They have advanced technology, magic arts, and a powerful industry that allows them to produce a surplus of military supplies."

"Yes."

"They establish outposts as they conquer territory to efficiently transfer men and supplies from their homeland and colonies, and put great effort into establishing routes to said outposts so as to create a reliable logistic network."

"Uh, um, what? I think, yes..."

"They have a powerful navy and control the seas, especially the eastern sea known as the White Sea. This allows them to dominate all naval trade routes and obtain treasures and necessary materials from other lands."

"Uh..."

"It also allows them to receive men and supplies by sea, strengthening their logistics prowess even further."

"How in the name of the gods do you know all this!?" Gozzag screamed. *Aren't greyborns forced to live their lives in the shadows of the cavern? How did he learn all this?!*

In response, Lev simply tilted his head and smiled. "I have my ways." In truth, he'd gathered information regarding the Brizilum Republic from his companions in the ruins, mostly from Shahn. He'd pieced together the bits of information to create, in his mind, a complete picture of the republic's strength and methods.

"Still, even if you know them well, how can you even think about fighting them?"

"You mean how *we* can fight them."

Gozzag stared, unblinkingly, straight into Lev's pupils. "You've got a lot of convincing to do. To fight the Brizilum Republic for you? That's a lot of risk."

"I wasn't just talking about us bogeys and the Dragma."

"So, the other tribes, clans, and kingdoms? Forget it! Why would they listen to any of us? Well, some might listen to us Dragma, but why would anyone listen to you bogeys?"

"People will always listen, as long as the benefits are there."

"What benefits?"

"Volker."

Volker handed Lev a large scroll.

Gozzag looked at the scroll and saw the weapon's design. "A Brizilum siegebow? No... this looks more similar to one of the Jiira's designs."

"It's my design."

Hearing that, Gozzag's eyes immediately turned towards Lev. "You made this?"

"I did."

"Does it work?"

"It's called a crossbow, and it does work. We already have some in the field, so feel free to ask one of my men outside to show your craftsmen how it works."

Gozzag nodded, still examining the crossbow design schematics. "I'll send this to our craftsmen to verify. Still, this isn't enough to fight the Republic."

"But the Jiira?"

"Hm..."

Lev placed a bag on the table near Gozzag.

"Haze crystals, huh? Well, I guess it should've been obvious that you'd pay us with these."

"I can get you a full crate, to be delivered at the conclusion of our war."

"A crate," Gozzag muttered as he calculated the price of the haze crystals in gold. Then he shrugged his shoulders. "If this crossbow of yours works well enough and you can handle paying a crate, then sure. That covers the bill and more. For the Jiira, at least. I'm not yet sure I want to antagonise the republic."

Of course you agree. Your people have always needed more ranged support, Lev thought. Grasha always complained about his people's weakness when it came to ranged combat. Dekas were strong and sturdy, but were not built for magic or long-range combat. Not to mention, no matter the race, it took any fighter years to master the bow.

Gozzag handed the design to a guard before returning to the tent to discuss the settlement and the Dragma's future cooperation with Lev's group. After nearly an hour of chatter, the same guard rushed inside the tent as the sound of excited voices neared.

"What happened?" Ban asked.

"The craftsmen are here. They said the design's great," the poor fellow muttered before Gozzag handed him a jug of water.

The craftsmen's voices turned louder and louder. Apparently they wanted to meet the designer.

Lev turned to Gozzag and raised his hand. "Do we have a deal?"

"A pinskin's agreement, huh? Deal."

* * *

After the meeting, Lev, Volker, and Ban made their way to another tent where a table had been set with large wooden cups filled to the brim with mead. As they entered the room, they saw that a few old expedition members and Lev's men had already started drinking, probably bored of all the waiting.

As the three entered the room, however, the partying quickly came to a pause as they turned their attention to their respective leaders.

"Now look at that," Ban said. "Looks like you were right, Lev. We've been talking for too long."

"S-Sir, I can explain! We were just checking the quality of the mead. We didn't want your guests to have a disappointing visit," one of the seated dekas said, looking at his feet. His mates stayed silent, too drunk to even form coherent words.

Ban didn't respond. He took an empty barrel, walked towards the storage room, and filled it up.

"You guys should've told us to stop talking! Here Lev, this one's for you!" Ban said as he took the next empty barrel, filling it up as well.

"Volker, you better stand your man in front of Lev. Don't want to lose now, do you? Even the new leader of the goblin girls can down a few rounds. Where is she anyway?" Ban pondered as he looked around.

"You mean Ruune? The moment one of our men told her that Rapha's alive, she bolted towards the cavern. Hopefully she's able to avoid the angry bogey hordes. Even the old harem guard won't be spared right now. Tempers against the goblins are high."

"That's a shame. We could've seen her drink you under the table," Ban said with a laugh.

"Shouldn't we be leaving, Lev? We got our answer," Volker asked, looking nervously at his cup of mead.

Lev didn't respond. Volker looked around, only to find that Lev had already seated himself among the others and was guzzling down mead like a champion. Ban and the other dekas laughed and sang old ballads as Lev drank another cup empty.

"Hits the spot, doesn't it?" Ban said with his ears and nose purple.

One of the deka drunkenly leaned over to whisper into Volker's ear, but forgot to whisper. "Oy, Volker, isn't it time for you to start that cup?"

Just as Volker touched the rim of the cup to his lips, the flap of the tent swung open and in walked Gozzag.

"Ah, the king himself has joined us! Meeting got you thirsty as well, didn't it?" Ban shouted, slack-jawed. He stumbled forward and grabbed a piece of Gozzag's pants and tried to drag him towards the table.

"You told me we were going to get a drink, so I'm here to—"

"You can't talk to us before finishing this barrel!" Ban interrupted as a barrel slid from his hand, falling pitifully on the ground at Gozzag's feet, splashing his pants wet.

"Thanks for joining us, Gozzag. But first, let's leave this room before Ban makes a mess of it. I enjoy drinking among friends, but Ban has... lost it," Lev said, still lucid, even after having finished all of his drinks.

Volker left the room together with Lev and Gozzag, taking his still-full cup of mead with him and leaving behind Ban and his drunk dekas. Most of the greyborns had passed out.

As they hustled away from the tent to escape Ban's drunken singing, the air around the trio grew cold as the merry mood stayed behind.

"A storm is coming, Lev. It won't be pretty," Gozzag said whilst leaning on a newly built wooden wall.

"I know, but we'll be prepared. As long as we both do our part, and our men are prepared and armed, we'll be fine in the coming battle."

"I hope you're right Lev, I really do."

CHAPTER 18
OLD BLOOD

While Lev and his men had made their way towards the deka camp, two other greyborn forces had gathered in a tunnel. One was more than a hundred and fifty strong while the other group was only a third of their size. Sparks flew between the two sides whilst their leaders argued to no end.

"Why are we even talking to these shits? Isn't that guy the boss is talking to just their leader's pet?" A short greyborn with a cloudy eye and short messy hair asked his much older, bald comrade. He'd joined Vyrga's forces only a year ago, while the older bogey had already been present when Vyrga had killed his parents and taken over.

It didn't take long for the younger bogey to notice all the murderous glares from the older members of the gang. Had he misspoken?

"What did I do wrong? All I did was talk about Rak's—"

"Watch your mouth," the older bogey growled. "He's got history with us."

"Really?"

"Yeah, we've known him since he was a brat," the bald bogey added.

The one-eyed thug returned his gaze at the arguing leaders, even more confused than he'd been before.

"Don't be a damn idiot!" Hem yelled at Vyrga.

"You're making it sound as if I'm in danger," Vyrga replied. "I only need to retake my position, see a wayward child, and ask him a few questions."

"And those questions are what? How to get killed? You know what he did to Os!"

Vyrga glared at Hem. "That's one of the reasons why I need to go. It's not something he would do."

"Ha! That's rich. Don't your teachings revolve around doing whatever you want, no matter the consequences?"

"There are always consequences, Hemgall. But I believe that if you can accept them to do what you desire, then you should do it. With how unfair this world is, there's no reason for us to play by its rules."

"Even if it leads to this? Is Heimo following your example and Os's death acceptable to you?"

Vyrga said nothing.

"I figured as much. Maybe that's why I never liked you at all. You regret teaching him your shit, right?" Hemgall scoffed.

"No, I only regret this outcome."

"Stubborn as always. Hey, shortstack," Hem growled at a short, spear-wielding greyborn standing close to Vyrga. "You're just gonna let him go through with this?"

"How many times did I tell you not to call me shortstack!?" the spear-wielder, Ludger, yelled at Hem.

"Well, you got rid of that stupid hairstyle, so I can't exactly call you tailhead anymore. More importantly, stop him before he gets himself killed!"

"I'm going with him. Heimo did something he shouldn't have," Ludger replied, tightening his grip on his spear.

Hem sighed. "So Vyrga's not the only one going numb in the head. Great, just great."

"This is what you call it? Going numb in the head? He killed Os, Hem! Yeah, we didn't always get along and his strict attitude was shit, but he was a brother to me, to us! I'm not going there to make peace with that traitor. I'm only going there to find out why he went so far before I shove my spear up his ass!" Ludger yelled.

Before he could go on a tirade, a large but timid-looking greyborn patted him on the back. It was another one of Vyrga's children, and Ludger's biological brother, Bolo.

"Calm down. Just like Hem said, I think we need to think this through."

Ludger turned to his brother and scowled. "Like when you thought I should let Heimo go after I'd cornered him? Look where that got us!"

"We were surrounded by his loyalists. We would not have made it out alive if we'd killed him. Besides, when you attacked him, he had a look like he'd accepted the outcome. I know Heimo more than you, Ludger," Bolo retorted.

"Accepted the outcome? Are you kidding me? It's all in your head, Bolo. You're just trying to defend him because you and Gelmar were his closest friends. You two, along with the deserter over here, were the first to approach him."

"I was his best friend, but Gelmar was a brother to him. We two were the only ones who accepted him and managed to get him to open up."

"A miracle, if you ask me. That kid was a freak. Still is, by the looks of it!"

Bolo frowned. "You just don't know what he went through. The emptiness of his eyes back then—"

"And neither do you. Only four people know how bad his life was before he became one of us." Ludger glanced in the direction of Hem and Vyrga. "And one of them was put down for biting the wrong hand. That's what Heimo deserves."

Vyrga cast down his eyes. He'd wanted to test Lev and get rid of Gelmar before the latter turned dangerous, but hadn't realised how much the fellow's death would hurt him. His ambitions required him to terminate any possible threats, even those close to him. How was Gelmar's death different?

Why, though? And why do I want to speak with Heimo? He's a bigger threat now than Gelmar ever was. Have I grown attached? Or is this due to lingering guilt over Gelmar? Did I make a weakness for myself? Vyrga shook his head, then looked up at the arguing bogeys.

He only needed to snap his fingers once to grab everyone's attention.

Vyrga frowned at the two arguing greyborns. "I've heard enough, and I'm not going to back down. This needs to be done."

"It does. But will you give Heimo what he deserves?" Ludger probed.

"As I said, I'll do what needs to be done."

"That's not an explanation," Ludger argued.

"No... Does that mean you'll kill Heimo?It must have been a mistake, so give him a chance to explain himself," Bolo pleaded.

"You better back down, Vyrga! You won't like the ending of this damned tale!" Hem argued.

"Enough!" Vyrga roared, silencing the three.

"But—" Ludger began to retort, but Vyrga's steely glare frightened him to a halt.

Vyrga sneered. "But what, boy? This farce has gone on long enough. I thought I'd taught you all that the only thing you should never do, is defy me. Should I teach you again what happens to those who ignore me?"

All of them, with the exception of Bolo, who'd been too young at the time, recalled a certain event.

There was once a greyborn named Rasha.

Rasha was one of the original members of Vyrga's crew. Due to his strength, charisma, and loyalty to Vyrga, he received his approval. Given command of thirty men, he'd been tasked to defend their limited territory during a gang war while Vyrga dealt a final blow to the enemy's base of operations.

The veteran bogey, indignant that he'd been ordered to perform such a trivial task despite his years of servitude, had ignored his orders and led his forces to join Vyrga in attacking the enemy base, leaving their own defenceless in the process.

Vyrga and his men were still in the midst of battle when they heard the unfortunate news. Their base had been conquered by a small force, cutting off their supply chain. Vyrga's men lost their morale as they worried for their families, many of whom lived in and around the base. In the end, Rasha's insubordination led to Vyrga's first defeat in battle, and the loss of many able men.

Ludger shuddered as he recalled two things. First, while retreating from the battle, Ludger and the rest of Vyrga's disciples had been forced by Vyrga to take shelter so that they'd be able to escape in the aftermath of the battle. Despite their best efforts, four of them were found and killed. The rival gang's men had been but a few steps away from finding and slaughtering the rest.

Second, and this is really what made him shudder, was what had happened to Rasha.

It didn't take long for Vyrga to rally what remained of his men and chase the invaders off his territory. Once he did, he searched every nook and cranny till he found the man responsible for his defeat.

The bogey had had his ears, eyes, and tongue cut off. As if that weren't enough, Vyrga even crucified Rasha on the very spot he'd ordered him to defend their territory. There, Rasha was further humiliated by the families of those who'd been butchered, kidnapped, and raped during the enemy's attack.

By the time Rasha finally passed away, he'd been covered in shit and rot. Eventually, his body was eaten by corpse-eaters, and people moved on.

Whether it was from the grief of losing four of his brothers or his dislike of Vyrga's methods, it didn't take Hem long to leave after that, eventually joining Rak.

Ludger and the others knew that Vyrga wouldn't do such a thing to them, but he wasn't foolish enough to talk back to an angry Vyrga. Neither were Hem and Bolo.

"Heh. Same attitude as the old times, huh? People like you never change. Fine, do what you want. Don't say I didn't warn you. I'm not risking the life of my men for the likes of you," Hem said with a glare before turning towards his men.

Vyrga frowned as he watched Hem and his men leave.

Bolo was torn by the sight. He managed to gather his courage and asked, "Is this really ok? He's also—"

"Enough, Bolo. Just enough," Ludger interrupted before turning a weary look to Vyrga. "I might not like Hem for leaving us, but I get his point."

Ludger paused. "I'll join the fight. I'll do as you say, but Heimo has to pay."

"Come on, then. Let's leave," Vyrga replied. He signalled his men to march.

Bolo could only follow the duo and make sure they and his men were safe.

Vyrga, Ludger, and Bolo organised their forces and left towards the westernmost cavern entrance where Heimo had set his base.

The march was unremarkable, filled with loud yells and jeers from the men. While he did choose to pass through an area controlled by his allies and clients, Vyrga found it suspicious how the commoner bogeys they passed on the way did their best to ignore the massive force of greyborns. The fact that they weren't approached by any overseers, guards, taskmasters, or nobles made him even more weary.

Our relationship aside, shouldn't they be trying to prevent any infighting at the moment? We were given the order to forget grudges and focus on the Jiira, so why would they let us through? I can't think of a reason...

It suddenly hit him. He turned around and looked at the back of his formation to see the commoners condensing around the area, blocking their earlier path. *Unless we were betrayed.*

Vyrga chuckled. *Well played.*

Ludger noticed Vyrga's strange behaviour and approached. "What's wrong, Vyrga?"

"Keep an eye out and tell the men to prepare for a possible ambush."

"From where?"

"Everywhere. The bogeys here could be enemies. They may be looking to flank us or cut off our escape route.

The shocked spear-wielder looked around. With what Vyrga had told him, he noticed some new details he hadn't before. He noticed how the better-equipped green bogeys, presumably commanders in the war against the Jiira, were keeping an eye on them. And he, like Vyrga, noticed the blockade forming behind them.

"So we're doomed?"

"Depends on what Heimo offered them. At best, they won't interfere and are just here to prevent us from running away. At worst, they'll ambush or join in the attack."

Ludger wanted to yell, but doing so would alert the traitors. "Why didn't you choose a less crowded path?" He hissed as quietly as he could.

"There are no empty paths. Even the smuggling routes were blocked to prevent leaving any backdoors to the Jiira."

"Dammit..."

"What happened?" Bolo inquired. Ludger's voice was too loud and tense to ignore.

Ludger approached his brother and whispered everything to him, causing the latter to click his tongue in frustration.

"Let's not worry yet. I doubt he's gained enough recognition from the higher-ups to make them waste their men if we go to battle."

"There's obviously going to be a battle. Why would he have cut off our route back otherwise?" Ludger queried.

"To have the higher ground in a negotiation," Bolo answered.

"His force should be smaller than ours. Most who joined him left once they heard that Vyrga was alive and back."

"Are any of them currently with us?"

Vyrga shook his head. "No. I divided them up and put them on patrol. I'd be a fool if I had them march with us only to have them stab us in the back."

Both Bolo and Ludger nodded in agreement. "So what should we do now?" Ludger wondered.

"Tell the men to be on guard for any cheap tricks," Vyrga ordered.

"Wouldn't that make things worse? Don't need them getting scared and breaking rank."

"The smart and observant ones probably understand the situation already. The latter might be spreading rumours. It's better for us to tell them, so we have some semblance of control. If anything goes wrong right now, it'll be a disaster," Bolo answered his brother.

His brother's words made sense, so Ludger promptly relayed the command to the group. The men efficiently adjusted their formation from one for marching to one for fighting. Their apparent discipline greatly surprised the bogeys surrounding them.

The commoners and nobles hadn't thought much of the greyborn force to begin with, but to underestimate them would be a mistake. Due to Vyrga's presumed death during the expedition, his current force wasn't as strong as Rak's, or as disciplined and trained as Lev's, but these were still Vyrga's best and most trusted men.

Unlike the rabble in Gelmar's group, most of Vyrga's personal forces had served in battles against other powerful gangs. Some had followed Vyrga since the beginning of his climb to power, while the younger members were the smartest and strongest of their generation.

All of them knew exactly when to follow orders and operate as an army.

The group advanced onwards until there were no more commoners in sight, then proceeded through several more tunnels. As they reached their destination, they found their opponents standing in rank, waiting for them.

To their surprise. Heimo and his men were wearing sets of bronze armour... accompanied by goblins.

CHAPTER 19
NEW BLOOD

Vyrga, tailed by Bolo and Ludger, stood a distance away from Heimo.

Vyrga could see the goblins standing behind Heimo's men, which numbered less than Vyrga's. Twenty of them were fully clad in bronze armour, wielding short spears and shields. Five were lightly armoured with hardened leather and carried strange bows. Five more were wearing no armour at all and held haze-tipped focus staffs. There was also a gigantic hooded figure covered in chainmail that gave Vyrga chills when he stared at it. Something about that figure felt... off.

To Vyrga, Heimo looked different. Even from a distance, and with most of Heimo's face covered by his horned bronze helmet, Vyrga could tell that he seemed older and paler. Heimo's right hand seemed to be twitching. Vyrga almost felt concerned for his old protégé until he took into account the Jiira standing a short distance away behind Heimo's formation.

Vyrga's lips curled. "So you sold out your own people."

"I'm doing this *for* our people. The greyborns," Heimo retorted.

Ludger spat in Heimo's direction. "What a sick joke."

Bolo silently shook his head.

Vyrga could barely contain his incredulity. "Doing what?" he spouted. "Keeping us as slaves? You'd keep us under goblin thumbs and say it's for *us*?!"

"We need these goblins' cooperation if we want to get anywhere out of here!" Heimo shot back.

"Don't be a fool, boy! 'Cooperation' means submission to them, no matter what they deliver in return! The Jiira would never accept us as their equals."

"Things have changed. Many among the Jiira nobles are discontent with how things are run. These goblins can take out the Jiira chief and his cronies without spilling any greyborn blood!"

"That doesn't refute what I said. Replacing their ruler doesn't guarantee us a good position in their new order. What makes you think that those who stabbed their liege, as idiotic as he was, would keep their word? After all is said and done, we'll still be toiling in this cave, dying to hivelings while lining another tribe's pockets!"

Heimo shouted back. "Supporting a doomed revolution won't help us either. You should know that what we faced during the last revolution wasn't even the full might of the Jiira. Compromises need to be made, and I'll bet on their side. In return for our service, not only will greyborns reign at the top, but these goblins will help us get our magic back so we can wipe out the hivelings together! This is the path with the least tragedies for our race!"

"I don't give a shit," Ludger interrupted.

"What?" Heimo asked.

Ludger glowered. "I said, I don't give a shit. Neither of you will budge. Why did you kill Os?"

Heimo lowered his head and turned silent.

"Answer the question, Heimo!" Ludger yelled.

"Please tell us why," Bolo cut in.

One look at Heimo was all that Vyrga needed. That look of guilt and hesitation gave away what had happened.

"I wanted to believe that it wasn't you, that it was the goblins or a mishap, but it seems otherwise. He got in your way, didn't he?"

Heimo looked at the three and answered, "You wouldn't believe how much Os's death ate—eats at me. I tried to spin the truth in my head.

How it'd been an accident, how it wasn't my fault. But it doesn't matter. I still killed him.

"It had to be done to prevent him from leaking information. If it means anything to you, I tried to bargain with him... but he chose to fight."

Ludger growled, Bolo lowered his head in defeat, and Vyrga took out his bow. "Seems this discussion is over. I have raised a disloyal dog, with each of its legs stuck in a drudging quest for power. You turned out to be such a disappointment, boy."

Heimo sneered and took out his own bow. "Like my brother, huh?"

"If only. At least Gelmar had conviction, while you've become a goblin bootlicker." Vyrga drew his bow. "Just tell me one thing. When did you side with them?"

"During the expedition, when you made peace with Gelmar's killer instead of going for his head like you promised," Heimo replied in a cold voice, his own bow ready in his hand.

"I see."

"Do you, now?"

Both leaders rapidly nocked an arrow and fired. Vyrga dodged to the left, while his arrow struck the horn on Heimo's helmet, leaving a dent before it fell to the ground.

Their armies charged each other head-on.

Vyrga withdrew to the back of his formation. Drawing four arrows from his quiver, he nocked one, targeted one of the goblins archers, aiming slightly ahead of him, and shot.

The arrow sped through the air and hit the enemy archer in the throat. The goblin struggled to dislodge the arrow until he took another arrow to the abdomen.

Vyrga cursed under his breath, then dodged one of the goblin archers' giant arrows as he nocked another of his own. He aimed for the goblin that had just targeted him and released. His arrow made contact but unfortunately bounced off the goblin's helmet.

Before Vyrga could shoot again, a bronze-tipped projectile whizzed over his shoulder. An instant later, another was blocked by a friendly shield. Its owner groaned as he withstood the tremendous might of the javelin-sized arrow.

"Are you all right?" Bolo asked. Vyrga nodded.

Brothers against brothers, Vyrga observed dryly. Though his own men were more experienced and loyal than Heimo's, both forces fought with the same brutal frenzy.

Vyrga turned back to Bolo. "Things aren't going according to plan. Heimo's benefactors are unexpectedly hardy."

"I don't mean to be rude," Bolo started unsteadily, "but, low ceiling or not, we should've brought more archers. You're a great archer, but I don't think even you can take them all out. Besides, those weird giant bows are doing a solid number on us."

A shattering noise alerted Vyrga to another attack. Four of his men were soaked in a viscous liquid, shielding their eyes in pain. Shards of a clay flask had scattered on the ground near them. Vyrga winced as Heimo's men finished them off.

Poison! I should've known Heimo would play dirty.

"Boss. Do you have any special arrows?"

"Poison-tipped copper arrows."

"How many?"

"Six."

Bolo repositioned his shield to help protect Vyrga from the oncoming arrows, blocking another arrow. Vyrga fired another of his, missing the archer but hitting a goblin shaman behind him. "I doubt that'll be enough."

"Bolo, you know good poison is hard to get, even for me. And I can only hold so many arrows."

"How many arr—"

Another arrow hit Bolo's shield, almost breaking his stance.

"This isn't the time, Bolo. Focus on the fight!" Vyrga continually fired arrows whenever Bolo gave him an opening, while Ludger scoured the battleground for Heimo.

Ludger thrust his spear at a charging axeman. The spearhead penetrated well past the back of the axeman's eye socket before Ludger yanked the spear back out.

He dodged a spear thrust from another of Heimo's men. One of Ludger's men grabbed hold of the incoming spear, pulled its owner in with it, and bludgeoned the man's bronze-helmed head with his mace, leaving behind a few flakes of metal in the resulting cavity.

Ludger was blankly inflicting another casualty upon Heimo's men when he heard a loud roar from his left. He turned to face the chainmail-adorned hulk of a greyborn, easily two heads taller than Rak. With glowing blue eyes; the giant held an oversized axe and shield and stared at him. He grinned viciously, as if he had marked his next prey.

He let out a roar and straight at Ludger, holding his gargantuan shield up high to cover his face and upper body.

Ludger immediately thrust low, but the behemoth slammed his shield feetward, deflecting Ludger's attack. He then utilised his shield to slam Ludger onto the ground.

Ludger coughed and gasped for air. His spear slipped out of his grip. He quickly reached for the shortsword at his waist, but just as he unsheathed it, the gargantuan greyborn kicked it out of his other hand, far out of reach. The giant giggled, mirth spilling out of his bizarre blue eyes. Ludger had never seen a bogey with blue eyes before.

The behemoth raised his axe high to deal the killing blow. Suddenly, Ludger heard a loud *Clang!* and the behemoth froze, an arrow embedded in his helmet.

Stunned, the giant dropped his axe. Ludger had just barely enough time to roll out of its way. Two belaboured spear-thrusts later, Ludger had knocked off the giant's dented bronze helmet. Ludger then raised his spear high over the fallen giant, but once it came down, the spear ricocheted off the giant's chest plate into its armpit.

Try as he might, Ludger couldn't get it out. It was stuck there.

To his surprise, instead of reacting in pain, shock or anger, the giant instead grinned maniacally. It then erupted into roaring laughter and turned its attention away from Ludger and to the spear. With a single pull, it removed the spear from its armpit and snapped it in half.

The giant's eyes scanned for another, easier prey. Its eyes landed on one of Vyrga's other men. As it rumbled away, Ludger collapsed and laid on the ground, adrenaline still rushing through him.

One of his own soldiers, a bald man wielding a mace, ran over to him and helped him back up. "You alright, boss?"

"Willibald!"

"Hah! The one and only."

A now-familiar roar followed by sounds of greyborn distress drew Ludger's attention. The giant had tackled a spearman, one of his own, and embedded his greataxe narrowly between the man's mouth and nose. With another series of mad giggles, the giant began to punch the spearman's face over and over, even as the sounds of blunt force gave way to squelching noises.

"What a freak!" Willibald cried.

"A freak I'm gonna kill," Ludger seethed with renewed vigour. The beast's back was turned to him. Ludger picked up a bronze sword from one of the fallen goblins and sneaked closer.

The beastly giant released a satisfied sigh as he peered down at his latest victim's remains. As he opened his mouth to inhale once more, a sword emerged from between his jaws like a lopsided bronze tongue.

With both hands, Ludger pushed the blade further and snapped the behemoth's cervical spine, leaving the sword in the titan's nape. Sweat dripped down his blood-spattered body as he retrieved his spear. From what he could see, severe losses had been dealt to both sides.

Ludger could not grasp how Heimo's men, even with superior equipment, had lasted this long. Nor how they had managed to take out so many of Vyrga's most experienced soldiers. He surveyed the battlefield. Blood, piss, and smoke from the fallen soldiers covered all he could see. The stench of dead men mingled with that of charred flesh. *Charred flesh?* Ludger noticed a shaman pointing a focus staff at him.

"Dodge!" he yelled at Willibald before jumping out of the way, narrowly avoiding a large fireball that made impact where his feet had been. Ludger felt the hairs on his skin singe.

"Blasted shamans! My daughter made this tunic for me!" Willibald lamented. He hurriedly tried to pat down the flames that had caught on his tunic.

Ludger, meanwhile, could no longer see Vyrga shooting arrows from the backline. He scanned the corpses around him, fearing for the worst, until Vyrga interrupted him with Bolo in tow. Vyrga was wielding an extravagant sword Ludger had never seen before. Its pommel, carved in the form of a wolf, was a design unfamiliar to bogeykind.

Two hands pushed Ludger down as a large moving object smashed behind him. A quick glance showed it to be a large stone spike.

"Stay sharp if you don't want to die!" Willibald growled as he got up, glaring at the goblin shaman who had launched the spell.

He then turned to Ludger. "So, boss, any idea on how to deal with these overpowered spell lovers?"

"I don't know. Besides, Vyrga's out of arrows. He's fighting with a flashy sword now."

"Well, shit."

Ludger looked at the Jiira's numbers and shrugged. "At least their numbers were reduced considerably."

From what he saw, there weren't many goblins, nor bogeys left on Heimo's side. Two shamans, one archer, and a few of their guards were all that remained.

"Not that I care much, but most of Heimo's lot died horribly," Ludger muttered.

Bolo nodded. "Agreed."

"Could've been worse," Vyrga responded in a bone-chilling tone.

"Hey, boss," Willibald nervously greeted, receiving a nod in return.

"Let's end this. I've had enough of this farce." Vyrga growled as his gaze met Heimo's.

Ludger grinned. "Damn right."

"Let's hope nothing bad happens. His men might've given up already, but Heimo hasn't." Bolo cut in.

"You're such a downer, Bolo. And weren't you against killing Heimo a while ago?"

Bolo released a tired sigh and looked at his brother. "I still am, but there isn't any other option. He's made his choice. I can't risk my loved ones for someone who'd kill family."

Family, huh, Vyrga thought to himself before shaking his head. "Let's go," he commanded.

Screams filled the air as the free-for-all continued as the last of Heimo's men were slain or fled.

Upon seeing their leader and his disciples once again joining the fray, morale soared for Vyrga's men.

Heimo hesitated as he looked at the scant numbers on his side. He bit his lip in frustration, then raised an amulet with a shining green crystal. Each remaining goblin heeded his signal, seizing a vial of a substance similar in colour to the crystal. Heimo put down his bow, picked up his now haze adorned short glaive, and seized his own vial. Together, they drank the accursed liquid Bodobert had given them.

Magic is at play, Vyrga thought.

Heimo sneered. "You left me no choice, father."

Vyrga suddenly noticed Heimo's eyes. His usual yellow pupils had been engulfed by an intense blue glow. The same happened with the remaining goblins.

"Let me show you the power that will help us Greyborn rise to the top!" Heimo bellowed, pointing his finger at Vyrga.

Vyrga perceived little more than a split-second flash, a crackle, and a sizzle that burned his skin as he was blasted backwards into a stalagmite. The leather armour he had been wearing had burned to a crisp. He struggled to breathe as his muscles convulsed.

"This concoction increases my strength and allows me to use volatile magics without a focus amulet. Pretty great, wouldn't you say so?" Heimo gloated. "I wish it augmented my abilities as much as I've seen in some of my men, but it seems like this is my limit. Be glad I didn't use my glaive as a focus, I wouldn't be wasting my breath if I did."

"Vyrga!" Ludger blubbered. He rushed, spear drawn, at the greyborn he had once considered his brother. "Heimo, you damned soul, who taught you magic!"

Heimo nonchalantly chucked his short glaive in Ludger's direction. "That's none of your concern, brother."

Ludger dodged the weapon, but it hit Willibald in his shoulder. Willibald bleated in pain.

As Ludger approached, Heimo grabbed his former brother's spear with both hands. With a grunt, he hoisted both spear and owner into the air before slamming him into the ground near Vyrga.

"Impossi... ble," Ludger muttered before losing consciousness.

CHAPTER 20
OUTRAGE

Heimo heard a war cry behind him. He dodged a flying bronze axe and sidestepped another strike from Willibald, only to be stabbed in the arm with his own weapon.

"Should've worn some armguards, fucker!" Willibald taunted, bringing his mace down at Heimo again. Heimo hopped backwards and swiped the bronze axe from where it'd landed right as Bolo bashed him with his shield, knocking him to the ground.

Bolo shakily made his way forward, straddling the fallen Heimo, and raised his own mace above Heimo's head. With an impassioned cry, Bolo drove the mace groundward.

Heimo grabbed Bolo's arms, stopping the incoming mace, and kicked Bolo's knee. After a sickening snap, Bolo's knee bent backwards. Bolo roared in pain and fell to the ground, allowing Heimo to roll away.

Heimo jumped to his feet. He flung out his hand at an approaching Willibald and conjured a bolt of lightning at him. Willibald, too, fell to the ground, burnt and struggling to breathe.

Heimo made a quarter turn. "Guess it's just you and me now, Bolo. Old friend. After I'm done with you, it'll be the rat king's end."

"Heimo! Stop this madness! You'll never forgive yourself if you go through with this!" Bolo pleaded.

"It's too late for that, brother. I don't want to hurt you. But them?" Heimo glared at the fallen Ludger and Vyrga. "They brought this upon themselves."

"Really? Ludger? *Vyrga?!*"

"Especially Ludger and Vyrga!" Heimo retorted. "Your brother is too stubborn for his own good. As for him." Heimo glowered at Vyrga, "I admired him. I always told Gelmar we were more than tools to Vyrga. We were his children."

"And you're right! We are his children!"

Heimo shook his head. "No, Gelmar was right. Our *father* ordered him to die."

"Gelmar wouldn't listen to reason and was secretly preparing to start a war. Vyrga had no choice!"

"Then why did he make a truce with that snake, Lev? The guy that got him betrayed and slaughtered by his own men? He promised vengeance yet what did he give us? Gelmar's traitorous captain, and the one who first ran away from the battle! Face it, he's a piece of shit that deserves to die!" Heimo's fingertips crackled with lightning. "Open your eyes, Bolo! We're nothing but tools!"

Heimo sighed. "It doesn't even matter at this point. It's not like I can convince you, especially with our *dear father* and that daft brother of yours crawling around. I wanted to make them suffer... but it seems best I end them quickly now."

Bolo's heart skipped once he saw Heimo grab his short glaive back from the downed Willibald, and point it towards where Vyrga and his brother lay.

"Maybe you'll see reason after that," Heimo mumbled.

"No!" Bolo roared. Despite his broken knee, he leapt forward and swung his mace at Heimo again, only for Heimo to sidestep the swipe and roundhouse kick Bolo to the ground.

"I won't... let you hurt... them," Bolo gasped.

Heimo groaned. "Look. If I promise to spare Ludger, will you just stay down?"

Bolo gasped for air. "No. Vyrga... saved you, too," Bolo continued. "Thanks to Vyrga... We had real meals out of a... bowl, not out of the...

trash." Bolo struggled to stand, but his knee, along with a sharp pain in his chest from Heimo's kick, kept him down.

Heimo sneered. "So he fed us moss and lichen instead of carrion. And for that, we should die for him?"

Bolo was stunned. "Are you kidding? Out of all of us, he made sure to never put you in harm's way. He even taught you how to use a bow! If you feel so 'used,' why didn't you just leave like Hemgall did? Nobody would have stopped you!"

"You're really starting to piss me off— gah!" A wayward javelin knocked Heimo's horned helmet off his head.

Heimo whirled around. All of his men were either dead or captured. He was surrounded, the goblins nowhere in sight.

"Looking for these?" a large, muscular greyborn called out. He tossed a goblin's decapitated head at Heimo.

"Hemgall! *You're* back?" Heimo snarled in frustration.

"Damn right. Heard you took out Oswald, but not that old bastard Vyrga. Good for you—Vyrga's mine."

"Well, this is unexpected," Bolo muttered with a relieved smile on his face.

Hemgall ran towards Heimo, his steel double-headed axe raised high. Heimo readied a finger to blast Hem with lightning, but Hem's axehead wedged itself in his shoulder before he could.

The axe head started to glow as Heimo's lightning spell destabilised and shocked him. Though he managed to avoid Hemgall's incoming axe swipe with a well-timed backwards leap, he could not rip the axe out of his shoulder.

Heimo did a double-take. How had Hem produced another axe? Then he noticed—the axe Hem was holding now had only one head. "How did you—"

"You like my axe? When I first saw it, I wondered, 'What kind of idiot would waste good metal to make an axe with two blades and a weird handle?' Turns out this axe can split into two! Hahahaha!" Hemgall circled around Heimo, watching him sweat and struggle to maintain his grip on his short glaive. "Neat, huh? Ainshard's time was something else!"

"Ainshard?" Heimo's eyes widened in shock.

"Yup. Iron stronger than bronze? All that stuff turned out to be real."

"Gelmar... Gelmar believed more than anyone else that Ainshard had really existed." Heimo spat. "And yet you were the one to discover proof?"

A twinge of pity crossed Hemgall's face. "You've grown bitter, kid."

"Bitter? No. I'm just tired. Tired of being betrayed, tired of being abandoned, tired of this world where people trample on my dreams for their own! Getting rid of scum like Vyrga won't fix the world, but it sure as hell will make sure I won't be someone's puppet again!"

"I don't know what to tell you, kid. Vyrga warned us that this world is shit and that he'd use us. I'm sure that deep down you know that the goblins won't be any better."

"He acted like he cared! That's why we all agreed! We all wanted a family, yet how many times did our *father* throw us in the mire to test us!?"

Hemgall shrugged. "That's one of the reasons I left. Whether he really cared or not, I don't know. I just know I was sick of that life and that I don't want to live like he does."

"Vyrga wouldn't have tested Rak if you hadn't left, you selfish bastard!"

Hemgall was at the end of his wit. "I don't know how else to explain this to you. Rak knew I'd followed Vyrga before I followed him. Rak knew Vyrga was someone with ambition. Rak knew that someone like

Veit would betray him eventually, he just didn't want to believe it. Just… give up."

"As long as I still have a chance, I'll fight! My dream won't end like this and I won't lose!"

Hemgall sighed. "But you already did, this isn't a story where you're a hero who can slay entire armies by yourself. Look around you. Just give up already."

Heimo's eyes shone brighter. "Never! Never, never, never, never!"

"What happened to you, Heimo?" Bolo muttered between laboured breaths.

The glow from Heimo's eyes intensified, then spread to the rest of his face. It continued to spread through his veins until his body shined as bright as the artificial sun on the sixth floor of the cavern.

"I won't be stopped! My dream will come true! I'll save everyone! I'll protect everyone! I'll, I'll, I'll-ah!" His screams were cut short as a sword pierced him in the chest.

"I'm sorry. I wish it hadn't come to this. I should've been better towards all of you." A haggard Vyrga muttered in the struggling Heimo's ear. In a fatigued, clumsy motion, he grabbed Heimo by the neck and pushed his blade through Heimo's heart.

Heimo's eyes shook as his glow dimmed. His shaky hand grabbed Vyrga's arm, the one grabbing his neck, and tried to scratch it. "I-I hate you…" Heimo muttered through his gasping breaths.

Vyrga looked apologetic. "I hate myself, too, but I really did… love all of you," he whispered. "Now sleep. Gelmar's waiting for you."

A single tear dropped down Heimo's cheek. "Vyr… ga," he rasped. His convulsions came to a halt, but his body began to glow with a blinding blue light.

"Ahh! My eyes!"

"What the hell is happening!"

"Is there a fire?!"

Heimo's body spontaneously erupted into blue flames. Vyrga hurriedly doffed his already-singed cloak to beat the flames down, but they licked and crackled all the more until they had fully engulfed Heimo's body. With a final burst, the flames gave off another blinding flash of light, heralding a concussive shockwave that knocked Vyrga unconscious.

* * *

Vyrga opened his eyes and looked around. Everyone was still lying unconscious on the ground, with Heimo's body was nowhere to be found.

What happened? What happened to Heimo? Vyrga thought to himself. He suddenly heard Hemgall groan.

"Ugggh, what just happened?" Hemgall asked, gradually regaining awareness in his limbs.

"Heimo's body disappeared," Vyrga replied.

"Somebody stole him?"

"No. There aren't any footprints or tracks from his body being dragged away, nor evidence of corpse-eater activity. The bright light must've scared them off."

Hemgall chuckled. "So lights can kidnap bodies now. Makes sense."

Vyrga turned to face Hem head-on. "How much of what we've been through recently has made sense?"

Hem reflexively prepared to argue with Vyrga, but something about the other's expression shocked him. He sighed instead. "So what's the plan now?"

"Reorganise and prepare myself."

"For the coming battle?"

"For when we let the goblins through."

"What!" Hemgall yelled. "Have you lost your mind!?"

Vyrga sneered. "It's like you don't know me at all! I have a plan, and you, Rak, and Lev will help see it to fruition."

As Vyrga shared his plan with Hemgall, the latter was lost in his thoughts.

"Well?" Vyrga inquired.

"... Huh. Sounds deceptively simple, but it could work. Will they fall for it, though? We've taken out a good chunk of their forces already so they won't underestimate us again."

"Their main army will. Now run along and explain it to Lev and Rak while I get a healer for Bolo and the others. Ludger will be the end of me if Willibald dies."

"Who said I was gonna play messenger for you, Vyrga?"

"If it's you, Rak will listen."

Hemgall groaned. "Fine."

"Thank you," Vyrga muttered, surprising Hemgall once again.

Hemgall stopped in his tracks for a moment. "You owe me one. Now wipe your tears before the others wake up."

Tears? Vyrga thought. He touched his cheek; it was moist.

Vyrga sighed. He cleaned his relic sword with a rag he had kept tied to his belt, and slipped the blade back into its sheath on his left. He then plucked out a smaller cloth and wiped his eyes, missing a tiny blue spark as it swiftly appeared and faded within his sword's haze crystal.

CHAPTER 21
TOMORROW'S GAMBLE

Inside a large, decrepit building, hidden alongside a side tunnel in the slave quarters, many greyborns were in hiding. The majority were women, children, and elderly who were spending their time sleeping, discussing their current situation or reminiscing about better times. Many were praying, trying to comfort themselves in these troubled times. A few armed able-bodied men guarded them, making sure no one would discover their location.

Along one wall was a blonde girl trying to wake up her friend.

"Ghorza... Ghorza. Hey, Ghorza!"

"Mmm, Gherm?" Ghorza mumbled.

"Ha, nope. It's me, Abelarda," the blonde replied with a toothy grin.

Ghorza sat up from the cloth-covered haystack upon which she had slept. She realised once again that she was still in the hideout. "So it was just a dream," she muttered in disappointment.

Abelarda frowned. While she hadn't known Ghorza for long, she already considered her a good friend, and didn't like seeing her down.

I wouldn't be a good friend if I left her by herself. I'm sure she wouldn't like it if I tried changing the subject, though. Abelarda thought.

She snapped her fingers. "Did ya dream your brother was back again?"

"Yeah. And we weren't in a war... and he'd quit his gang... things were like they used to be."

"Ghorza. If it weren't for that gang of his, we wouldn't have had anywhere to hide. Rak's guys are only here because Rak respects your brother."

"Speaking of brothers, how's Volker?" Ghorza asked.

Abelarda sighed. "I heard he kicked goblin ass yesterday. I still wonder what Gherm did to give him a spine."

"You're not still mad at Gherm, are you?"

Abelarda waved her hand dismissively. "Nah, it was Gul's fault for getting Volker involved in the first place. I already gave him a black eye when he returned from the expedition."

Ghorza smiled. "Thanks for not blaming Gherm."

Abelarda grinned. *There we go. Talking always makes the pain a bit easier.*

"How could I? You care about him too much."

"No more than you care about Volker," Ghorza teased.

It didn't take long for Ghorza to notice the other two girls were missing. "Have you seen Reeza and Lore today?" she asked.

Abelarda shrugged. "Reeza's playing with the kids to cheer them up. Lore went out."

Ghorza gasped. "She what!? Isn't that dangerous?"

Abelarda chuckled. "Trust me, she'll be fine. Her family's full of smugglers and she learned the family trade. Who do you think gets us our dyes? That girl could hide from the gods themselves if she wanted to."

"Th-That sounds incriminating."

"She's the one who told me to tell you. Your brother's a gang leader, right?"

Ghorza nodded wordlessly.

Abelarda patted her on the back. "It'd help her family a lot to be on good terms with him once he's back."

Ghorza's eyes widened in surprise, her face sporting the brightest smile Abelarda had seen from her for a while. "Finally. Someone else believes in him!"

"I didn't before. It's not like anyone's pulled it off. But if he's kept my idiot brother alive, well, maybe he can achieve something after all."

"If you say so, haha!" Ghorza laughed. She had not felt this relieved, however temporarily, in a long time. *Even Thorst doesn't believe Gherm's alive. He's been trying his best to console me instead.*

"By the way." Abelarda added. "Why does he call himself Lev? Wasn't Gherm a good enough name? Surely, some pretty words from an old hag who thinks water in a cup can convey the will of a god isn't the main reason."

Ghorza turned away. "It's a long story. Hey, is that kid trying to eat Reeza's tunic?"

Abelarda rolled her eyes. "Alllllrighty then. Keep your secrets. I'm hungry. Let's get Reeza away from those brats for lunch."

The two made their way to the other side of the building. Young greyborns were running about, trying to catch others. Reeza was one of the unlucky targets, and she was proving difficult to catch for the younger greyborns.

Abelarda called out to her friend. "Wow, Reeza. You're fast!"

Hearing her friend's voice, Reeza instinctively looked around for Abelarda. While she was distracted, three greyborn children tackled her to the ground.

"Ugh," Reeza groaned. "Thanks a lot."

"We finally did it!" one of the children yelled excitedly.

"This doesn't count," Reeza whined.

"Yes it does."

"No it doesn't."

"Yes it does!"

"No, it doesn't!"

So the argument continued. Neither Reeza nor the young greyborn conceded until Abelarda dragged the brunette away herself.

"I lost because of you," Reeza muttered.

"Stop being a sore loser and grow up," Abelarda retorted.

"Same to you. How's gambling?"

"Shut up."

"Why should I?" Reeza teased with a mischievous grin.

"Ghorza and I will eat without you."

"You wouldn't. You'd get bored too easily," Reeza said with a smirk. "It's not like Lore's here, either."

"I heard she's away on family business," Ghorza replied.

Reeza shifted uncomfortably. "Y-Yeah, that's it, family business—"

"She knows," Abelarda said. "Did you forget who her brother is?"

"Oh, right. Sorry Ghorza."

Right as Ghorza was about to reassure her, Abelarda cut in. "Let's go eat already. I'm starving."

The three of them picked up their morning rations. Instead of heading to their usual eating spot, they sat against a wall covered in glowing moss.

"Why did we decide to sit here? The moss stinks," Reeza whined.

"Can't have you be the only one stinking," Abelarda announced.

"Gee, thanks. I feel relieved," Reeza grumbled, her nose scrunched. "It'll take forever to wash the smell off."

Each meal consisted of a bowl of grain porridge, mushrooms, a few insects, and a raw turnip. Rations were never extravagant.

Much to Reeza's irritation, Abelarda went down on her meal with gusto. Every sip of the porridge was a loud slurp and every insect that went into her mouth was followed by a loud voracious crunch.

Reeza put down her own bowl and stared daggers at her blonde friend. "Can you keep it down? You're eating like a starved hiveling again."

Abelarda shrugged. "It's how I am. Didn't stop me from tying the knot so no reason to change it."

"What do you mean?" Ghorza asked.

"Got married once and the righteous idiot couldn't wait long before turning me into a widow. Thankfully, no kids. Don't know how I'd be able to take care of them on my own." Abelarda replied nonchalantly, shocking Ghorza.

"I'm so sorry."

"Don't apologise. It's not like you killed the damn fool. He had to play the hero and got stabbed to death by Vyrga's lot."

The resulting silence was palpable. At least, until Abelarda lowered her bowl. "If I wanted silence, I'd eat alone." The annoyance left Abelarda's face after another bite. "So, have you heard?"

"Heard what?" Ghorza returned to her meal.

"About the outside world. All the conscripts talk about is how breathtaking the view outside is. Guess that's the one upside to risking their lives every day."

"Blue skies, a giant ball of light, and a 'forest,' right?" Reeza rolled her eyes. "These 'forest' things can't be much more than overgrown moss and vines tangled with sticks!"

"I really want to see the outside," Ghorza said.

Abelarda stopped mid-chew. "Why? If you want light, there's more than enough if you stand under a sky hole."

"It's a whole new world, full of food, water, and life. Half this entire settlement's food supply comes from 'outside,' and 'outside' food is just so different, so colourful, so... exotic," Ghorza replied, her eyes on the turnip on her lap.

"Nothing wrong with food, I'll give ya that. I just wish we had more of it," Abelarda replied, munching on her own turnip.

Reeza slurped up the last of her porridge. "Maybe you're right. Maybe tomorrow we'll beat the Jiira and suddenly have more outside food than we'll know what to do with."

"Hah, you must be joking," Abelarda chirped. "You didn't even let it end with that kid earlier. What makes you think armies would act any differently?"

Reeza lowered her bowl and glared at Abelarda. "Tch. Way to get my hopes down."

"She got my hopes up, at least." Ghorza was optimistic.

"Abelarda also believes my brother might return. Maybe he and Volker can kick the goblins out eventually."

Reeza smiled. "I hope so, Ghorza. I really do."

The discussion had long since pivoted to other topics when Thorst entered the chamber and immediately ran towards them. The three women briefly panicked, as they feared the hideout had been discovered, but there were no signs of other messengers, much less any sort of ruckus.

Abelarda was the first to speak up. "By the gods, Thorst, you scared us. What's got you so worked up, lover boy?"

Thorst took a few moments to catch his breath. Ghorza could not tell whether he was red-faced from running or from seeing her for the first time in a week.

"Gh-Ghorza," he panted.

"What? Did something happen?"

He wiped the sweat off his forehead. "Gherm's back. He's alive!"

Ghorza stood up. *Crack!* Her bowl had slipped out of her hand. "Is... Is he really back?"

"Would I lie to you, Ghorza?"

Ghorza's sudden, tight embrace made Thorst wonder whether he was dreaming, but the sensation of her tears upon his shoulder planted him firmly back in reality.

"Thank the gods," she sobbed, Thorst's arms wrapping around her ever more tightly. "Thank the gods."

When her breathing was steady again, Thorst felt her unwrap her arms. He released his embrace in response.

"So where is he, Thorst?"

Thorst froze, avoiding eye contact.

Seeing his reaction caused Ghorza to turn pale. "Thorst? Don't tell me—he was conscripted, too?"

"Gherm is—"

"Thorst, please!"

"He's—"

"Just answer her already, numbnuts!" Abelarda demanded. "You're not doing her any favours right now!"

Thorst wanted to lash out at Abelarda, but knew she was right. He turned to Ghorza. "He's joined Volker on the battlefield. Voluntarily."

Ghorza froze. It took a while for her mind to process what she'd just heard. She was fuming.

"He *what*? I need to go."

"Please don't."

"So I'm supposed to sit here quietly like a good little girl until then?" she argued.

"Just... Hang tight. The Jiira are done. We just need to clean them up. I don't want you dying out there, and I know Gherm wouldn't either."

Although she felt nothing but urgency, Ghorza effortfully flattened her forehead and relaxed her face. "Thorst, you're really good at knowing how other people feel, especially Gherm. But let me ask you this," she said, locking eyes with him with an intensity he had never seen before. "Do you have any idea how I feel?"

"I know you want to see him. Even a child could guess that. But it's dangerous outside, so staying here is best. For both of us."

"No. I want to see my brother, the only family I have left, alive and well. I've spent months thinking he was dead, Thorst," she cried. "I need to see him. I need to see my brother, I—"

Thorst shuddered as Ghorza's tears began flowing down her face again. He caressed her cheeks. "Okay, okay. I understand. I'll take you to him."

"Thank you." She slipped out of his grip and gave him a kiss on the cheek and hugged him to conceal the smile forcing its way across her face.

"Get a room, you two!" Reeza shouted.

"Yeah, I'm not going. You two run along now," Abelarda jokingly sneered. "Can't have my friend's boyfriend mesmerised by my charms."

"Charms?" Reeza and Thorst said in unison.

While Ghorza giggled, Abelarda smirked. "Very funny."

Thorst took Ghorza's hand and the two left, trying to ignore the whistles and catcalls from Ghorza's friends.

Abelarda turned to Reeza. "You and Lore owe me some alcohol. I want wheat beer, not that mushroom swill."

"Oh, come on. That was a joke! Who gambles on whether their friend's brother is dead, anyway?"

Abelarda laughed. "Someone whose prediction came true. Now buy me that beer."

"Your gambling habit's gonna bite you in the ass someday."

"Wanna bet how long that'll take?"

"Nope. Not betting against you again, ever."

CHAPTER 22
A DEVIL'S CONTRACT

"Just die already!" a goblin in a decorated set of iron scale mail screamed as he brought down his axe aiming at his adversary's neck. The enormous insectoid creature thrashed, deflecting his attack and directing it to the thick chitin covering its head instead.

"Dammit! Stop struggling already, you damned oversized bug!" he cursed loudly before striking at it with his axe once again. He wanted nothing more than to deliver the finishing blow.

The creature let out a miserable screech as it struggled. Killing the goblin would normally be a simple task, but the twenty spearmen surrounding it had already disabled more than half of its legs.

The goblin relentlessly swung his axe until the warrior hiveling's head finally fell to the ground. Once the light faded from its eyes and its body stopped thrashing about, the goblin shouted his cry of victory.

"Finally!"

He surveyed the battlefield. Littered as it was with goblin and hiveling bodies, it was impossible for him to count their losses.

"Raban!"

"Yeah, Barra— I mean, war chief?" a warrior asked as he pillaged one of his dead comrades' bodies. This was normal, even customary behaviour, for the Jiira believed every deceased person needed only a decent grave and a burial cloth to secure safe passage into the afterlife. Only for Jiira of noble lineage or with extraordinary achievements was it socially acceptable to be buried with treasure. For everyone else in the Jiira, it was far more standard to "redistribute" what little wealth they had during their lives.

Barra, the newly appointed war chief, frowned. "I need you to prepare two teams. One to scout where the insects came from and one to count casualties on both sides. How are they even this far out of the cavern? Did they wipe out the bogeys and decide to wreak havoc in my lands?"

Raban shook his head. "I've led an expedition before. Bogeys put up a hell of a fight, so that's not likely what happened."

"Then why are they outside?" Barra was puzzled.

Raban stroked his short, unkempt beard, trying to think of a reason.

"Today, Raban," Barra growled.

"Don't rush me," Raban growled back before realising his mistake. "Uh, apologies, war chief."

Barra narrowed his eyes and sneered. "You're lucky we need you. Otherwise, I'd have tied you to a tree, whipped you until you were bathed in your own blood, and left you to be eaten by wolves. You're forgiven... this time."

Raban barely stopped himself from rolling his eyes at Barra's empty threat. "Thank you for your mercy. Now, to answer your earlier question, I have no idea. Judging from the tracks they left behind, I can only assume there's another surface exit we didn't know about."

Barra scratched his head in confusion. "Another?"

"Hivelings can dig through stone, so they could have dug their way out. What's weirder is that they never tried to get out of the bogey cavern before."

Barra tapped his axe as he thought of the possibility. "Could be. But if so, why now? I'm about to lead my first campaign as the Jiira War Chief to crush those damn bogeys! It's taken long enough to muster a force that can suppress them, and we're not even halfway there! We can't be delayed any longer, and we definitely can't lose our fighting force beating back these bugs along the way."

"Well, at least we finished them off and can collect their haze crystals," Raban answered.

"Crystals, eh? Tch, there's not enough time to harvest a good amount and it's way too inefficient without greyborn bogeys handling those corrosive crystals. Those same bogeys could be arming themselves and building fortifications as we speak." Barra mused. "We've only got four months' worth of supplies left. We need to crush their petty rebellion as quickly as possible so we can rejoin our other forces in fending off the Kur."

"Or we could use the crystals to trade for supplies with the locals. We could even buy their services as mercenaries or have them support our supply routes. We're going to need all the builders, healers, and other support personnel we can get."

Barra scoffed. "More mercenaries, after what happened with Bulgu and my uncle before him? Besides, the locals have sworn fealty to the Jiira already. Why buy what we should be getting for free? They're our vassals, they're obligated to support their liege!"

Raban crossed his arms. "That's how you think, but that's not how they think. We have our hands full dealing with one rebellion. Can't have you starting another. Besides, the mercenaries did their job. They protected Bulgu during his failed expedition like we paid them to do. What happened after the expedition wasn't in the contract."

Barra's left eye twitched. "Maybe they should've kept their client alive so he could hire them again in the future!"

Raban wanted to shake his head. *Ainshard will return before any mercenary sacrifices themselves for that pig. We all heard the same thing from the survivors—it was his own guys, not the mercenaries, who poisoned him. Maybe if he wasn't such a miserly, prideful dolt we wouldn't be in this mess in the first place!*

Instead, he tried to change the topic. "Look, we've got snow coming in a few weeks. We better quash this rebellion quickly."

"Boss!" called the foreman of the body-count team.

""How many casualties?" Raban asked.

"We lost seventy men to forty of these insects. Ten of those things were elites and thirty were scouts. The elites consisted of five spitters and five warriors."

Barra groaned. "That's more than I'd imagined. I've never heard of scouts being supported by such a large number of elites."

"That's right," Raban said. "Elite hivelings mostly roam around alone or, moreso with warriors, with a couple of workers in tow. These hiveling aren't behaving normally. At most you'd face two elites together, maybe three on the lower floors of the monster caverns."

Barra sighed. "Whatever. The real problem is that we're down to six hundred and eighty men."

"We're going to need some support if we want to cut our losses," Raban advised.

Tapping his foot on the ground, Barra thought over Raban's suggestion.

Even before Ainshard, mercenaries were ubiquitous, comprising much of the fighting forces of all sorts of tribes, clans, and even kingdoms. Leaders in those days preferred to lose gold over their own people, who could otherwise tend the fields. At its founding, Ainshard's eventual empire did the same, but when Ainshard had decided he had cultivated enough home-grown martial prowess, he'd stopped hiring mercenaries entirely.

Many local powers had thought the nascent empire's decision foolish. Ainshard's realm was now responsible for providing weapons and training in combat, and if too many Ainshardian soldiers died, the people they left behind would turn against Ainshard himself.

Even so, Ainshard recognized the advantages of a standing army: loyalty and quick mobilisation when peace turned to war.

To this day, the Jiira believed themselves the true successors of Ainshard's empire and sought to emulate Ainshard's practices. From the tribe's founding, the Jiira had kept a standing army and rarely ever hired mercenaries, meeting their domestic needs through a combination of slave labour and vassal tribute. Jiira, as well as the Ajin clan, were also encouraged to bear many children to keep the military well-staffed. A typical Jiira family had six to twelve children, not counting bastard children born from slaves.

Thanks to these practices, the Jiira had been able to maintain this tradition over the past centuries, until recently that is. Due to Barra's grandfather and his expansionist policies, they'd bitten more than they could chew and found themselves waging war against their neighbours on several fronts.

In the beginning, they not only managed to repel their adversaries but even annexed large swathes of land. It didn't take long, however, for the trophies of their conquests to become their biggest burden.

After generations of reckless expansion, the Jiira found themselves without enough men to guard all their territories, new and old. Their soldiers were simply stretched too thin. To acquire the money to expand their army, they'd increased taxes, which had angered many vassals. Eventually, this had led to the previous bogey rebellion.

Besieged from inside and out, the Jiira had lost a number of battles, leading to the current situation.

Barra spat in disgust. "What a sickening choice we have to make."

Raban held back a groan and smiled. "Trust me when I say that you're making the right choice. For the time being, hiring mercenaries is our most efficient option. They do cost a lot up front, but it'll keep more of our people alive. "

"Warchief Barra!" yelled a returning scout. Barra brightened upon hearing the scout's voice. Hopefully he had intel on the remaining hivelings' presence in the west, and maybe even how they had exited the cavern.

The scout ungracefully tripped over a rock in his haste. Coughing and gasping, he jumped to his feet. Before Raban could offer the scout his waterskin, the scout spoke frantically, fear visible in his eyes. "Danger! Hivelings! Sky devils! We need to get out!"

"What?" Barra muttered in confusion.

"We need to leave immediately! Before night falls!" the scout shrieked

Raban stepped in before the scout could further irritate his superior. "Calm down! What's this about danger and hivelings? And what do those damn jelly-like creatures have to do with the insects? Have a drink and explain things calmly."

Accepting the waterskin, the goblin gulped a few mouthfuls and took a moment to calm his nerves.

"So, can you explain what you found or are you going to waste more time acting like a scared rodent?" Barra started.

The scout hid all his distaste and nodded. "We found over two hundred hivelings."

"Two hundred!?" Barra screamed in shock.

"They were all dead and you won't like what killed them"

"From what you said earlier, I presume it's the sky devils' doing. I know it's getting colder, but isn't it still too early for them to migrate?"

"Looks like they decided to migrate earlier this year," the scout answered.

Raban nodded and turned towards Barra. "So what're we gonna do?"

"Tell everyone to prepare to leave. Meanwhile, we'll gather a few men and check on the corpses."

Raban stared at Barra with wide eyes. "Don't tell me you want to harvest them. Weren't you against wasting time on harvesting crystals?"

To Raban's dismay, Barra grinned. "That was when it was forty hivelings, but now it's two hundred and forty. You wanted me to hire mercenaries and play nice with my vassals, right? We can use the crystals to do that and add something extra for ourselves."

"With those tentacled beasts waiting for the sun to set and eat us? Why in the hells should we do something that dangerous?"

Barra smiled. He raised his hands to the sky, like a priest praising the heavens. "I'm sure Ainshard's will sent them down to save us from annihilation. How could they hurt us?"

Raban was dumbstruck. "You think the devils were sent by Ainshard's *will* for our sake?"

"Could be," Barra replied. "You said it yourself not so long ago. They're not actual devils, just high-flying versions of their sea-dwelling counterparts. Sky devils barely use magic for more than sustenance for their watery bodies. Speaking of which, our alchemists could use some sky devil gel for medicine right about now."

"You're not thinking this through, Barra. Sky devils could kill half our army if we're caught off guard at night," Raban retorted with narrowed eyes.

Barra chuckled. "Sky devils glow at night. We'll easily spot them from a distance."

"Not if we happen to camp near them during the daytime. If they wake up near us, it'll be too late for us by the time we see them glow!"

Raban and Barra glared at each other, unnerving the soldiers around them. Most favoured Raban, but Barra was their war chief, chosen by the council of elders and the Jiira chief. Their, and by association, Barra's orders, could not be ignored.

Seeing how tense the troops had gotten from their debate, Barra relented. "Fine. We don't need to harvest them all. We'll just harvest as many as possible before dusk. Happy now?"

Why in the world are you this stubborn? Raban thought before shaking his head. "Barra, please. It's not worth the risk."

"That's not your judgement to make. Ready the men."

"Barra!"

"That's an order. Are you going to make my clan disown your family?" Barra threatened.

"You can't do that! That's for the council to decide!" Raban barked back.

Barra shrugged. "I'm greedy and ambitious. It runs in the family."

* * *

After a short trip, Raban's crew arrived to a shocking sight. The remains of now more than two hundred hivelings littered the area, all entangled in unmoving tentacles. Numerous insect-like heads protruded from under giant, mushroom-like shells.

"Those are sky devils alright," Raban whispered.

"How on earth did they defeat the hivelings?" one of his men muttered.

"Why can't I feel any magic here?" a nearby shaman questioned.

Raban looked at both of them with irritation. "You want me to answer those questions?"

He pointed with his axe at the first goblin. "Since you were the first to ask, I'll begin with you. Tentacles."

"Tentacles?"

Raban lowered his axe. "On each tentacle are hundreds, if not thousands, of needles. Those tentacles shoot out their needles at the first hint of a threat, usually when something gets close or disturbs their surroundings. Sadly, those are the only part of the damn things that don't degrade under direct sunlight, so watch your step. There are always a few sticking out of their morning shells."

The first goblin spoke up. "If I cut the tentacles off, the sky-devils can't hurt us, right?"

"That's the thing. Severed tentacles can still release needles. If you're lucky, they'll just prick you. If you're not, they'll be venomous, too."

The shaman was more inquisitive. "Sir, how do we know whether they're venomous?"

Raban shook his head. "You don't. In the daytime, sky devils encase themselves in shells to protect from the sun."

"That doesn't explain why there's... no magic around here," the shaman muttered.

"Sky devils constantly feed on magic. Usually they just absorb magic from the air, but when there's a concentrated source of magic, they'll go for that instead."

"Like hivelings carrying haze crystals," the first goblin noted.

Raban yelled to his superior. "Did you hear that, Barra? These things might be after us if we don't look out!"

"Not if we get away in time. They're dormant for now!" Barra yelled back, earning yet another scowl from Raban.

Raban turned back to his men. "You heard him. Let's get this done quickly."

His men first grabbed long spears and shoved away all the tentacles they could before dragging out and cutting open a hiveling. They carefully opened the sac, avoiding its pressurised acid, and retrieved the crystals from inside.

They laboured until sunset, and were able to cut open sixty hivelings and gather about two hundred crystals. All it'd taken was twenty-eight casualties. Eight dead and twenty injured. Two had died from acid spurting directly onto them; the rest had stepped on sky devil tentacles.

They managed to run away before the creatures' protective shells cracked open. The dark skies filled with a bright, rainbow-like glow.

"They look beautiful from afar, don't they?" Barra asked Raban.

"From afar? Yes. When you're near the damn things? Not so much," Raban replied. "So, are we going to meet up with the rest of our men or what?"

Barra shook his head. "You really need to learn how to enjoy your surroundings."

"This isn't a playground, Barra."

"Fine, fine. Just go tell everyone to get ready."

The group advanced towards their camp, close to the road that led to the bogey caverns. During early dawn, they would continue on their way.

Along the way, they passed through thirty villages. In most of them, Barra "negotiated" deals to resupply for a pittance and gather more men. Two villages tried to resist; Barra simply burned them down.

As news spread to the remaining villages remaining along the Jiira's path, those villages sent messengers requesting help from other nearby settlements. Unfortunately, Barra's scouts caught wind of this newfound coalition, and the ensuing battle was more of a massacre, as a measly five hundred villagers were routed by Barra's now thousand-strong army.

The prospect of another victory brought Barra some amusement.

I guess Raban was right for once. Maybe hiring mercenaries isn't so bad, he mused upon hearing that most of his losses were from his new sellswords.

Three days after the scouts' report, Barra's forces were halfway through crossing a river when something unexpected occurred.

Arrows rained down upon them from the woods nearby in a single volley.

Next came the charge. Barra's men caught glimpses of their attackers: some with grey, dark skin; some with green skin, wearing scraps of armour and leather; some clad in eerily familiar bronze armour.

The bogeys had arrived.

CHAPTER 23
A DEVIL'S RESOLVE

"Watch out!" a man yelled, his voice almost muted under the heavy pattering of the rain.

Flaming pitch-covered logs rolled down the nearby hills and smashed into those of the Jiira who couldn't escape.

"Don't these guys ever take a break? Protect the rear!" Barra yelled. He jumped out of the way of a falling log and landed in boggy ground with a sticky splash.

With the end of the falling logs came a rain of lead shots and bronze tipped arrows.

"Shields!" Raban commanded the men as an arrow bounced off his own.

The Jiira soldiers, for the umpteenth time, formed two walls of shields and covered their shamans, archers, and crossbowmen behind their formation. They had learned the hard way that chasing the attackers into the woods was a terrible idea, and breaking formation made them more liable to getting hit by arrows.

They had also tried approaching the bogeys in a shield wall, but the Jiira could never close the distance. The only thing that worked for the Jiira was answering the bogeys' ranged barrage with ranged attacks of their own, especially from shamans.

"If only it weren't for this damn rain," Barra cursed.

During these skirmishes, the Jiira shamans had relied heavily on fire spells, setting the entire wood ablaze and flushing the bogey slingers out of the trees. For a time this had managed to push the bogey ambushers back, but the torrential downpour negated that advantage. The rain extinguished the flames and prevented any foliage from catching fire afterward.

"Rain or not, the bastards will retreat soon, just before our shamans shoot their spells." Raban seethingly predicted.

Just as the Jiira shamans fired their spells, the rain of arrows stopped. The Jiira shamans, with the rest of the Jiira army, stood guard for what became an entire half-hour.

"Collect any projectiles you can find so the bastards can't get them back, and more importantly, keep an eye on the rear. We don't want what happened two days ago to ever occur again!" Raban roared. Two days ago, deka horsemen had attacked their supply wagons with axes, spears, bottles of pitch, and torches, killing twenty goblins and setting five wagons of supplies ablaze.

"Once we're done here we'll make the Dragma pay for their betrayal." Barra growled.

"Yeah, yeah. Let's focus on surviving first. Gods know it's hard to go back thanks to their 'gift.'"

"Fucking sky devils. I swear those blasted jellyfish are following us." Barra spat with a sneer. A few days ago, despite covering a large distance and staying away from the sky devils' migration routes, Barra and his army were horrified when they realised the creatures were still heading in their direction, and to make matters worse, their numbers were far greater than their last encounter a few months ago.

"Something is wrong, Raban. The sky devils are purposefully trying to prevent us from going back, I know it!" Barra cried.

Raban couldn't argue with him. The tentacled beasts covered an area large enough to make any form of withdrawal or cancellation of the attack improbable and likely very costly. A group of ten or twenty might be able to escape if they were lucky, but not an entire army. That the sky devils were getting closer by the hour didn't help, either.

"We need to take shelter. But where?" Raban pondered.

Barra sighed. "Hell if I know. I thought we might be able to hide in a cave 'till they leave, but there had to be a hiveling outbreak. Considering that the bogeys are still around, the bogey caverns must still be safe somehow. We need to take it as soon as possible.

"Speaking of bogeys, they sure seem like they aren't worried about those flying magical parasites," Barra continued.

"Those bogeys have been penned in this cavern for generations. They wouldn't know the terror of the sky devils even if their more worldly cousins told them," Raban answered.

"Hah, please don't call those bastards our cousins," Barra scoffed.

"Aren't they our distant cousins, though? We're pretty similar."

"We goblins have standards. Just because we could birth half-breeds with their ilk doesn't mean it's right."

Raban rolled his eyes. "Whatever you say. More importantly, considering it'd take a while before we reach the cavern, not to mention conquer it, what should we do about the sky devils?"

Barra tapped his foot on the ground in defeat. "I don't know. There just isn't a good place to hide. If there was, we'd be able to wait for the sky devils to take out the bogeys. How long until we arrive, anyway?"

Raban looked north, towards a jagged mountain in the distance. From afar it resembled an open hand with six fingers pleading to the heavens for help. Winding around three of the finger-like projections were rivers flowing down towards the bottom. From what he remembered, the cavern was located near the mountain's palm, covered in woods.

He turned back towards Barra. "At our current pace, I'd say three more days before we arrive."

Barra grit his teeth. "Three more days of arrows and fire, huh? Just wait, you bogey bastards. I'll get the last laugh in your pitiful play."

Contrary to Barra's assumptions, the bogeys were not enjoying their victories. Instead, they were wearily assisting women, children, and the elderly in marching as far away from the bogey caverns as possible.

Lev stared at the makeshift wagons making their way across the dirt towards the east. *How did it come to this?* he asked himself.

Hivelings. They ruin everything, Gherm replied.

Why now though? This isn't the first time the bogeys have revolted against the Jiira so I doubt they're trying to take advantage of our weakness. What could be so different this time? Lev asked Gherm, or perhaps himself.

Who knows what the hivelings are planning? Gherm replied.

Lev shrugged. *No matter what they do, I think we can still survive this. We could rid ourselves of the Jiira to boot.*

'Think'? We're luring the Jiira army into the hivelings' path while keeping our own safe. All should be fine.

We'll rid ourselves from a few major liabilities. The bogey chief retainer, a couple of nobles, and their closest, equally survival-minded associates.

I still disagree with this. We shouldn't just leave them to die, Gherm protested. *Nobody deserves to be fed to hivelings, not even them.*

You're naive, Gherm. Once society stabilises, any upper-crust bogeys we save will claw their way right back to the top at our expense.

How would you know? They'd owe their lives to us!

From experience. Humans "forget" debts just as easily as they can accrue them.

Lev could sense Gherm's displeasure. *We aren't humans, Lev. We're bogeys,* Gherm argued.

Lev chuckled. *Humans? Bogeys? They're the same on the inside.*

Those nobles aren't even armed. They don't pose a threat to us! Gherm cried.

All the better for those nobles to claim we threatened them. Then again, I don't know how long manipulators like that would last in combat.

Lev could have sworn he felt Gherm gulp. *What are you going to do, Lev? Don't tell me—*

Who said I'd do something? Vyrga's the one with the perfect opportunity. He had a plan after all.

And if he doesn't go through with it? It's his own blood!

Then I have no choice but to take matters into my own hands.

Don't! You'll prove the nobles right that you are a threat. And if they can't get you, they'll go after Ghorza!

Lev shrugged. *No matter the optics of what we greyborn commanders do, the green-skinned commoner masses have been indoctrinated to do what the nobles say. After we get rid of the troublesome ones, all we have to do is curry some favour with the remaining nobles. The sensible ones will listen.*

Because we'll help them escape?

Lev smiled at Gherm's response, but continued to explain the situation. *After asking around, we found out that Vyrga is the bastard son of the chief retainer himself, right? With his father's sudden death, he'll make contact with his supporters in the upper echelons. They'll bring the rest into the fold.*

And that will benefit everyone, how, exactly? Vyrga's a conniving bastard!

He's no idiot. He needs our help and he has the connections we need. It'll go smoothly.

They've always ordered him around. Why would they listen to him now? Gherm questioned.

Because there is a clear hierarchy and they know how brutal Vyrga can be when necessary. Fear isn't optimal, but it can be quite a persuasive element for the short-term. They also had the most contact with the goblins so they must know the terror of the sky devils. They'll comply, for their families' sakes if nothing else.

"Sir! Volker's arrived!" yelled one of Lev's men as he pointed towards the southeast.

Lev looked into the distance and saw Volker separate from the arriving ambush party and head towards him.

Families!? Wait, Lev! Don't—

Lev quickly severed the connection between his and Gherm's consciousness, just as he had been practising. He felt Gherm struggle inside his head. "Sorry, Gherm, but it's better to deal with such issues as early as possible," Lev muttered before stretching his back and turning towards the approaching Volker.

"So how many did we lose?" Lev asked.

"Five men, sir. Not everyone was able to escape."

"Tell Rapha to record their names. We'll need to build a memorial once we finish off the Jiira's forces."

"Rapha? It's been barely four months since one of Zeja's healers fixed her left arm, and she's got another half year before she can wield a weapon again. Wouldn't it be cheaper if we had one of those independent green shamans do the healing instead?"

"Trust me, earning Rapha and her band of shieldmaidens' favour is worth more than some crystals. It will help us in the long run."

"Well, that's good to hear," Volker replied with a smile. It didn't take long, though, for it to turn into a frown. "On another note, I still can't believe we're cooperating with the likes of Vyrga."

"We're doing what's necessary to survive."

"Sir, I understand the extra manpower is a big help, but it still doesn't sit right with me."

Lev sighed, a hint of frustration in his eyes. "We lost thirty people fighting hivelings at the second-floor outpost. I don't like the situation any more than you do, but we need to work with Vyrga. For now."

He paused, a grim expression on his face. "Most of those we lost had only just joined us. We'll need to recruit more."

"I'm just happy Gul managed to come back alive."

Lev nodded. "Indeed. It's unfortunate that Rogg wasn't able to escape."

"You're sad for the old bas— uh, the late witch doctor, sir?"

"Why wouldn't I be? Witch doctors, healers, herbalists, they're all useful in keeping our men out of hiveling stomachs. He was far from the best, but would've been useful to have around. At least his son is still alive."

Volker pursed his lips in tacit agreement.

"Now, what's our enemies' status?"

"They haven't noticed the convoy yet and are about two to three days away from the caverns. Their men are exhausted, tense, and scared from their own shadows. They'll suffer even more since it's Hem and Rak's turn to pay them a visit. As for how many soldiers they still have left... estimates are at about five hundred and forty."

Lev grinned. "So they've lost about half. Glad to hear it. I'll look forward to seeing Hem and Rak giving them hell."

"Thank you, sir. May I go take a break?"

"Two things first."

"Sure."

"Bring Vyrga. There's something he needs to do."

Volker managed to stifle a groan. "Is he really necessary? Can he be trusted to do it?"

"I believe he will not disappoint. At least, not in this scenario."

Volker chuckled. "I don't think he'd enjoy hearing himself talked about as a pawn, sir."

"I consider him an ally, not a pawn, for the time being."

Vyrga took a moment to process his thoughts before responding. "I'm kind of weirded out how someone like him managed to earn your respect."

"He's more interesting than I'd expected." Lev admitted. "At first I took him for some ambitious scoundrel, but he's much more complex than I thought. At least much more nuanced than the rumours give him credit for."

"You expect me to be civil with him, then, sir?"

"Can you manage it?" Lev inquired. "I know your distaste for the man, but sometimes you need to shake hands with those you hate."

"I—yes, sir."

"Good enough. In the meantime, tell the blacksmith to bring me the special gear I ordered. I'll join the final battle against the Jiira."

CHAPTER 24
PATERNAL SINS

In the desolate hours of the night, under the gaze of the stars, a band of mismatched wagons trudged through an unkempt road.

With their recent victory against the Jiira and the destruction of the goblins' outpost, a feast was held to raise morale for the real fight.

Yet, once most of the guards were drunk or asleep, the organisers of the feast fled the caverns in the middle of the night. They were some of the most prominent families amongst the blue bogeys. The cowardly abandoned their kin, only bringing along their treasures, their most loyal servants, and almost all of the refined haze reserves left in the caverns.

Within the fanciest of the wagons, one safe from the elements by its ornate red coverings, sat five bogeys. Two blue bogey men, two young green bogey women, and an old green bogey priestess of Zeja.

"This is a disaster." Reingard, the former chief retainer and now self-proclaimed chief of the free bogeys, grumbled. His fingers tapped the side of his empty cup.

Bodobert nodded. "Indeed. We should've brought more men," he replied, causing Reingard and the two young women sitting next to him to laugh.

Reingard shook his cup, but not even a single droplet fell out. "I was talking about the lack of wine, my friend. Where we're going, there's no need for soldiers."

Unable to stand this tomfoolery any longer, the priestess, Kathaga, rebuked with a sneer, "How foolish of you to abandon your followers, much less for the promises of the Kur."

Unaffected by her words, Reingard grinned. "And yet here you are. Instead of dying valiantly for the sake of our people like Zeja intended, you chose survival. You should thank Bodobert for allowing an old crone like you among us. I would've preferred if he picked a younger girl, but it's Bodobert we're talking about, so I'm not very surprised. We don't need a goddess of a bygone era. The Kur don't believe in that nonsense, and neither should we."

"Oh, really? Did you forget all of Zeja's blessings?" Kathaga remarked, "Without the aid of this old crone and her goddess, becoming the head of the bogeys would've been far more difficult for you."

"Oh, how can I forget her blessings? Zeja helped me become chief amongst mice, hurray for me," Reingard snidely replied. "If it weren't for your blasted temple stoking the flames of my ambitions, I might've been happier in life!" He furiously yelled.

His outrage was met with silence. The only sounds heard were the howling of the wind and the creaking wheels of the wagon.

Seeing the hollow look in his eyes, Kathaga couldn't hide her disappointment and eventually let out a weary sigh. "It's a shame how much you've changed, Reingard. Your fire is gone. What happened to that young boy I met? The one who wanted to redeem his family after they were framed for starting the previous rebellion? The ostracised boy who dreamt of a free and unified bogey race?"

Hearing her words, Reingard grew morose. His earlier scowl slipped away, making way for a tired smile. "Once he reached the top of bogey society, he found out how pointless change is. Zeja's ways are wrong, Kathaga, and every blue bogey knows it. I saw what the Jiira are capable of once I became their retainer."

"I greeted their armies when they passed by, heading out to war with the Kur. What we faced was merely a token force, a joke meant to guard compliant slaves. Our parents and their fathers tried to rebel, but no matter how hard we fight, we can't free ourselves from the powers that rule these lands. By the time we reach the Kur, the Jiira's main force will have crushed all bogey resistance in the caverns."

He motioned for one of the girls to fill his cup. Once the cup was filled to the brim, he downed it in one shot.

Not wanting to argue with the old priestess, he turned to his oldest companion and smiled.

"On the bright side, we made the right choice. I'm glad that you got your head straight and joined me, Bodo. I was sure a warmonger like you would have stayed behind."

Bodobert laughed. "You weren't my first option, no doubt. I'd be busy slaughtering the Jiira if that old fool hadn't decided to stay behind. The last thing I want is to die with Meinrad."

Reingard sneered. "Good riddance! I hope that hypocrite's corpse rots among the greyborn. He always acted high and mighty, spouting that he knows what's best for bogeykind. But has he ever take action?"

"Have you two forgotten the support he gave you in the past?" Kathaga chided.

"You mean the support he stripped away when I no longer acted according to his views? He saw me as a mere tool, one to be thrown away when broken." Reingard spat back.

"You did break, Reingard. You became decadent once you grabbed the reins of power and stopped caring for others. Meinrad has always done things by the law, so of course he wouldn't tolerate what you became. Especially when you had a child with a greyborn, only to throw her and your child away."

"I'm a blue bogey, Kathaga. Just because I was curious and had fun with a grey harlot, he expects me to raise her spawn? Besides, I gave the bastard enough support once he grew up."

"Bodobert did, not you," Kathaga argued.

Reingard curiously glanced at Bodobert. *Speaking of Bodobert, he seems awfully silent. That man never wastes an opportunity to flap his tongue.*

Reingard smirked once he noticed a creeping smile on Bodobert's lips. *Hah, is our argument that amusing to you, Bodo? Well, I'm happy to oblige and put Zeja's pet in her place.*

He turned back towards Kathaga and sneered. "Which wouldn't have happened without my permission. Thankfully, Bodobert was right once again, and—" Reingard's argument was cut short as the wagon abruptly stopped.

He would've tumbled off his seat if it weren't for the two bogey girls beside him.

His ears twitched as he was about to go on a tirade. "Are those… shouts?"

Screams, clangs, and the iconic boom that followed magical flames. All sounds that Reingard did not want to hear, especially now.

The shadows on the red cloth covering the wagon didn't help ease Reingard's mind.

Reingard turned towards the front of the wagon, to the wooden wall separating them from the driver, and yelled, "What's happening!? Did the Jiira find us!?"

Yet to his dismay, no one answered. In a mix of panic and rage, he got up and kicked at the wall. "Answer me! I am your chief!" he yelled at the top of his lungs.

Reingard waited, only to be met with a suffocating silence.

"Damn it all!" He cursed under his breath as he drew his dagger.

Seeing his reaction, Bodobert stood up with a smile. He took out his favourite mace from his belt and placed it on his shoulders. "Seems you've still got some fire in you. Are you ready to fight?"

"No, you fool! This isn't the time for conflict!" Reingard scolded. To Bodobert's irritation, he used the dagger to nick open a hidden compartment before sheathing it away. Hidden in the compartment were numerous bags full of high-quality haze crystals.

"I don't understand how you and that stupid priestess adore as barbaric an activity as mindless violence! There's no honour or grace in the spilling of blood! Only greyborn revel in it!" Reingard continued.

Bodobert frowned. "We spilled blood for our ambitions. Don't forget that."

Reingard stood up and, with no regard for his friend's complaints, began counting the crystals in one of the bags. "Maybe it was enough to meet your ambitions, Bodobert, but not mine. Hitting things with a bronze stick wasn't what got me to power. Coin, influence, and connections did that. You were the one gifted with a silver tongue, yet you wasted your abilities on your buffoonery."

Reingard paused before speaking up again. "It's not due to a lack of intellect or cunning, but due to your sick, twisted desire to sow chaos and feed off its sorrows. That's why most blue bogeys, including your kin, don't like you."

Bodobert shrugged. "Maybe you're right. Done counting?"

"Yes. We need to escape before the Jiira reach our wagon. Have the girls inform my wife and kin that once they escape, they should keep their eyes on the ring of stars. That constellation will lead them south, and there should be a few outposts belonging to the Kur."

With the sound of violence getting nearer, Reingard began to panic. "Are you all coming or not? The Jiira won't wait all day."

He didn't wait for an answer before making way to the exit.

"Have you ever thought that it might not be the Jiira?" Bodobert abruptly asked, causing Reingard to halt in his steps.

"D-Don't be foolish, Bodobert. Who else could it be other than the Jiira? Who else would have any reason to attack us?"

Kathaga chuckled. "Those who suffered at your actions the most. One of a few actors, who thanks to your sacrifice, will play a great role in upheaving bogeykind on the world stage. Someone born from a mere curiosity."

Reingard's ears spasmed at this revelation. "The gods be damned! All of you be damned!!"

"Bodobert!" Kathaga yelled.

Just as Reingard was about to make his escape, a sickening crunch rang out in the wagon, followed by excruciating pain assaulting his now mangled knee.

Reingard let out a horrific shriek. He wailed on for minutes before he could shakily muster the strength to look at the one who'd betrayed him. "Bodobert... Why? Is this the gratitude I get after all I've done for you?"

"It's simple, really. You're no longer the man I followed. You bore me," Bodobert said with a pitying smile.

Reingard gnashed his teeth and yelled, "That's it? I bore you!? That's the reason you chose a damn priestess of a mad goddess and some grey wretch!?"

Bodobert chuckled and made his way to the door. "Well, there are a few more reasons, but I'll leave it to you to figure them out. If you'll excuse me, I don't want to get in the way of your family reunion."

"R-Reunion?" Reingard muttered in fear.

"You'll know soon enough," Bodobert replied before heading out.

The two green bogey girls giggled as they emptied the wine flask onto Reingard's head before making their way to the exit.

"I hope you do better in your next life, Reingard," Kathaga advised before following suit.

Reingard tried to stand up, but his knee gave in and flared with pain. He grovelled on the ground, silently bemoaning his fate, before shakily grabbing the closest flask.

The sound of fighting eventually died down as Reingard lay alone in the wagon, surrounded by shattered cups, haze crystals, and empty wine flasks.

In his drunken state, he heard the sound of approaching footsteps, yet he only grumbled. The wagon's flaps opened, revealing a blood-covered Vyrga.

"You don't look so good, my dear father." Vyrga jested, his now-iconic wolf sword in his hand.

"You were a fucking mistake." Reingard threw back.

Vyrga sighed. "To you, maybe. Only time will tell of my fate. I can only guarantee it'll be better than yours."

"How would you know?"

"A child would fail if he doesn't learn from the sins of his father," Vyrga replied.

He placed his sword on Reingard's neck. "Any last words?"

"Your mother was my worst." Reingard spat. Those were the last words of a man who sold his people for power. And from his death, a new leader emerged.

CHAPTER 25
A DEVIL'S TREACHERY

From atop a tree-covered hill overlooking a river, two greyborns and their men awaited the Jiira, whose next move was to ford the river. Between the two leaders sat a large contraption Lev had had the craftsmen build for this very occasion. Four other contraptions like it were concealed in scattered groups of Lev's men.

"Rak, you've done so much already." Lev admonished. "Shouldn't you go back and rest a bit?"

"I've been feeling ignored lately. That won't do if I want to grow my following after this," Rak answered.

"Once we're free, you won't need numbers."

Rak grinned. "Because we'll all be allies? You're not naïve enough to ditch your own army, so don't expect me to be."

"Heh. Everyone promised to cooperate, yet everyone's prepared to fight for power themselves." Lev chuckled.

"I just want men to enforce our contract and keep the others, especially Vyrga, in check. Speaking of keeping everyone in check, I like that idea of yours. Beats that 'nobility' nonsense the old guard loves."

"You mean forming an elected council? Agreeing upon and codifying exact positions and rules will take some time, let alone effort, but for now it's in our common interest to plan for one. Ironically, a bunch of blues led by an old man called Meinrad were in favour of the idea," Lev mused.

Rak shook his head. "I don't know if they think people will actually choose them as their leaders or if they're planning something. Wasn't there a fat blue bastard being chummy with Vyrga? What was that about?"

"Likely an alliance. Some blues prefer Vyrga to become our leader considering his amicable relationship with them and his noble blood."

"Noble blood, hah! He's a bastard, why would anyone want him to lead?" Rak argued.

"When I was stuck with him in the lower levels, I learned that he has the forethought and patience to play the long game. I'm sure many of those politicking higher-ups know that. And he's been building friendly relationships to grab that leadership position. Doesn't mean he'll get what he wants without a fight, though." Lev smirked. "Because I'm not backing down."

"And if you lose?" Rak asked.

"I have a contingency plan, but someone reliable needs to manage the military," Lev replied with an expectant look in his eye.

Rak smirked at Lev. "Sorry, but I can't. I hate him and don't wanna do anything for him. But I've agreed to a ceasefire for now."

"Are your men okay with this?" Lev questioned Rak, knowing his lot's grievances with Vyrga.

"When I returned from our little trip, I found my sister feverish and bedridden. Not a single healer I knew could cure her. Not without materials either the Jiira had seized for themselves or the nobles and affluent merchants had bought up," Rak said. "As luck would have it, many of my men came home to similar circumstances."

Lev frowned. "Let me guess. Vyrga was able to source those ingredients?"

"Bolo was. Through Vyrga's connections. I keep telling myself that unlike his old man, Bolo doesn't have the heart to do it. But... I still wonder if he used those same connections to choke out the bogeys' supply of medicines before we came back. Sadly, no one's found any proof. If they do, I'll execute him on the spot."

"Could have been a coincidence. Everyone knew supplies were drying out, but few could've guessed that there'd also be a disease outbreak."

"Yeah, well, I'm glad we arrived before the snow. If we'd been a few months late, my sister wouldn't have stood a chance against the cold weather, even with all the medicine in the world."

"Okay. Medicine. Is that all you needed from Vyrga?"

Rak grinned toothily. "No. I'm going to manage all the pleasure houses."

Lev was dumbstruck by Rak's response. "What— You? Pleasure houses? I thought you forbade your men from that kind of work."

Rak merely grinned.

"Well, yeah. I've been thinking about it." Rak's grin left his face. "You'd be surprised what folks can get up to in them. Someone needs to bring order to those establishments before innocent and desperate folks get hurt."

"Speaking from experience, huh?"

A half-laugh escaped from Rak's throat. "What're you trying to say?"

"You tell me," Lev said, amused.

"Well, I'm saying the pay's good for folks who don't want to fight for their lives every day, and for those who don't have many options. Least I can do is create a safer environment."

"Whatever you say. I'm not here to judge."

Lev was content to let Rak prattle on about the state of the bogey sex industry, but a raised flag in the distance changed his mind. "It's time," Lev announced.

He grabbed his glaive and walked to the back of the contraption to access the ropes. He surveyed the other pockets of bogeys, where each squad's leader was positioned the same way he was.

"One, two... Now!" he barked as he cut the rope on the traction trebuchet.

The Jiira were stunned to see boulders raining from the heavens.

Just as the second catapult launched its projectiles, the Jiira loosened their formation to protect themselves against the projectiles.

Just as planned, Lev thought with a smile. He grabbed his glaive while his squadmates reloaded the catapult.

With a vicious grin, Rak looked towards Lev with Gelmar's bronze axe in hand. "Ready for some action?"

"Is that even a question? Let's do this."

Rak laughed and turned towards the Jiira army. He raised his axe high and roared; his men roared with him in unison before shoving burning piles of logs down the hill. They then charged out of the woods towards the panicking goblins.

"Form a wall!" yelled a black-haired goblin wearing ornate, bejewelled armour. "They won't risk crushing their own. Hold your positions!"

That must be their leader. Let's end things quickly. Rak thought. He and his men charged towards their enemies.

Wait, wasn't he supposed to have red hair? Lev pondered but it was too late to warn Rak. Searching for him now would only confuse his men.

The Jiira shamans and crossbowmen tried to intercept the bogey attackers, but a never-ending rain of stones, lead bullets, and arrows from Lev's ranged support forced them to take cover.

Unlike Rak's forces, who charged with chaotic zeal through the trees, Lev's men marched in orderly formations while the rest of his forces continued providing ranged support.

Before the Jiira could finish forming their shield wall, the rain of projectiles stopped, and Rak's men crashed into them. They ecstatically began the slaughter.

The exhausted Jiira were tired and unresponsive thanks to the constant ambushes, guerrilla tactics, and night attacks they'd suffered over the past week. The bogeys, on the other hand, were mostly in top condition.

It was all going according to Lev's plan.

Only fools would fight fairly when disadvantaged. What good is better training and better equipment if you're too exhausted to fight? Lev thought, readying for a group of Jiira who were trying to break through and escape.

From the second line of the formation, Lev thrust his glaive at an approaching Jiira axeman, stabbing him in the mouth, breaking his teeth. The tip of his glaive exited the back of the goblin's head, bits of flesh still clinging to the blade. Lev twisted the glaive forcefully and swung it upwards through the skull, with some resistance, the glaive's blade broke free.

Lev then hooked a Jiira shield with the edge of his glaive, dragged its owner to the front of his formation, and released him to three eager spears.

Master, this is dull, the glaive wailed.

Did you expect me to charge alone into enemy lines? You're a glaive. You belong in a formation.

Where's the glory in that?

Survival beats "glory." Go watch Rak if you want flashy heroics.

Lev glanced in Rak's direction just in time to see Rak ram through two Jiira and swing his axe at a third one. Lev chose to ignore both the *fwip* of a clean slice and the wayward goblin head flying into the air.

Rak stomped the ground and roared, stopping an approaching sword-wielder in his tracks. He kicked the sword-wielder into the ground, stomping on his face until the cracking noises under his foot stopped.

"You savage!" a Jiira warrior cried.

Rak laughed. "Funny, coming from one of you!" he yelled back, barely skipping a beat on his rampage.

The Jiira commander approached, hefting his sword and shield. Rak eyed the sword. It was made of iron.

"It's wonderful, isn't it?" the black-haired goblin exclaimed with a smile. "Won it from a noble out east! Surprisingly easy to handle, too," he said, swinging the blade with an audible *whoosh*.

After sizing up his much larger opponent, the goblin readied his stance; bent at the knees and nimble upon the balls of his feet. "You're quite big for a bogey, aren't you? My name's Raban. Pleasure to meet you," he calmly said.

"Name's Rak!" Rak roared before charging.

Raban dodged to the right, saving his left shoulder from Rak's axe, and countered the attack with a slash of his own. The attack glanced off of Rak's axe, which, as Raban was surprised to see, was now wielded in Rak's other hand.

"Quick hands, eh? And here I was, hoping for some dumb berserker," Raban muttered with a scowl.

Barely able to finish his words, he ducked, evading another cleave that would surely have lobbed his head off clean. He then leaped forward to close the distance between them, going for Rak's abdomen.

But Rak's reflexes were faster yet. At the cost of his balance, Raban halted just short of Rak's raised foot, which would have turned him to mush, much like his fallen allies. He wasn't able to fix his posture from the sudden change in manoeuvre, which caused him to lose his balance atop the slipper snow. He ingloriously fell, buttocks first, onto the ground.

Rak raised his axe over his head and took the opportunity Raban had inadvertently given him.

Unable to roll out of the way fast enough to avoid the attack, Raban instinctively raised his shield to block the incoming blow.

What is this guy made of? Raban wondered. To his horror, his shield hand quivered as sweat flowed down his arm. There seemed to be no end to Rak's successive attacks.

Rak swung again. Raban rolled out of the way to the left, hopped to his feet, and summoned a burst of strength to catch Rak off-guard.

Rak barely managed to deflect the lunge but Raban's blade still dug into his right upper arm. "Aaargh!" he snarled.

Raban slammed his shield into Rak's face, and with nary an extraneous breath, pulled his blade out and swung his sword around to slice Rak's neck from the side.

Amazingly, Rak managed to block the iron blade with his right forearm, lodging the blade into his bone.

"Aaaaargh!" Rak roared again. This time, Raban struggled to dislodge the iron blade; Rak angrily headbutted him to the ground. Raban's head bled in concert with Rak's arm.

Raban groggily tried to roll again, but Rak stepped on his arm, pinning him where he was. Rak rested the blade of his axe on Raban's neck.

"I don't want to kill you. Order your men to surrender."

Raban's jaw relaxed. "Rak. Any last words?"

"Huh? What do you mean—"

A loud scream cut Rak off. Lev appeared barely a killig away soon after.

"He meant someone was about to kill you," Lev replied. He withdrew his glaive from the corpse of a goblin, shortsword still clenched in the goblin's hand and mere inches away from Rak's back.

"Shit," Raban muttered.

Lev grinned maniacally, walking ever closer.

"Stand up, great Jiira commander, and look around."

Rak moved out of the way. Lev pressed the cold metal of his glaive onto Raban's neck and held it there as Raban gingerly returned to his feet.

For the first time since he had encountered Rak, Raban surveyed the battlefield with his own eyes.

Raban quickly made up his mind and sighed. "Give me the horn on my belt, the bone one on the left."

Lev retrieved it for his black-haired goblin foe. "How do we know this is surrender and not another Jiira trick?"

"Talk about tricks! Others might, but I'm not going to waste my soldiers' lives. I swear to Ainshard and my honour as the war chief."

"Is that so?" Lev responded.

"Lev." Rak interrupted. "I believe he's telling the truth."

"You what? What kind of steroid did he give you, Rak?"

"He's unlike any Jiira I've met before. I can tell after trading blows. And what's a steroid?"

"Never mind that." Lev sighed. "It'll be your life on the line if he's lying."

"Deal." Rak took the horn out of Lev's hand and held it to Raban's lips. Raban blew the horn.

Just like that, waves of battle-weary Jiira heads turned to face Raban. A moment later, waves of worn Jiira weapons clattered to the bloodied dirt ground.

"What'd I tell you?" Rak said, taking away Raban's horn. "Still going to beat him up later for messing up my arm."

"Leave it to the healers," Lev replied.

Raban felt his energy draining, but there was a question he had to ask. "What will you do with my people now? Kill us? Imprison us? Enslave us?"

A silent moment passed between Rak and Lev. Rak chose to respond first. "I'd love to kill you all. Every single one of you. But killing unarmed captives feels cheap, and I'm not a fan of enslaving others. Nor do I have the patience for babying prisoners. I'll leave the decision to Lev."

Lev gave him a grateful nod before facing Raban. "My decision depends on whether what remains of your forces will cooperate with me. We bogeys have somewhere we need to be."

"Doesn't Vyrga have the thing that's supposed to take us there?" Rak asked Lev furtively.

"Yes, but if things go as they did last time, I might need to open the gate. Let's not discuss this here."

Raban was confused, but knew not to expect to earn an answer from the bogeys. "Your secrets are yours to keep, but could you at least tell me what you're proposing?"

"As requested," Lev said. "Instead of enslavement for the rest of your lives, we'll ask for ten years worth of service."

CHAPTER 26
FATE'S QUERY

There was silence after Lev's announcement. Both bogeys and goblins stopped fighting. Instead, they stared at Lev, unable to believe their ears.

Raban was the first to break the silence. "So, we'll still be slaves... but only for a few years."

"Yes." Lev nodded. "With a few exceptions. You'll be able to retain property and earn a wage that you'll receive once your time of service is complete. You won't have to worry about your children either, any born during or after the service will be free, and you'll have the choice to join our tribe or leave once the service is over."

Raban stared wide-eyed. "That's... That's quite generous."

"I wouldn't say that. Goblins don't live that long."

"Considering the Jiira's colonial legacy? We'd be fools to expect better. Even Brizilum doesn't give this many opportunities to those who willingly bend the knee."

"I have my reasons."

"You'd better," Rak complained whilst glaring at Lev and Raban.

"Now," Lev said curtly, "where's your leader?"

"Leader?" Raban questioned.

"You may be wearing his armour, but you were awfully close to the front lines for a commander. My scouts have told me the real Jiira commander is a goblin with red hair."

Raban scoffed. "Like I said before, I'm the war chief. My men needed a morale boost after your constant ambushes, so what's better than witnessing your war chief himself fighting alongside his troops? Besides, do you think a proud leader of the Jiira would run away with his tail between his legs?"

"Considering what happened to your clan and that it needs to solidify its position after generations of failed leadership, yes. Yes, I do. Crushing bogeys seemed to be low hanging fruit, but when the fruit turned sour, the logical choice was survival over pride. Many trustworthy eyewitnesses saw the red haired goblin. He bore a striking resemblance to Bulgu."

"If you had people watching us, then why don't you don't know where the 'real' commander is?" Raban asked.

"I chose my scouts well, but they still failed, I see. Since you're wearing his armour, I'm guessing he escaped with the deserters."

"I'm telling you, this is my armour," Raban argued.

Lev frowned and motioned one of his men to retrieve a wooden box. "The Dragma left me with a gift after their latest Jiira raid. Looks like they really did a number on him."

Raban saw Lev open the small box. "Does this look familiar?"

"What— How—"

Seeing the look of disgust on Raban's face allowed Lev to take another leap. "The deka aren't as generous as I am. We're all goblinoids after all, we should treat each other with a degree of respect."

Lev smiled. "Let me clarify it for you. You'll be a slave. Your men? Depends on your choice."

Raban glared at Lev. "And what if I say no? You'll kill them?"

"Those that defy us will be released after days and weeks of torture. We need insights into the inner workings of the Jiira, after all. It'll be quite easy to get it out of them. We only need them to drink some neurotoxins and apply the antidote to some knives. You can guess the rest." Lev said in a cold tone.

After hearing that, Raban spat near Lev's feet. "You speak of generosity, only to threaten us? For a moment I thought you were better than this. Someone decent. Think of what the Jiira would do after your little games! My choice here hardly matters."

"Yes, my people and I will be in danger. Lev began. "But fear is a great deterrent. I'll happily perform unscrupulous acts over and over again for those I care about. I figured you of all goblins should understand that the most."

Seeing the determined look in Raban's eyes, Lev sighed. "Looks like you've made your choice, then."

He waved for two greyborns to approach. "Rak, go clean your wound before it festers, then gather his men while we hold him here."

Rak nodded. "Be careful around him."

"Don't worry. I can handle him."

As Rak left, Lev looked at Raban with a frown. "It's a shame you sacrificed a better future for you and your men just for pride."

"Our pride is the only thing keeping the Jiira together."

"Can the war chief survive on his own with all the hivelings swarming the area? What about with all those glowing jellyfish approaching?"

"I slipped some good men in with the deserters. They'll find the war chief and escort him and his family to safety. I doubt you'll be able to find them."

Lev and Raban glared at each other for a while before the former started laughing. "You're a smart one, and loyal to boot. I'm impressed."

Raban sighed and rubbed his forehead. "I'm not really that loyal. If my men and I go with you, we need assurance that someone capable is looking after our families. You mentioned you bogeys are going somewhere? I doubt you're heading into Jiira territory. It's one thing to work for you, but endangering our folks is another matter entirely."

"Well, that's a reason I can respect, but I'm still going to interrogate your men."

"Can I persuade you to take it easy on them and punish me instead if they defy you?" Raban pleaded.

Lev shrugged. "It was mostly a threat. Don't misjudge me. I'm capable of using such methods, but in your people's case, it's overkill. No offence, but goblins, especially you Jiira, aren't exactly the most sophisticated of goblinoids. I'll be able to get my answers with some less...invasive methods."

"Or, maybe someone will reveal all that's needed after a drink or two." Lev added with a smug look.

Raban groaned. "What about that offer of yours?"

"If you'd immediately caved in, I would've increased the service period to fifteen years for you. If you all serve well, I might be able to shorten the period."

"That's a relief..."

* * *

"Gherm!" Ghorza ran into her brother's arms, crying.

Thorst looked on with a smile. "Told you he'd be safe."

"Of course I am," Lev replied warmly. "Are Vyrga and the others here?"

"The deed is done." Vyrga cut in, having approached Lev with Ludger in tow.

Rak spoke with almost nauseated hesitation. "You... killed your family?"

Vyrga sneered. "I was only related to them by blood. Not that they cared. Those craven parasites were nothing close to a family,"

Lev briefly raised his eyebrows, but returned his attention to the matter at hand. "That means we've only got two things left to do."

Vyrga took out the compass-like artefact he had pillaged from the armoury in the ruined city. It shined brightly once he pointed it towards the northwest.

"To gather our allies and begin our journey to the shrine we found. It'll lead us back to that old city." Vyrga finished Lev's words.

Back when they were preparing for the Jiira's attack, Vyrga had discovered that the artefact glowed whenever he approached what looked like the destroyed remains of a shrine near the cavern entrance, similar to the one they'd seen near the armoury.

Seeing that most shrines they knew of acted as teleportation nodes, he'd kept searching until he found an unscathed one. With Orva's help, they were able to activate it. It'd led them to another shrine at the top of a mountain, hidden behind a waterfall. The hidden shrine's platform was large enough to transfer many at a time—enough for a mass exodus.

Vyrga had then tasked some of his men to go through the shrine, and sure enough, they'd appeared in an area close to the city. In the days since, they'd been scouting the city to see if it was viable to seize it from the hands of the masked bird creatures.

"If everything works out, I'll finally get my own weapon, right?" Rak asked somewhat eagerly.

"We will need to purge the city of aberrations first." Vyrga reminded his former rival.

"And if we can't?"

"Then we'll build a settlement near the city and take them on once we're prepared." Vyrga replied.

"For now," Lev refocused, "let's give our Jiira guests a place to stay, celebrate our victory, mourn our losses, and start preparing for our trek tomorrow."

After catching up with Ghorza, Lev led the others away to gather all notable bogeys who were eligible to become council candidates. The birth of a nation was waiting on the other side of a grand exodus.

* * *

Deep within the cavern, a winged purple hiveling approached the gate where Lev had first encountered the stark white being. The hiveling raised its head, its eyes glowing brightly.

"How did it go?" Though his form was nowhere to be seen, the voice of the white being reverberated around the gate.

"There were some minor inconveniences, but the bogeys, and your champion, have proven themselves capable."

"My champion? Of course he would. I chose him myself," the voice gloated. "In a way, he reminds me of *him*."

"You mean he deigned to accept the contract you needed him to."

"Silence, Kram," the white being said with displeasure.

"I only tell the truth," Kram responded.

"Don't ruin my mood. More importantly, what is he planning to do now?" The white being asked.

"After I chased them away from the cavern, the bogeys found a gate to one of *his* frontier cities. An unsuccessful old playground of mine that's connected to the cavern."

Kram could sense the white being's glee.

"Splendid! And?"

"And what?" Kram asked.

The white being paused. "I thought you'd clean the city for their arrival. Isn't the city littered with trash from your failed experiments?"

The hiveling clacked its mandibles repeatedly as though it were expressing joy. "I wanted to test their prowess, so I waited till after their departure from the caverns. Still, I suppose your champion deserves a reward for enabling us to communicate once more. I'll chase away any threats to their exodus. I might even guide some lost souls their way. You can consider it a favour, but no more will come his way," the fragment of Kram said curtly, "unless he impresses me again."

"He will impress you, brother. Just don't abandon him as quickly as you did Ainshard."

While the hiveling started to scurry away into the darkness, Kram's voice faded. "As long as he's useful, brother... As long as he's... interesting..."

The white being's voice trailed off in turn. "He'll surpass your expectations... He has already surpassed mine."

Silence settled into the ruins once again, at least until the dawn of a new age.

BONUS CHAPTER I
FALSE IDENTITY

In the dark hours of midnight, the cold winter winds let out shrill howls throughout the desolate wasteland. In the midst of the blizzard, the only structure in sight was a giant wall, one that separated the lands between the Technocracy and the Empire.

Under the heavy snow, the metal that made up the great wall looked as if it had shrunk greatly. The cold, combined with the dimming of the nuclear fusion reactor in the frontline outpost had caused the wall to loosen its iron grip on the borders.

This wall split Canada, now known as Zone Five, in half. The western half served as a buffer vassal state for the empire; the eastern half served as a spearhead for Eurasian operations.

The Technocracy had heavily fortified the eastern half with landmines and countless military grunts in defensive formations. Additionally, the land in the eastern half was infertile and inhospitable without a generator.

Understandably, the Empire had yet to reclaim the eastern half since Eurasia captured it a couple decades ago. It seemed pointless to lose personnel over such hostile land. Accordingly, the Empire had seen fit to build a great wall to cut off the Eurasian-occupied zone from their own land.

* * *

"Another day, another limb," Ava joked, observing the white snowy wasteland that spread almost endlessly along the horizon. The only sign of civilization left in this freezing, callous desert was the wall and the small encampment behind the main gate.

Most of the guards had been sent home due to inclement weather. After all, Eurasia would have no advantage attacking during a blizzard. The rapidly accumulating snow was already too deep to move in heavy equipment. The supply lines, already neglected, were few and far away from the wall.

Liam smirked. "Another limb? You shouldn't say such things, Ava. You know what the corp thinks about us joking around all day."

Ava laughed. "Oh, and what's he gonna do? Cut off my arm? If this keeps up, it'll fall off without him!"

It had been rough for the settlement these past few months. Winter was settling in, and everyone knew what that meant. It was going to get cold—very cold.

The rattling and creaking of the furnace houses had always annoyed the guards on the walls. It seemed only the upper branches were allowed to enjoy the comforts of fusion energy.

"If only this furnace were made for more than one person," Ava said as she loaded up the old machine with coal.

"You know how things have been, Ava. Another important Imperial nitwit got killed in action outside of the wall. They're always suspicious of Eurasian activity. Especially since we're literally at the frontline."

"Of course. But we, the citizens of this accursed zone, are the ones who planned, assembled, and guard the border wall to this day. The wall is more defensible than Eurasia could ever predict. Those pencil pushers should have some faith in us." Ava grumbled.

"Still. It's strange, isn't it? We're so close to enemy territory, never see enemy activity these days. It seems like they..." Liam trailed off.

"Gave up?" Ava posited.

"Yes, that's right." Liam closed the furnace's lid and helped Ava clean up the coal chunks.

"Anyway, it's my turn to go up the tower." Liam sighed. He put on a second coat and left the furnace house to begin making his climb up to the surveillance tower.

* * *

Numb feet crunched against the snow as a man slowly trudged through the blizzard. His breath was heavy, his clothes torn by the harsh winds.

Liam was watching his every move. *What is this guy doing? We don't take refugees from the other side during the winter,* he wondered. *Wait. Is he—*

"Lotus. Do you copy?" Liam said into his walkie-talkie. He watched the strange figure approach the gates. "Is that an enemy? Over."

"Copy that, Centurion," Ava replied. "Look for an insignia and report back. Over."

Liam took out his binoculars. The figure was equipped with a shattered MCS harness and looked like a walking corpse straight out of an old horror movie.

"Looks like a soldier. No identifiable emblems, or anything, really. Over." *Dammit, Ava, why would he even leave an insignia on his MCS?* Liam wanted to say. To his bewilderment, the man did nothing to indicate he wanted to enter.

Liam tried to catch the man's attention. He lit a blue fare and tossed it near the gates.

The flare flew parallel to fifty metres of wall, taking an eternity to hit the ground. When it did, the snow extinguished the flare while the wind dissipated the blue smoke.

"Real nice, Centurion, you've just wasted a flare. Mister 'first contact' my ass. Nighthawk's gonna like this one for sure! Over."

How am I supposed to contact him? Fuck. Liam changed his radio frequency to ping HQ, and soon the corporal picked up.

"This is Nighthawk, are there any problems up there? Over." Johnson's tone did nothing to hide his annoyance with another round of personnel issues.

"Sir. We have a man approaching the main gate. He is not answering our calls. Over."

"Bullshit. Have you been drinking on duty, Private? I'll confiscate that booze myself. Over," Johnson said, amused. A cold drink on his subordinate's tab would surely ease his endless boredom.

"Please do, sir. Over," Liam replied with far less amusement.

The corporal took out his coat and left the officer barracks, slamming the door shut behind him. He took a cig from his chest pocket and lit it up, soundlessly cursing his authority. *Those damn recruits and their fantasies about war. I swear to God, if Liam's pulling another prank on me, I'm sending him to the coal mines.*

Upon entering the furnace house, the corporal wasted no time. "Where is he?"

Ava answered without looking up from her notes on Liam's observations. "From what Private Liam radioed me earlier, he seems to be a middle-aged man of Eurasian descent. He's equipped with a damaged MCS that looks like one of ours, but with no identifiable Imperial insignias."

The corporal extinguished his cig in a nearby ashtray and left the room without any further remarks. Ava scowled. *This man...*

Johnson ascended the surveillance tower where Liam was stationed and asked for his binoculars.

"Sir, do you see him?" Liam bleated. "This is serious. He doesn't look like your standard refugee."

The figure looked up at the gate, revealing a battered and scarred face, then raised his left hand to present a red badge. The corporal zoomed and refocused his binoculars to examine the badge more closely.

Then the corporal gasped. "You've gotta be shitting me. He's one of those hounds!"

"Hounds?"

"Dumbass! Let him in immediately or we'll both be hanged!" Johnson cried.

Liam was speechless.

"Are you deaf, Private? Open the goddamn gate and get this man to safety!" the corporal barked. He watched Liam descend the tower and pull the levers. The giant doors slowly opened just enough for the strange man to hobble through.

Shortly afterward, Johnson was explaining the situation to the encampment's supervising officer. "A fucking bloodhound! Can you believe that, George? We're in for a ride!" Johnson cheered.

"Now? In this season? What is he thinking?" the lieutenant complained. "I knew the upper brass were moving some forces around the walls, but what's a VIP like him hanging around in this wasteland?"

He took a sip of coffee to gather his thoughts. "Alright, John. Get him here ASAP. I need to know what they're up to this time around."

"Sure thing. Give me a minute."

Sure enough, a minute later the door opened and the strange man stepped, rather apprehensively, into the lieutenant's office. Liam followed closely behind, on guard.

"Come closer," the lieutenant bellowed. "I need to verify that badge up close."

The man edged closer, one faltering step at a time, and showed his red badge again. "Here," he said hoarsely. His cheeks were sunken. Shrapnel scars decorated his face and arms. As he raised his arm, he revealed that the abdominal part of his combat suit was almost entirely worn away, exposing countless bullet scars. In fact, his combat suit was barely recognizable to begin with.

"Jesus!" Liam exclaimed. "What happened out there? Are the Eurasians really going that far out for scouting? How did you—"

"Now is not the time for chitchat, Private," the corporal said with a glare. "Get back to the tower. There may be Eurasians tailing this guy."

Liam exited the office, and the corporal took off the man's dog tag to examine it. "Officer Moritz Antonius Bluthund of the eleventh spec ops division. That's you, huh?"

The man now identified as Moritz nodded, turned around, and reached for the doorknob.

"Hey, wait a minute!" the corporal started. "I still need to verify your badge!"

Moritz ignored his pleas and walked towards the furnace house.

"Liam, help Ava with that intel! Move it!"

Upon entering the furnace house, Moritz encountered a man sitting on one of the staircases. The man was wearing officer attire. He gestured for Moritz to sit down with him.

"George, didn't you want to meet him in your office?" the corporal asked, having entered the room shortly after Moritz.

"It's 'sir' now, John. We've got a visitor."

Finally, or perhaps suddenly, Moritz opened his mouth. "I need transport, straight to the capital." His newfound voice carried enough confidence and strength that George and John could hardly believe it was Moritz talking.

Not that Moritz was done. He turned to face John next. "I've come back from death to serve His Excellence once more."

The walkie-talkie sprung back to life. "Sir, we've identified the stranger. The sample we took from the badge matches the molecular structure of a bluthund badge matched to an agent who went missing a few weeks back. I'll need some time to ask for more intel from the imperial database but everything points to him being the real deal."

Hearing that, George grinned and offered his guest a seat. "Well then, Officer Moritz. I'll make sure you'll get the first ride to the capital. In the meantime, make yourself at home."

Eurasia, Two Months Earlier

Eric nervously paced around the room. "Invading Imperial territory is one thing, but espionage is another."

"Eric, I'm a private. I'm in no position to refuse," Lev sternly replied. "And if it means I get to see her, all the better."

It was obvious the general hadn't believed their story. And who could blame him? How could two lone soldiers survive two full days in the Neutral Zone? The general had demoted Eric for losing all his men and dishonourably discharged Lev from the levy program for his "cowardice". This job was Lev's last hope at completing his final year of military service to achieve freedom.

"That's not all that's bugging me, Lev. You've been a sole survivor for all these years, yet only now do they discharge you for it. Don't you find that odd?"

"It doesn't matter. Nothing I can do," Lev answered, "Besides, Maria's been sending us encrypted messages lately. She has intel on the upper echelons of the Empire. She wants to help us."

Eric shook his head. "You've gone mad after all! Leo, she's an imperial! She's part of the upper echelon—heck, she's even a member of the emperor's right hand! Why would she throw away such a valuable position just to help an old acquaintance? This mission is pure suicide. We should've deserted instead of reporting to that wretch of a general. Cowardice, huh. Can you believe it?"

"I still believe I can complete this mission. It's also a good chance to investigate Maria's motives."

"You're crazy."

Lev opened the door, his back towards Eric. "Try to enjoy your life, Eric."

"Leo—"

The door slammed shut.

* * *

I, Private Leonard Erand Vandersteen, have been assigned to Zone Five. My mission is to infiltrate the capital and send back vital military data through the encrypted channels provided to me.

I, Private Leonard Erand Vandersteen, have been made aware that in case of failure, the Technocracy shall neither assist in my rescue nor acknowledge my involvement.

By signing this document, I acknowledge that only upon successful completion, shall I receive full citizenship and all associated benefits.

Lev signed the documents.

"Excellent," his notary reported. "Most Eurasian soldiers in your position would serve their final six months in the ground forces, but that's not soon enough for a prodigy like you, is it? You must be very grateful for this opportunity."

Lev didn't react to his words. "What identity am I taking for this mission?"

"Moritz. Moritz Antonius," the notary answered. "He had a hideout near the borders of Zone Five, but we flushed him and his comrades out without alerting the Empire. As far as they know, he's missing in action. You'll receive all his equipment." The notary paused to breathe, then resumed reading off her clipboard. "There are no supply lines in place that far out, and heavy transport vehicles would be too conspicuous. You'll have to cross the wasteland yourself."

"When do I leave?"

"As soon as you're dressed, 'Moritz,'" the notary said cheekily. "We'll implant a universal language chip shortly before you depart."

"What about facial recognition?"

"Moritz had a history of facial augmentation. We'll just alter your bluthund badge to show your face."

Lev closed his eyes. *Maria, I'll see you soon.*

BONUS CHAPTER 2
RECKONING

Imperial inventions had always been far ahead of Eurasian technology.

The holo train, engineered for high-speed, long-distance travel, was one such example.

From the 180-degree viewing port, train passengers could observe the wonderful scenery behind and in front of the train. First-class passengers could flip a switch and instantly turn their train cars transparent, allowing them to watch the world go by before their eyes. Business- and coach-class passengers could get the same effect by equipping a holo lens, a device that was also used for "virtual reality"—or at least that's what Lev had read in the rider's pamphlet.

Service robots rolled up and down the aisles and in and out of the train cars, delivering various refreshments for a small fee. Lev watched the robots serving other passengers wine, beer, and snacks. His stomach noisily requested sustenance, but he already had all the stimulation his brain could handle and no Imperial money.

Holo trains levitated above a rail, and thanks to the near-absence of friction, their almost magical speed, smoothness, and relative quietude outclassed anything else Lev had ever encountered in Eurasia. Most magically, at present it was carrying Lev away from the horrors of war.

Lev was seated next to a guard Lieutenant George had appointed. The guard was to keep "Moritz" safe from prying eyes and escort him to the royal identification hub, where his badge and DNA would be scrutinised in higher detail. After all, Lev was not the first to try to infiltrate the Emperor's realm.

"Almost there. It must have been a long journey for you, Moritz."

Lev sized up his guard, Maik Falkenberg. Although he was younger than Lev, he gave off the impression of a veteran weathered by the hell that was the battlefield.

His face was scarred, aged beyond his years fighting for an expansionist Imperial cause from his first moments of consciousness. Yet, determination oozed from every scar. Every salute, every step, every breath was an oath to serve the Emperor to his end, and then some. He reminded Lev of Brutus.

Lev had overheard the wall guards talking about Maik.

"Is it true he's been to the Neutral Zone multiple times? He talks about it like it was just another vacation," a younger cadet had said.

"He's been mad for years. Man's probably done and witnessed ten times as much as I have," a middle-aged guard sporting an iron service cross had replied.

As far as Lev was concerned, if even iron cross veterans bowed to Maik, he personally stood no chance of survival if the truth came out at the identification hub.

Lev peeked out the window. The snow-capped trees and cosy mountainside cottages progressively gave way to the tall, slick buildings of the capital, and soon Lev could discern his destination's holo gate, a large circular device intended to decelerate the train without touching it—or so, again, Lev had read.

"We're here, Moritz. Follow me."

Lev disembarked the train. Maik kept pace behind Lev, watching his every move, as they proceeded to the identification hub.

Countless shining skyscrapers and flying vehicles bewildered Lev, who had expected to pass slums on the outskirts—as he had seen in the megacities of Eurasia—but had observed no such blight.

Lev knew that this was his last obstacle. His last obstacle before he would be able to see Maria again, complete his mission and leave the army behind him. He would be able to finally run for office and with a little bit of good luck, he would be able to enter the united council and bring change to this static world.

A world engulfed in perpetual war, fueled by the greed of those who stand above all. The emperor certainly was no better than the corrupt leaders that filled the seats of the Eurasian council.

"This shouldn't take long, officer. We just need to verify your badge and profile before we enter the inner sanctum and reward you for your service."

"Thank me for my service? Does that mean I'm no longer useful to the Imperial cause?"

Maik muttered something Lev could not hear before turning back to him. "It means you've gained the privilege to live in the inner city now, where you'll be safe for the rest of your life." He took Lev's badge with a beneficent smile. "I wonder, though... Did the war destroy your memory?"

"War changes people, Maik," Lev said, more brusquely than he had hoped. "You of all people should know that."

"Hmm, I see. Sorry for reminding you." Maik passed the badge to a service robot, which politely requested that the both of them follow it. Lev and Maik followed the robot through hallway after hallway in the gigantic, well-staffed hub until they arrived at one of many medical bays. The building's secondary purpose was to house and take care of Imperial casualties; after all, it was important for dead soldiers to be returned to their families.

Lev took a seat, extended his left arm, and clenched a fist. The robot deftly palpated his arm, drew blood, bandaged the venipuncture site, and disappeared to another room.

The robot returned an hour later. "The results are in. Officer Maik, please follow me," it said with a synthesised female voice.

Maik and the robot left through a sliding door, which closed more heavily than Lev had expected.

He tried to open the door, but soon found out it'd been locked.

For a few long minutes, Lev heard muffled, unintelligible noise from beyond the door. Finally the door opened again.

Maik stepped in. "We must make haste. They'll notice the disabled robot sooner or later."

Thank the Technocracy for their extensive Imperial spy network! Lev nearly cried out loud. "Wait. Won't they notice my blood's a mismatch?"

Maik paused, mentally running through the steps he had taken to disable the robot and tamper with the sample. "They won't. Anyway, we need to get going. As far as *they* need to know, *you* were never here."

"But the cameras—"

"Get going. Moritz changed his face often enough that only the wall people and I know what 'Moritz's' face should look like right now."

Maik and Lev returned the way they had arrived, pretending nothing was out of the ordinary. Robots occasionally glanced at Lev, but continued with their menial tasks. The two had just left the hub when Lev noticed a familiar face, whose forehead scar betrayed a long-held thirst for combat, in the distance.

"It's been a long time."

"Brutus—"

"I'm called Fynn here."

Lev thought it strange that despite the years they had spent together in various regiments of the Eurasian army, Brutus could wear Imperial attire almost naturally.

From what Brutus knew, their next checkpoint was located in a hideout, amazingly close to the imperial palace. The hideout was one of many that had throughout history housed spies and political dissenters.

While en route to the checkpoint, they observed Imperial citizens within the capital. Carefree children played on the pavement while their mothers chatted about the latest fashion.

Lev thought their lives were peaceful, ignorantly peaceful, considering the world was actively at war, and wondered what it was like to have known one's mother by name and face. Since Brutus, Maria, and he had had no parents, the three of them had been assigned the same surname: Erand Vandersteen, after the manager of Neue Berlin Kinder Orphanages.

A short walk later, they arrived at the hideout, a rather nondescript, single-floor dwelling that lacked any defining characteristics and definitely lacked any visible fortifications. The house blended perfectly with the surrounding Imperial architecture.

The party entered through the front door and barricaded the door behind them with heavy boxes that had seemed haphazardly strewn across the floor. They proceeded deeper into the house, farther away from the walls and windows that allowed natural light and prying gazes in, and arranged chairs and a table in the middle of a dimly lit storeroom crowded with yet more boxes.

Lev tore open a nearby box on a whim. It was filled with ammunition.

Maik sat down in a chair near the storeroom's door. "This place isn't great for our purposes, but it's the best we've got this deep within the capital. Now listen up—our mission is simple." Maik placed a bound stack of documents onto the table and slid it towards Lev. "We have a contact within the Imperium."

Brutus gasped in amazement. "How did you penetrate into the Emperor's closest circle?"

"Very carefully. I'm not sure how much longer they can hold out," Maik replied. "You weren't lying about what Lev could do, right?"

"Absolutely not. I'm just floored." Brutus wisely refrained from mentioning their childhood. He leaned backwards in his chair into one of the walls. "I didn't know how deep into the lion's den we were going. And your contact is—"

"Maria von Mitternacht. You got it. She's been part of the Imperium for years now. Stellar military logistician this side of the wall."

So that's what she did after leaving Neue Berlin. She fought for the Empire despite knowing there was a chance we'd meet as enemies on the battlefield, Lev thought. Taking Brutus' lead, he also refrained from mentioning their shared childhood.

"As you know," Maik continued, "Maria made contact a while ago. She's pulled strings for 'Fynn' and me to come work for her, 'hardworking Imperial citizens' that we are. We're going to join the lower ranks as logistics managers and work our way up."

"What about me?" Lev asked.

Maik visibly struggled to find his next words. "As soon as we get your badge fixed, you'll be going for the top. You're going to become one of the Emperor's hands, serving directly under his nose."

Lev's stomach dropped. He was all too familiar with suicide missions like this. The Technocracy's brass probably hadn't expected him to survive the cold wastelands, let alone get this far with an invalid badge.

Nonetheless, Maik walked Lev and Brutus through the process, explaining their infiltration step-by-step.

"Lev. Brutus. Welcome to the underground world of the empire. We're going to change the world, one despot at a time."

Yes, but maybe not the way you expect.

AFTERWORD

Here we are, at the end of volume two of *Lord of Goblins (Definitive Edition)*. It's been a wild ride for us ever since the original version of volume one was released.

Over the years, we found the bogeyverse unfolding before us, guiding our fingers on our keyboards and (almost) writing itself. The characters have pretty much come alive themselves! It was almost as though Lev had become the Lord of the Word Document!

We're excited to announce the release of the *Lord of Goblins* Webtoon, illustrated by Light Comic Studio. The future looks bright for *Lord of Goblins*!

And before we forget, another big "hooray" for Moonquill and their amazing publishing team.

All that aside, there's nothing quite like putting a physical copy of a book you wrote on your bookshelf next to other novels. We're grateful to all our readers for giving us this opportunity.

Thank you for reading!

ABOUT MICHIEL WERBROUCK

Michiel Werbrouck was born in Oxford, UK but grew up in the Belgian city of Leuven. He is currently studying Applied Computer Science while working as a freelance Graphic Designer and Marketing Assistant.

Aside from his studies, Michiel is an up-and-coming author, having started out writing short Sci-Fi stories on various online platforms before finally taking the next step. Since then he has improved his craft, honing his writing skills.

In his free time, Michiel enjoys playing grand strategy games, hanging out with friends and reading fantasy novels. As a tech fan, he spends lots of time developing apps and games of his own.

In the future Michiel sees himself developing games about his books, working on software/web IT solutions, writing more books and travelling the world.

ABOUT HADI Y. BENDAKJI

Hadi Bendakji has always been a fan of fantasy and science fiction, whether they be games or books. Since childhood, these interests spurred a desire to create his own works.

Hadi was born and raised in Beirut, Lebanon and graduated in Bir Hassan's Technical College, graduating as an IT-Software Developer.

Due to his studies and family life, he'd been unable to spend time on creative pursuits until after his graduation.

He now pushes himself to constantly improve his skills in order to achieve his dreams.

On top of his passion for creative writing and gaming, Hadi likes listening to metal, reading books, and watching historical documentaries.

Please consider leaving a review on the book's Amazon page.

Thank you very much for enjoying our work.

Thank you for reading a MoonQuill original novel. To experience more exciting stories, visit us at moonquill.com

To know when we release new books, join our mailing list from our site and receive three books for free!

We will never spam you!

To talk with other members of the MoonQuill community, check out our community Discord.

Finally, we would really appreciate it if you could take a moment to review the book. Every review greatly helps the author and supports their ability to continue writing fantastic books for us to enjoy.